W9-AYO-849

DISCARD

THE NIGHT CHARTER

THE NIGHT CHARTER

SAM HAWKEN

Little, Brown and Company
New York Boston London

The characters and events in this book are fictitious. Any similarity to real persons, living or dead, is coincidental and not intended by the author.

Copyright © 2015 by Sam Hawken

All rights reserved. In accordance with the U.S. Copyright Act of 1976, the scanning, uploading, and electronic sharing of any part of this book without the permission of the publisher constitute unlawful piracy and theft of the author's intellectual property. If you would like to use material from the book (other than for review purposes), prior written permission must be obtained by contacting the publisher at permissions@hbgusa.com. Thank you for your support of the author's rights.

Mulholland Books/Little, Brown and Company
Hachette Book Group
1290 Avenue of the Americas, New York, NY 10104
mulhollandbooks.com

First Edition: December 2015

Mulholland Books is an imprint of Little, Brown and Company, a division of Hachette Book Group, Inc. The Mulholland Books name and logo are trademarks of Hachette Book Group, Inc.

The publisher is not responsible for websites (or their content) that are not owned by the publisher.

The Hachette Speakers Bureau provides a wide range of authors for speaking events. To find out more, go to hachettespeakersbureau.com or call (866) 376-6591.

ISBN 978-0-316-29921-3
Library of Congress Control Number: 2015936945

10 9 8 7 6 5 4 3 2 1

RRD-C

Printed in the United States of America

For my wife, my very own action heroine

THE NIGHT CHARTER

CHAPTER ONE

CAMARO ESPINOZA AWOKE before dawn. She had fled New York City after the killing of five men exactly 364 days before.

The bright fluorescent bulb in the bathroom hurt her eyes, so she switched it off, choosing instead to shower in the dark. She left the bedroom unlit afterward, putting on her clothes without a shred of sunlight passing through the slightly parted curtains. Her small backyard, only just visible, was a square of blackness because there was only the sliver of a moon.

She packed a small ice chest with a couple of beers and a lunch she'd made the night before, then let herself out onto the carport where a Harley-Davidson snuggled up against the shadowy bulk of her pickup. A pair of bungee cords secured the chest to the back of the pillion seat, and she walked the bike down the driveway and out onto the street. When it started up, the rumble of the engine was remarkably loud on the quiet street. She gave the throttle a twist and pulled away. The morning air stirred her dark, honey-brown hair.

Her home was in the Allapattah neighborhood of Miami, and she lived fifteen minutes from the water. A pair of lights illuminated the sign at the marina, and beyond the open gates were the steady rows of silent boats waiting patiently for their time on the waves. Camaro parked up against the side of the marina's office. She took the ice chest with her out onto the pier.

The fifty-nine-foot Custom Carolina waited about halfway down, bobbing slightly as the water shifted beneath her hull. The boat was named the *Annabel.* It had taken nearly all of the money she had for Camaro to get it. The flying bridge stood tall and white against the slowly lightening sky. Camaro boarded onto the aft deck and lightly touched the fighting chair mounted there.

She stowed the ice chest in the cabin and cast off before she climbed the ladder to the bridge. The boat had an even throatier noise than the Harley did, but there were no sleepers to disturb. The marina was utterly still.

Camaro navigated out of the forest of boats and onto open water. She drove toward the rising sun and found a spot in the blue just as the last of the bright orange disk cleared the horizon.

There were poles on board and bait in a cooler she had stocked a day ago. Camaro let the *Annabel* drift in the Gulf Stream and cast a line. The bait sank a thousand feet. She sat in the fighting chair and relaxed with the pole in the holder between her legs, listening to nothing and feeling only the feathering morning breeze that carried across the waves.

She carried on until noon, pausing only to slather sunscreen on brown arms and drink a beer. She hid beneath a cap and a pair of wraparound sunglasses. Nothing bit, but she didn't much care one way or the other. Today was an empty day with nothing scheduled, no clients to meet, and no responsibilities. If she went ashore without a single catch, she would at least have spent the hours with the splendor of the sea around her and the luxury of absolute quietude.

By two she'd had a couple of nibbles but no solid hits. These were swordfish waters, but swordfish hunted by night. It wasn't unheard of to catch them in the full glare of the sun and see them rear out of the water at the end of the line, battling the hook and the tension of the rod. She could have set the bait lower, all the way down to two thousand feet, and maybe find a little action, but she preferred to let the fish come to her today. If there was going to be a fight, then there would be one, but she wasn't looking for it.

She reeled in at three and took her lunch inside on the vinyl-surfaced galley counter. The second beer went down cold and good, and even her sandwich tasted better for the wait. There was a bed in the bow, good for naps, and she considered it, but in the end she went back to the water and rod and line and the glare of the cloudless sky.

It was close to seven o'clock when she brought the bait in for the last time and set course for the marina. She'd drifted some forty miles, and the trip back was slow, the *Annabel* cresting the waves and carving them, the engine keeping her high. Eventually, the shoreline came into view, and the glitter of Miami was visible in the distance. Camaro felt a delicate sadness at returning to people and roads and cars and all of that. It was better out here beyond the skyline, absent all demands. She could stay here forever if the opportunity came. She'd buy a sailing vessel and take to the high seas and be free of it all.

The sun was failing, and already the lights were on as Camaro entered the marina, closed on her berth, and spotted the man coming down the pier.

CHAPTER TWO

He looked like a beach bum from where she stood, dressed as he was in long khaki shorts and a bright short-sleeved shirt. As she drew closer, she saw the sun-streaked dark blond of his hair and the deep tan of his skin. He waved to her with a newspaper in his hand, but she didn't wave back.

He waited for her as she killed the engine and tied the boat up, and then he approached her. "Is this the *Annabel*?" he asked.

"Yeah," Camaro said.

"Is the captain aboard?"

"I am the captain."

"Oh, sorry," said the man. He switched the folded newspaper to his left hand and extended his right. "Parker Story. I came because of your website. Coral Sea Sport Charters? That's you, right?"

"That's me. You been waiting long?"

"Only about an hour. I wasn't sure when you'd be back."

"I could have stayed gone all night."

"That would have been bad luck," Parker said. "I'm looking for a boat to charter."

"That's what I do."

"I didn't catch your name," Parker said.

"Camaro."

"Ha! That's a good one. Your parents must have been into cars."

"My dad was. Can you give me a minute, Parker?"

"Okay, sure."

She went below to get her cooler, and back on deck she dumped the melt water and ice over the side before stowing the empty beer bottles inside. When she came back to Parker, she looked at him more closely. She figured him for his middle thirties, or maybe a little older. He had a weather-beaten face, like he'd spent his life in the sun, and he wasn't soft like a lot of clients. Some women might even have thought he was handsome.

Parker did not stare at her chest, which she liked. He looked her in the eye when they talked, and he seemed solid, but he rolled the newspaper between his fists. Camaro watched him. "You have a nice boat," he told her.

"Thanks. There are some outfits that have nicer ones."

"I liked your website. Nice and simple. Seemed homemade."

Camaro stepped off the boat. The cooler dangled from her hand. "I'm not sure if that's a compliment or not."

"It is. Some of those places are way too flashy. You know they won't give you the personal touch."

"You want the personal touch?" Camaro asked.

"If I can get it."

Camaro nodded. "You can get it. I take you out to the good water, and if you don't know how to fish, I'll show you what to do. Rates start at forty-five dollars a person, and I can take up to ten. It gets a little crowded with that many, but it's all right."

Parker pointed to the boat. "Who gets the chair?"

"Whoever hooks the big fish."

"Do you do nighttime charters?"

"I do," Camaro said. "Is that what you have in mind? The rates go up."

"How much?" Parker asked.

"One seventy-five a person and we stay out for about eight hours or so. Depends on how everybody's doing and if the fish are biting.

If they are, we stay out longer. If they aren't, I won't waste your time."

Parker seemed to consider this. He slapped the newspaper against his leg. "We don't have a big party. Only five altogether. I'm not sure what that runs to."

Camaro did the math in her head. "That's eight seventy-five. When do you want to go out?"

"Well, that's the thing: we're not quite set on a date yet."

Camaro frowned. "I can't hold dates open if I don't know when you're going out. It's first come, first served."

"Right, I understand. Can I get back to you in a couple of days?"

"I'll need twenty percent up front. That's one seventy-five. I only take cash, no checks or credit cards. Is your party going to need gear?"

"We'll bring our own," Parker said.

"Okay," Camaro said, and she moved to walk past him.

Parker gave way and then hurried to keep up with her as she walked along the pier. "It doesn't bother you to go out with five guys at night?" he asked her.

"I've gone out with twice that many at night. I'm not worried," Camaro said. She was ready to stop talking now. All day long she'd enjoyed the perfect tranquility that could only be gotten out on the waves. Now the man was talking at her. She walked a little more quickly.

"I wanted to make sure," Parker said. "About how far out do you go?"

Camaro stopped. "I go out about twenty miles. The water's close to two thousand feet out there. It's a good spot for swordfish. You are looking for swordfish, right?"

"We'd be happy with anything," Parker said, "but swordfish are good. They're the ones who come out at night, right?"

"Lots of things come out at night. But if it's swordfish you want then, yeah, the night's a good time to get them."

She moved on. Parker stayed at her side. "Do you ever go out farther? I mean, out where it's really deep?"

"No need. You go out too far, you'll leave the good grounds behind, and then you won't catch anything. Don't worry: I know where to go so you'll get what you want."

"Been doing this a long time?" Parker asked.

"A while," Camaro replied.

They reached the Harley, and Camaro used the orange bungee cords to tie up her ice chest. The bottles rattled around inside. Camaro turned her back on Parker completely to shut him out, but he was undeterred. "Good Harley," he said. "Heritage Softail Classic, right?"

She looked at him again. In his sandals with his bare, brown legs showing out of his shorts, he seemed like the sort to drive an old VW Bug or a van with ugly art on the side. Camaro had seen his type a thousand times. "That's right," she said. "How'd you know that?"

"I like Harleys. I don't own one myself. My daughter asked me to stop riding, so I gave it up. She worried about losing me if I dumped it going too fast. I had a Honda cruiser before. Kind of looked like yours a little, but it wasn't the real thing. You know how it is."

"Sure," Camaro said. "Listen, Parker—if you get me that deposit by tomorrow, I'll hold open the next seven nights for you and your guys. After that, you'll have to take what I can give you."

Parker nodded. "Tomorrow? No problem. I can get it to you tomorrow. Where are you going to be? Here?"

"Come back to the boat tomorrow afternoon about three o'clock or so, and I'll meet you."

"I'll be here," Parker said.

"Good. I'll keep an eye out for you."

She swung a leg on the Harley, and when she turned the engine over there was no more talking to be done. Parker waved and mouthed a good-bye. Camaro watched him go before she circled around and pointed herself toward the marina gate. She saw his car—not a Beetle or a van but a little, rusted-out Toyota pickup with a bashed-in passenger door.

CHAPTER THREE

Parker watched Camaro go, and even when she was out of sight he could still hear the blare of her Harley's engine. He got behind the wheel of his truck and started it up. The little sound it made was a thoroughgoing disappointment. He left the marina parking lot and turned himself toward home.

Parker lived deep in the dense urban expanse that spread over Miami-Dade County. The house was small and rented, but it had two bedrooms, and that was enough. The lawn was a patchy little square of crabgrass and dirt, and the property was too small for a garage or a carport. Parker left the truck at the curb out front and went inside.

The smell of food wafted through the front door when he opened it, and he came in to lights and the sound of the television turned too loud. "Hey!" he called. "I'm back!"

Lauren poked her head out of the kitchen. She smiled and his concerns lifted. Never in his life would he ever have said that one look from a fourteen-year-old girl would be enough to put him at ease, but it was true, and he was glad of it.

He turned the TV down in the front room and then went to the kitchen. Lauren fussed with a pair of insulated gloves as she opened the old, olive-green oven to get at the Pyrex dish inside. Immediately there was a stronger odor of spicy meat. "What are we having?" he asked.

"Chuck-wagon casserole," Lauren said.

It was Kraft macaroni and cheese mixed with corn and browned chunks of Italian sausage. A meal that could be made on the cheap but was filling for two. Parker hugged Lauren as she stripped off the gloves. "Smells terrific," he said.

"Fifteen minutes to cool down?" Lauren asked.

"Fifteen minutes," Parker said.

He turned to leave her, but she brought him up short with a question. "Where did you go? I thought maybe you were going to get us ice cream for dessert."

"You know, that would have been a good idea," Parker said, "but I completely forgot. I had to run an errand for Uncle Matt. We're gonna go out fishing soon."

Lauren's face turned down at the mention of Matt. "You're not getting in trouble again, are you?"

"No, of course not. Why would you say that?"

"Mom said Uncle Matt is the kind of guy who gets everybody in trouble."

Now it was Parker's turn to frown. "Your mother wasn't exactly an authority on anything. You'll notice she's not around to eat this great food. And she's not running out to the store for ice cream, either."

"Sorry, Dad."

"Don't worry about it. Set the table, and I'll be back in a few."

He left her and went to his room. He closed the door until it almost caught, and then he listened for the sound of Lauren fiddling in the kitchen. When he heard it, he went to the closet and opened the doors. His few nice clothes hung there, and his single pair of dress shoes rested on the floor beside an empty suitcase. These last two things he moved aside to expose the wall behind them.

Parker crouched in the closet and caught hold of the wainscoting at the back. An eighteen-inch section was loose enough to get fingernails behind, and rocking it gently pulled it completely free of the wall. A flat attaché case was revealed. He pulled the case out.

When he unzipped it, a bundle of bills fell out, and he picked it up. It didn't have a paper strap like a bank would use, but was simply collected inside a tight rubber band. He unwound the bills and counted off two hundred in fifties before putting the band back on again. The bundle went back in the bag.

Parker put the attaché case back into place and then stopped. He pulled it out again and emptied it to count. There were fifty bundles of a thousand dollars each, and they were all there, minus the little bit he'd just taken for the deposit. His sudden fear satisfied, he put the money away and secreted the case in the wall before replacing the wainscoting. He closed the closet and put the two hundred on the nightstand.

He had a phone in his pocket. He used it to dial Matt. It rang three times. "Who is it?" Matt asked.

"It's Parker."

"Parker? Why isn't your name coming up on my caller ID?"

"I don't know. Maybe something's wrong with your phone."

"Man, there's nothing wrong with my phone. It has to be *your* phone."

"Okay, I'll check it."

"All right. So did you go out there and get us a boat?"

"I talked to the lady who runs the charters."

"A chick?"

"Yeah, but it's okay. She seems to know what she's doing."

"Did you talk to her about what we want?"

"Not yet," Parker said. "I just told her we wanted to do a night charter for some fishing. It didn't seem like the right time to get into the rest of it. I'm going back tomorrow to give her the deposit."

"Don't wait too long to get down to business," Matt said. "We don't have a lot of time."

"I'll do it. Let me talk to her a little bit and see how it goes."

"Dad! I'm putting it on the table!" Lauren called.

Parker put his hand over the phone. "I'll be right there," he said, and then he spoke to Matt again. "Don't worry about anything. I have it covered."

"All right, man. Talk to you again tomorrow."

Parker killed the connection and put the phone back in his pocket. His mind was weighed down again, but then he went to the little dining room and Lauren made him forget about all of it.

CHAPTER FOUR

IN THE MORNING Camaro took a half-dozen businessmen out into the deep water to search for mackerel or swordfish or anything else that might be biting. One of them managed to hook a wahoo early on, and he wanted to keep it, but it went back into the water. "What am I supposed to show off at home?" he asked.

"Take a picture," Camaro said, and that was all. Camaro's trips were strictly catch-and-release. Everyone knew this going in.

They got lucky here and there over a few hours, but the men were as interested in drinking as they were in the fish. Camaro did not let them get sloppy and put a curb on them when they went to their cooler one time too many. There was more grumbling and talk about refunds, but she reminded them it was money up front and no refunds. They were more subdued after that.

She got back to the marina a little after two and let the men off. She thought to warn them about driving off buzzed, but they had probably heard enough from her already. If they wanted to end up wrapped around a pole or in the back of a police car that was their business and not hers. Camaro's responsibility stopped the moment they stepped off the boat.

When they were all gone, she broke out the hose and cleaned off the deck. She got an old towel and wiped down plastic and wood and metal alike. She checked the bait locker and made a mental note of what she had to stock. Afterward, she got a sandwich out of her personal cooler and ate it in the shade with a little bag of chips. Watching the men put away beers had put her in the mind for one, but there would be no drinking while she worked.

She lay down for a short nap. It was four when she heard Parker calling from the pier, and she got up to meet him. He stood beside the boat in a different shirt and nearly identical shorts, his feet tanned in his sandals, the barest hint of white flesh peeking out from underneath one strap. Camaro saw herself reflected in his sunglasses. "Hey, there," Parker said. "Sorry I'm late."

"You're not late," Camaro said. "I told you three o'clock or so."

"Well, I'm here now."

"You want to come aboard?" Camaro asked.

"Sure," Parker said, and he stepped over onto the deck. He looked over the fighting chair and made an admiring sound. "I can't wait to sit on this baby. Is that teak? Is this thing an old classic?"

"No," Camaro said. "It's just a nice chair."

"I'm gonna land the big one," Parker said.

"That's what everybody says. Come on in. Let's get you out of the sun."

They went inside and stood in the little galley. Parker dug in his pocket and came up with four fifty-dollar bills. He laid them in front of her on the counter. "That should cover our deposit," he said. "But I don't know what night it'll be yet. I'm sorry about that."

"I said you get a week, so you get a week," Camaro said. She took the money and put it away. "It's your charter."

Parker fiddled with his thumbs and looked around the small cabin. He took off his sunglasses, and Camaro was glad to see he didn't have the strange, pale shadow around his eyes that some men got down here. To her they looked like raccoons of the wrong color. "This really is a nice boat," he said.

"It cost enough," Camaro said.

"Expensive?"

"Yeah."

He put his hands flat on the counter. "Listen, I might be able to swing some extra money your way if you're interested. It's not strictly charter stuff, but it could be worth something to you."

Camaro looked at him. "I just do fishing charters," she said.

"Right. Of course. I'm only saying that we might be able to arrange some extras to give you a bigger payday."

"My paydays are plenty big," Camaro said. "This is my business, remember? If you want extras, there are plenty of places that do extras. This isn't a party boat."

"Sure, sure," Parker said. "I'm sorry I said anything. Don't be insulted."

"I'm not insulted," Camaro said. "I like to keep it simple, that's all. Boat. Water. Fish. That kind of thing. Maybe that means I lose some clients once in a while, but I don't mind too much. There's always someone out there who wants service without frills."

Now Parker smiled, and Camaro read both relief and tension in it. He was fiddling with his thumbs again. She could not tell what was driving him on. "This is my first time chartering a fishing boat," he confessed to her. "I don't know all the rules."

"They're not really rules," Camaro said. "I think they're like habits. Sometimes you break them, but most of the time you do what feels right. I like doing what I do."

Parker stood up. "I guess I should go, then," he said.

Camaro looked at him again and saw the nerves prickling out through his skin. "Are you busy?" she asked him.

"Me?"

"Yeah, you. Are you doing anything right now?"

"I didn't have any plans."

Camaro got up. “I already ate, but I could use some dessert. There’s a diner up the road. Want to have a coffee or something?”

Parker blinked. “You want to have a coffee with me?” he asked.

“Yeah.”

“Okay.”

CHAPTER FIVE

AT THE DINER, they sat across from each other. Instead of coffee, Parker had iced tea, but Camaro had a hot cup with cream, along with a slice of key lime pie. The tartness and sweetness combined with the mild bitter flavor of the coffee played games on her tongue, and she enjoyed it. Parker added far too much sugar to his tea.

"What do you do?" Camaro asked him.

"Me? Oh, I'm a business consultant. I go around to businesses and tell them how to improve their operation. Efficiency. Stuff like that."

Camaro grinned a little. "That so?" she asked.

"Yeah, sure."

"Do business consultants work outdoors a lot?" Camaro asked.

"What? You're talking about the tan, right? I like to do yard work and gardening on the weekends with my daughter."

She shook her head. "You are an absolutely awful liar," she said.

"I'm not lying," Parker said. "I'm a business consultant, and I'm going to take a few clients out fishing to butter them up a little before we make a deal. Try to jack my fee up, you know? That's how you make a living."

"I believe you're chartering a boat," Camaro said. "And I believe you have a daughter, but I think the rest of it is bullshit."

Parker opened his mouth and then closed it again. Then he said, "I do have a daughter."

"How old?" Camaro asked.

"She's fourteen. Going on forty. She's trying to turn me gray, but

I think I can keep a handle on her for a couple more years. When she hits sixteen, I don't know what I'm going to do."

"What about her mother?"

Parker made a gesture with his thumb, whisking the thought away. "She's long gone. Out the door when Lauren was seven. The old, 'I'm going to get some cigarettes,' thing. Never called again, never wrote. She was just out of there. So it's the two of us, me and Lauren."

"Any other family?" Camaro asked.

"I have a brother, but he's not local. I think he's seen Lauren once. No, twice. You?"

"A sister."

"Huh," Parker said.

"What do you really do?" Camaro asked.

Parker rolled the moist glass of tea between his palms for a minute. The condensation made a smeary puddle on the tabletop. "Can we hold off on that question for a little bit? I'm kind of happy with the whole 'business consultant' thing right now."

"Okay," Camaro said.

"How about you? Maybe I can ask you some questions."

Camaro shrugged. "Ask me anything you want."

"You from around here?"

"No."

"Where'd you come from?"

"California originally."

"How'd you end up in Florida?"

Camaro smiled to herself. She took a forkful of pie and held it between them a moment. "I rode my bike," she said.

"Now who's telling lies?" Parker asked.

"No lies. Go ahead and ask me another."

"If you're from California, what are you doing running a fishing boat out of Miami? Why aren't you off surfing somewhere or something?"

Camaro ate the piece of pie and followed it with coffee. She considered the question. "When I was growing up, my dad liked two things more than anything else in the world," she said. "He liked fixing cars, and he liked fishing. Fast cars were his favorite. Muscle cars? Forget about it. He'd fall in love with anything that had a big engine. And when he wasn't under a car getting oily, he was saving up his money to get on a fishing charter and go after barracuda, calico bass, yellowtail . . . whatever."

"So you have fishing in your blood."

"Something like that. I know how to put together an engine, and I can tell you where the fish are. That's what my dad gave me."

"Can't be a cheap business to get into. You said the boat cost a lot."

"I had some money to spend."

"You make a good living?"

"Good enough. Keeps me in my house, and I don't starve. I make what I need and a little extra to put away. I keep up the boat myself and that saves a bundle. Whatever it takes to go on."

"And you still don't want more than you're charging me," Parker said.

"Nope. The price is one seventy-five a person and that's it. More if you need gear. I told you: I like to keep things simple."

"I can respect that," Parker said.

"I'm glad. Some guys don't."

"I get the feeling those guys don't last too long around you," Parker said.

"They don't," Camaro told him.

Parker was quiet awhile, and Camaro thought he'd finished talking, but he spoke up again. "So you have a sister, huh?" he asked.

"Yeah."

"I'm surprised she doesn't help you run the business."

"She doesn't live around here. Besides, I don't think she liked fishing as much as our dad did. She was the one who always got seasick."

"That's funny," Parker said.

Camaro finished off the last of her pie and drained the coffee cup. The waitress came by with the pot to top it off, but Camaro put her hand over it and asked for the check instead. "I have a night charter tonight," she told Parker. "We're headed out around eight."

"What time is it now?" Parker asked.

"About five. That gives us a couple of hours."

"A couple of hours for what?"

The waitress put the check down between them. Camaro took it up and counted off the cost from the bills in her wallet, plus a twenty percent tip. She weighted it all down with her coffee cup. "I don't want to go back to your place, and I don't want you back at my place," Camaro said. "But there's the boat."

"I'm still not following," Parker said.

"Hey, listen: I know you're a bad liar, but don't tell me you're slow on the uptake, too," Camaro said.

She got up, and Parker followed her out.

CHAPTER SIX

THEY LAY NAKED together in the forward compartment, the sheets twined around them messily. Parker slept, his breathing slow and even. Camaro slipped free of the bed and went to where his shorts lay on the floor. She came up with his wallet and leafed through it. There were fifty-seven dollars in cash, his driver's license, a trio of business cards from other fishing outfits, and a photograph.

She looked at the picture. It showed a young girl of eight or nine on a beach, corn-silk hair blowing in a sudden gust off the water, and a more youthful Parker half-caught in the frame. The girl was laughing, and he was laughing, and the entire moment was washed in sun and pleasure. Camaro touched the girl's face once and then put the picture away. She returned Parker's wallet to his shorts and then climbed back into bed.

Parker murmured slightly and took a shuddery breath through his nose. Camaro looked down at Parker's feet, at the colorless bands of skin that marked where his sandal straps lay, and she nudged one foot with her own. She felt him wake. He chuckled. "Watch it," he said. "I'm ticklish."

"Where?" Camaro asked.

"All over. Don't get me started."

"I won't."

She could feel him watching her, but she didn't look back at him, choosing instead to look out past their feet to the galley beyond and the wooden door that closed off the back deck from below. The door had a circular window, and through that she could see the fighting chair waiting.

"You know, when I said you could earn a little extra, this wasn't what I was talking about," Parker said.

"I know."

"I can't really remember the last time somebody... you know, gave me an invitation."

Now she did turn to him, and she saw that the nerves were gone from him for the first time. His features were softer, the stress lines shallower. He was more handsome that way. "I don't do that for everybody," Camaro told him.

"I wasn't saying anything."

"Okay, then. Don't."

Her left leg was above the sheets and Parker pointed at a spot on her midthigh. It was a long scar with a head like a comet at the end, and it stood slightly raised from the tan skin, marring her. "What's that?" he asked.

"A scar," Camaro said.

"What kind of scar?"

"A bullet scar," Camaro said.

"A bullet scar? You got shot?"

"Yeah. I have another one right here, on my shoulder. See that there on my side? That's one, too."

"Holy shit. When did you get shot?"

"In the war," Camaro said simply. She glanced at the scar once, then looked away again. She examined the roof of the compartment and the rows of little lights, switched off now, that gave off a soothing yellow glow in the night.

"Which war?" Parker asked.

"Both of them," Camaro said.

"Both...? You mean like Iraq and Afghanistan both?"

"Yeah. I was there. Two deployments each."

"What branch were you in?"

"The army."

"But you weren't a *soldier,* right? I mean, women don't serve in combat."

"Tell that to the Taliban," Camaro said.

"So you were shooting it out with them? Like with a real rifle and everything?"

Camaro glared at him. "What do you think women do in the army? We're not all secretaries. Some of us picked up a weapon once in a while. Some of us picked up a weapon a *lot.*"

"What did you do?" Parker asked. "In the army, I mean."

"I was a Sixty-Eight Whiskey," Camaro said.

"What's that?"

"It's a combat medic. I went out with frontline troops and got it done. Sometimes I got shot at. Sometimes I had to shoot back. If the enemy figured out what I was, I'd be the first one to take fire."

"Why?"

"You shoot a soldier, you put down that soldier. You put down the medic, and suddenly you put down two, three, four other soldiers. It didn't matter if it was Iraq or Afghanistan. They both had the same idea."

"Jesus," Parker said. "That's crazy. And you did this for how long?"

"I was in twelve years," Camaro said. "I enlisted right after 9/11. My dad was superpissed. I think he got over it after a while, but... I don't know."

Parker was quiet. Finally, he said, "I never served."

"Lots of people don't."

"It's not because I didn't want to. I used to play football in high school, you know? Anyway, I didn't get a bunch of concussions or anything, but I did manage to tear the hell out of my ACL. That was the end of that. No more football, no army, no marines, no nothing. I still can't run right."

Camaro sat up and searched for her watch. She found it at the foot of the bed, swathed in sheets. "I'm running out of time. You're going to have to get out of here," she said.

"What time is it?"

"Seven thirty."

Now Parker sat up and made an angry noise. "Goddamn it, I didn't tell Lauren I was going to be late tonight. I'm surprised she hasn't called me already."

"Then go. My charter's going to be here any minute."

Parker tried to kiss her, but she turned her head. She got out of bed and put on her clothes. She noticed him watching as she put on her boots. "Is that a knife you have in there?" he asked.

"Yes," Camaro said.

"You don't take any shit from anyone, do you?"

"Hurry up and get dressed."

She went up on the deck while Parker scrambled for his clothes. The day was bleeding away, the sun already low in the west. They would be on their way to the good swordfishing waters by the time it was full dark, and then it would be ten hours out where there were no lights except those of the boat and the distant blink of ships passing miles away on their way to port.

Parker stumbled out from inside after a few minutes, still buttoning his shirt. His hair was mussed, and it made him seem younger than he was. He dragged his fingers through it and cleared it away from his face. "I hope this isn't the last time we, uh, run into each other like this," he said.

"No promises," Camaro said.

"Okay," Parker said, and she could hear his disappointment. "I guess that's it for me, then."

Camaro climbed to the flybridge. "Let me know when you're ready to go out with your people," she said without turning toward him. "You have the number."

"Right," Parker said. "I will. Good night."

He left. Camaro did not watch him go.

CHAPTER SEVEN

THE NEXT DAY was a half-day at Lauren's school, and Parker waited at the bus stop for her return. He knew she was old enough to make it the two blocks from the stop to the house. But he had been meeting her after school as regularly as he was able since she was very young, and he didn't feel the urge to stop now. Sometimes she told him not to come, that her friends would make fun of her. He came anyway, because that's what dads did for their daughters.

He saw the yellow bus rise out of the silvery heat coming up from the asphalt, and he put on a smile as the bus came closer. It slowed and stopped, and its shadow fell over him. Parker waved to the bus driver, and the driver gave him a little salute. Parker was aware of the eyes of young teenagers watching him from the windows. Lauren came off, and he saw that she was aware of them, too. She clutched her books to her body and hunched her shoulders without looking at him.

"Hey, there," Parker said to Lauren as the bus left. She was already walking, and he hurried to catch up. "How was school today?"

"Fine," Lauren said.

"Just fine? Learn anything new and exciting?"

Lauren regarded him with a sour eye. "It was the last day of school, Dad. We're not learning anything on the last day of school."

"Yeah, I guess not. Still... there's got to be things going on."

"Nothing, Dad," Lauren said.

"Absolutely nothing? You guys sat there and stared at the walls all day?"

He caught the slightest hint of a smile, but she stanched it. "They gave us busy work. I had to write an essay on what I'm doing this summer. That's the kind of thing *kids* do."

"That's tough," Parker sympathized. "They should have asked you about how we can have world peace."

"I'm *serious,* Dad! It's stupid. If they don't have anything for us to do, they could cancel classes and let us all go home a week early."

"I don't know if I'm ready to have you home all day right now," Parker said. "I could use another week. How about summer school? You ever think about summer school?"

Now Lauren did smile, and she punched Parker in the arm. "That's not funny. Only stoners and juvies go to summer school. You want me to lose *all* my friends?"

Parker threw his arm around her and squeezed her shoulders. "I want you to be happy. That's all. Whatever it takes to make you happy."

They walked like that part of the way. Lauren put her head against him, and Parker was glad. She was so tall now. In only three years she'd grown like a weed. He remembered holding her hand to balance her as she walked for the first time. "Dad?" she asked.

"Yeah?"

"Did you find a job today?"

The pleasant feeling fled Parker. He sighed. As if it was a signal, Lauren slipped away from him and put her gaze on him. He felt shrunken in her sight. "No, I didn't find a job today," he said. "But I looked. I really did look."

"I guess that's good enough," Lauren said, but she did not come back to his arm again. They walked apart the rest of the way.

Parker got the front door unlocked and held it for Lauren before he heard the rumble of the engine. It was as distinctive as a fingerprint. "Hey, go inside and relax a little while," he told Lauren. "Uncle Matt is coming."

"Ugh," Lauren said. But she did as he said and vanished indoors.

He waited on the front walk until he saw the familiar yellow-and-black Charger coming down the block. Matt had the windows down and a tanned arm propped in the window as he cruised the old car to a stop at the curb. He cut the engine and climbed out. "*Hola,* Parker," he said. "What's up?"

"Not much."

"Catch you at a bad time?"

"No. I was just getting ready to fix Lauren a snack."

Matt approached him. He was a lean man, so much so that his skin seemed tight over his flesh and bones. His hair was lank and brown and came down floppily over one eye. Matt was always brushing it back, but it fell in the same place every time. Parker did not know why he didn't cut it. "Lauren, huh? Maybe I should go in and say hello."

"It's okay," Parker said. "She only got off the bus a few minutes ago. She needs some downtime."

"Sure, whatever," Matt said, and he brushed his hair from his face. "I came to talk business anyway."

"What about it?"

"Well, do you have the charter all set up?"

"I'm still working on it."

Matt frowned. The expression pulled taut skin even more tightly. "Parker, we don't have all the time in the world. Now is this lady going to take our money or not?"

"I don't know. I'm trying to work my way around to it."

"There's no more time for that. The Cubans are getting antsy, and they want to get this done soon. They're waiting on us to give them a window. I can't stall them forever."

"I'll get on it," Parker said.

"Okay," Matt said, and the frown vanished. "And there's one other thing: I wanted to throw the guys a little bit of money to keep them happy. So I need about a thousand right now."

Parker stood with his back to the door, aware of the house and Lauren and everything inside. He did not let worry cross his face. "I can't do that right now. You know how it is."

"Hey, come on, Parker, who's the man in charge of all this?"

"You are."

"Right. So I need some of the money. Like right this minute."

"It's not where I can get at it," Parker said.

Again Matt swept the hair back. Again it fell into place. His eyes had darkened. "Where did you put it?"

"Somewhere safe. Even I can't get at it right away."

"Did you put it in a safe deposit box or something?"

"You told me not to say," Parker said. He thought of the loose piece of wainscoting. Even if Matt looked, he would not see it. "You told me to take the case, put it somewhere where only I knew where to find it, and sit on the money until it was time to divide it up. So that's what I did."

"How are you paying the rent on this place?" Matt asked.

"We get assistance. And I had a little money saved up. It's enough to get us through until this pays off."

"Until it pays off," Matt said. "I guess that's all up to you now."

"I'll get us the boat."

Matt scrutinized him. The darkness had not gone away. "I want to meet the captain. Can I do that much, or are you keeping her all to yourself?"

"Sure, you can meet her," Parker said. "Just don't . . . don't push too hard. I get the feeling she'll say no if you push too hard."

Now Matt smiled broadly and spread his hands as if to take Parker up in a hug. His arms were spidery, the muscles long and raw. "Hey, do I look like the kind of guy who'd screw up your thing? I put all my trust in you, man. We're partners for life."

A tension eased in Parker's chest, and he breathed a little more deeply. "I'll call her up and see when we can see her. Maybe tonight. I'll have to check."

"You call me with the time and the place, and I'll swing by to pick you up," Matt said. "Okay?"

"Absolutely," Parker said.

"I can't wait to lay eyes on this chick. Is she hot, or what?"

"Yeah, she's good-looking."

"Does she have big, giant titties?" Matt asked, and his smile turned wolfish.

"They're okay," Parker said. He imagined Camaro beneath him and above him. He imagined her beside him in the little bed at the bow of the boat. These were things Matt could not know.

"All right, then. See you later, bro."

"Bye," Parker said. He went inside and closed the door, and then he watched Matt through the peephole until the Charger drove away. He relaxed only when he couldn't hear the engine anymore.

CHAPTER EIGHT

When the *ANNABEL* was within cellular range of the shore, Camaro's phone vibrated in her pocket. She checked her calls and found three from a number she didn't recognize and one message. She dialed into voice mail. It was from Parker. She was glad it was not an invitation to a second date, a real date with dress-up and flowers and dinner by candlelight. He wanted her to meet one of his clients, and he wanted the meeting soon. Camaro deleted the message.

She looked to the back deck at the three men and their wives, each taking turns snapping pictures of each other in the fighting chair as the sun went down. There had been plenty of snaps earlier when one of the women managed to land an eighty-pound swordfish, and much disappointment when it was time to return the fish to the sea. There were sailfish and mahi-mahi and blackfin lining up to be caught thereafter, and everyone was happy again.

The *Annabel* was close to the marina when Camaro called Parker's number. He picked up right away. "Is this Camaro?" he said.

"It's me," Camaro said. "Sorry. I didn't get your call until now."

"I thought maybe you were avoiding me."

"I can't avoid you," Camaro said. "You paid me a deposit, remember?"

"I meant because of... you know. The other thing."

"Don't even think about that," Camaro said. "I had fun. You had fun. That's all it had to be."

"Right. Sure. Okay."

He was quiet a bit, and Camaro angled closer to shore. "You needed to talk to me about your client?" she asked.

"Oh, yeah, absolutely. Matt, he's one of the guys I'm chartering the boat for, wants to meet you. I was wondering if you had time tonight for us to come by and check the boat out, say hello. That kind of thing."

"What's he worried about?" Camaro asked.

"What do you mean?"

"I mean what's so important that he has to see me right now?"

"He's a real picky guy, that's all. Wants to make sure we have the right boat."

"Do *you* think you have the right boat?"

"Yeah, I think so. I think so. You know, there's some stuff I want to talk about, but we could maybe do that some other time. I don't know what kind of food you like."

"I told you: I'm not looking for any boyfriends," Camaro said. "You want to talk to me, you can call or stop by the marina. I'm around. And you still have a few days to schedule your charter."

"Will you be around in an hour?" Parker asked.

The marina was close now, the dense thicket of boats clearly visible in the dying sunlight. "I will. Come on by, and bring your client."

She hung up. On the aft deck the clients were all done taking their pictures and stood around glumly waiting for the charter to be done. The fun was over, and now there would be the drive home and tomorrow's pain from arms and necks that didn't get enough sunscreen.

They said their good-byes and tipped Camaro a hundred dollars, and then they were gone. Despite the time and the growing darkness, she hosed down the deck and set to cleaning up once again. What she did tonight she wouldn't have to do tomorrow.

She heard a deep-throated engine a half-hour later and climbed the flybridge to see out toward the parking lot. The yellow-and-black Charger was distinct under the lights. She recognized Parker when he got out, and saw the second man come from behind the wheel. The two walked together down the pier. When Parker saw her, he waved, but she did not wave back.

He stopped by the boat. He looked, as always, like a castaway on some beach in the Keys. The other man wore a short-sleeved shirt open over a white tank top and worn jeans that had light patches over the knees. His boots were steel toed and heavy. He watched her with critical eyes.

"Permission to come aboard?" Parker asked.

Camaro came down from the flybridge where she could be closer to the second man. When he looked at her, she looked back, and they went on like this until he blinked and glanced away. "I think you're good," she said finally.

She caught a moment of unhappiness on Parker's face, and then it submerged. "Camaro, this is Matt Clifford. He's one of my clients," he said. "Matt, this is Captain Espinoza."

"Nice to meet you," Matt said, and he held out a hand for her to shake. She took it. He was stronger than his frame suggested. "Parker said you had a nice boat. Sure looks good to me."

"She gets the job done," Camaro said.

"I was kind of hoping to see the whole thing."

Camaro hesitated. She sensed the old nerves from Parker again, but Matt was languid, at ease like a loosely coiled snake, his eyes hooded. He had tattoos coiled down his arms, some of them crude, done by amateurs. Prison ink. A long minute passed in silence. She beckoned him forward. "Come on then," she said.

They boarded, and Matt prowled the deck while Parker stood aside. Camaro watched only Matt as he poked a head into the cabin. "Real nice," Matt said at last. "Clean."

"I saw your ride," Camaro said. "The Charger. A '70?"

He looked at her sharply. "Yeah, that's right."

"Got a 440 under the hood."

"Yeah. You know cars?"

"Some cars."

"She's a classic," Matt said. "I restored her myself."

"That so?"

"That's so."

He stood still, and they looked at each other again until Matt broke the spell a second time. Camaro marked him as he began to walk the deck again, touching the rods on their rack, drifting a hand over the back of the fighting chair. She had Parker at her back, and he had not moved.

When Matt stopped, he did not look right at her, but past her. "I think you're gonna earn your ten thousand just fine," he said.

"What ten thousand?" Camaro asked.

"The ten thousand," Matt said. "Parker didn't tell you about the ten thousand?"

Camaro glanced back at Parker and saw him looking at his sandals. A muscle in her jaw flexed. "I didn't sign on for anything paying ten thousand," she said. "It's eight seventy-five for a one-night charter. You're going swordfishing."

"Right. Swordfishing," Matt said.

"Yeah," Camaro said, and she fixed him with her eyes so that he could not look away. "That's what I do. I take people out to fish. If you're looking for something else, you have the wrong boat and the wrong captain."

"Didn't he pay you a deposit?"

Camaro rooted around in her pocket until she found the folded bills. She counted off two hundred dollars and turned on Parker. "Give me your hand," she told him. He complied, and she thrust the money into it before looking back to Matt. "There's your money, and that's the way off the boat. I suggest the two of you go."

Matt put his hands up for peace. "Hey, listen, I'm just saying—"

"I don't give a shit *what* you're saying. Get off my boat. Now."

Parker spoke up. "We should go, Matt."

Matt's gaze flared, and for a moment Camaro thought he might round the fighting chair and take a swing at her. The tension was in his body, the lazy snake a hard spring. She dropped a foot back and settled her weight. The instant passed. "Okay, let's go," Matt said. "I'm sorry you wasted my time."

"Whatever," Camaro said.

They disembarked. Parker stole a glance in her direction, and she glared at him until he looked away. As they retreated down the pier, she felt pain in her hands and realized they were balled into fists. She forced the fingers to come apart.

After a minute the sound of the Charger's motor rolled down to her. Then they were gone.

CHAPTER NINE

Parker called her in the morning. She let it ring through to voice mail twice, but when he tried a third time she answered. "Fuck off," she told him.

"Wait, listen," he said, "I can explain."

"I'm not interested," Camaro said.

"Can you at least give me a chance?" Parker asked. "I'm asking for fifteen minutes. Hell, give me *ten* minutes! I can lay it all out for you, and if you're still a no, then I'll leave you alone, and you'll never hear from me again."

"Or I can hang up the phone and never hear from you again," Camaro said.

"Look, I'm not saying you owe me anything, but I thought maybe we had a connection the other day. All I need is a few minutes and that's it. I'll come by your boat if I have to."

Camaro looked around her kitchen. She took a knife from its block and held it in her fist reversed, edge out, and point down. She cut the air. "I have a gun, Parker."

"Please," Parker said.

She didn't say anything, and he was quiet. His breathing carried down the line, quick and nervous. The memory of him standing by while Matt walked the deck came to her unbidden, and the sense of his discomfort in the presence of the man he called his client. "Okay, I'll meet you," she said. "But if you're wasting my time, I will *not* be happy. Do you understand?"

"Absolutely. Where do you want to go?"

"The diner. I'll see you there around one o'clock."

"I'll be there."

There was time enough to work out on the back porch, but she chose to dress for running instead. Her neighborhood was nothing but mile after mile of flat ground and cheap little houses occupied by people who worked hard and lived paycheck to paycheck. Mostly Cuban families, speaking nothing but Spanish at home. When she went running, they would sometimes watch her from their yards as they watered their plants or simply sat in folding chairs letting time and the world slip by them. Their children played in the street, riding old bikes or kicking a ball around.

In the end she ran five miles and then soaked in the shower for twenty minutes. She dressed and took her bike to the diner. She arrived ten minutes early and got a booth without Parker, ordering two iced teas and telling the waitress to hold off on taking their order until she was sure she would stay.

"Blind date?" the waitress asked.

"Something like that," Camaro replied.

He came right on time and spotted her through the front window. If he'd worn a hat he would have held it in his hands as he approached the booth, but instead he was shamefaced and timid, and it made Camaro want to knock him over. She pointed him into his seat.

He started immediately. "Thank you for seeing me," he said.

Camaro looked at her watch. "It's one minute past one," she said, and she turned the bezel to mark ten minutes. "When we hit eleven minutes, I walk out that door unless you have something amazing to tell me."

She expected an argument. He gave her none. "Okay," he said.

"Start."

"I'm not a business consultant," Parker said.

"No kidding."

"I had to tell you *something*."

"How about the truth?" Camaro said.

Parker began to tear open sugar packets, one after the other, and dump them into his tea. "The truth is that I'm thirty-four years old, and I'm a convicted felon. Now I don't know if you know what that means exactly, but if you're a felon in this state, you have about zero things going for you. People don't hire you, you can't vote...all of that."

"What were you in for?" Camaro asked.

"Motor vehicle theft. I did five years. That's when Matt and I crossed paths. He was on his way out, and I was on my way in. We did some time together."

"Tell me about your daughter."

"My daughter's name is Lauren," Parker said, and the name sounded like a plea. "She's fourteen. Just like I said. With her mother out of the picture, I worked my ass off to get custody of her after I got out of prison. She was living in foster care, but now she's with me. She's everything I have."

Camaro thought of the little girl in the photograph. The laughter and the gusting wind that caught her hair. She leaned forward, and she saw Parker withdraw the same distance. "I'm gonna tell you something," Camaro said. "I have a history of getting caught up in things that end up going the wrong way, so I don't need to get involved in some ex-con's scam, whatever it is. You worked hard to get your daughter back? I worked hard to get what I have, and I'm working hard to keep it. So if you're looking for someone to run drugs or something, you can stop talking right now and go."

Parker chewed the inside of his lip. "It's not drugs," he said.

"But it's a crime," Camaro said.

"Not really. Not when you think about it."

Camaro slapped a hand down on the table and made the glasses jump. People looked their way, and she glared at them until they turned back to their own business. She spoke quietly. "I said no bullshit. It's a crime or it's not. Which is it?"

"Okay, it's a crime. But it's not what you think. We're not smuggling drugs or guns or anything like that. We're bringing in a person. It's an escape from Cuba. This guy is desperate, and he has to get out of the country. Some people are willing to pay us good money to get him out of there and back to Miami in one piece."

"Cuba," Camaro said.

"That's right."

"Why not just leave on a plane? People can do that now, right?"

"It's a whole thing. The government has a say in who's allowed to come and go. They'll never let him leave."

"So he has to go out in secret."

"That's right."

"How much are they paying?"

"A hundred thousand dollars. We got fifty up front, and we get the rest on delivery. So you're getting ten percent just for driving the boat. It's in and out. We don't see anybody, and nobody sees us."

Camaro caught the waitress' eye and nodded. She saw the woman take up two menus and head their way. Parker ignored his when the waitress put it down. He watched Camaro's face with desperate eyes. She picked up her menu and looked at it carefully. "You ever been to Cuba?" she asked Parker without looking at him.

"No."

"You ever run the waters between Miami and Cuba? At all?"

"No."

Now she fixed him with her gaze. "So how the hell do you know it'll be as simple as scooting in and scooting out? Is that your whole plan?"

"Well, yeah," Parker said.

"Jesus, you guys are in trouble," Camaro said.

"That's why we need an expert!" Parker said quickly. "Somebody who can captain a boat and keep it on the down low! I bet you've been halfway to Cuba more than once or twice. What's a few more miles?"

"It's over two hundred miles to Cuba from Miami," Camaro said. "How far out do you think I go?"

"You see? We need expertise! You're smart, and you know what's up. With you on board, we can get this done no problem."

Camaro put her menu down and folded her hands on top of it. "Parker, I'm not interested."

"Please," he said. "I have to go back to Matt with something."

"If you have to go back to Matt, you need to go back to him and tell him to get the hell out of your life," Camaro said. "Anybody can tell he's bad news."

"You don't understand," Parker said. "I need the money his deal is going to earn us. I can't find work, and if I don't get a job I'm not going to be able to keep a roof over my head. I'll lose my house, and then I'll lose Lauren all over again. That can't happen. This is my big chance to land some serious money."

"How much is your end?" Camaro asked.

"About twenty-three grand."

"That won't last."

"It's something, and that's more than I have right now. I'm already a month behind on rent."

Camaro flagged the waitress down a second time. "On second thought, I'm just going to take the drinks," she said. "Can I pay for them right now?"

"Sure," the waitress said, and she waited as Camaro peeled off a few bills. Out of the corner of her eye, Camaro could see Parker reddening behind his tan. She hoped he would not cry.

"I'm going to go," Camaro told him when the waitress was gone.

"Camaro, I'm begging you."

She paused. "I'm not saying no," she said.

"What are you saying?"

"I'm saying I'll think about it."

"Camaro, I have to be able to tell Matt something. If I don't have anything to tell Matt, he's—"

"You worry about *me,* not Matt," Camaro said. "I'm the one who matters right now."

Parker nodded, attentive. "Right, right. I'll hold off on telling him anything until you make up your mind. But if he asks, can I say you're interested? Maybe I can get him to swing a few thousand more."

"I'm not looking for more money," Camaro said.

"What *are* you looking for?"

"A reason not to say no. I'll call you, Parker."

She got up to leave, and Parker caught her by the wrist. She gave him a look that made him let go as if his hand were burned. "I'm sorry," he said. "I just wanted to say... this is for Lauren. I don't care if you think I'm some kind of ex-con bum, but I have a little girl, and she needs me. I'm all she has."

"I'm going," Camaro said. And she left.

CHAPTER TEN

In his head, Parker turned over the time in the diner again and again on his way back to the house. He regretted putting his hand on her most of all. She was the kind of woman who let a man touch her only when she allowed it. He had violated an unspoken rule. They were not so close.

He imagined saying things a different way, and he considered arguments that hadn't occurred to him in the minutes he sat opposite her. Sometimes he could tell what she thought and other times she was closed. Today she had been a whirlwind of both, and he felt bewildered even trying to tell them apart. She demanded the whole truth from him. He could only give her what he knew.

Matt's Charger was on the curb in front of the house when he pulled onto his street. Parker's hands closed around the steering wheel, and the plastic squeaked in his grip. He nosed in behind the car and parked. Matt was not sitting in the driver's seat. There was no one in the car at all.

His hand shook slightly as he used his keys on the front door. He came through into the short hallway that opened onto the front room, and Matt was there on the couch with Lauren beside him. "Hey, it's the man," Matt said.

"What are you doing here?" Parker asked.

"What kind of a question is that? I came by to talk. Lauren let me in. She's been telling me about school. Man, I don't miss school *at all.* I couldn't wait to drop out."

Parker closed the door. "Lauren, why don't you go to your room?"

Lauren got up from the couch, and Matt reached out as if to catch her hand, but he touched only air. "Bye, Uncle Matt," she said.

"See you later, sweetie," Matt said. He looked to Parker. "Wow, she is really growing up, isn't she? Getting curves and everything. I don't envy you one bit, bro. Guys are gonna be all over her."

Parker swallowed. "Do you want a beer?" he asked.

"A beer? Sure thing."

He retreated to the kitchen and fetched two bottles from the refrigerator. Back in the front room he handed one over to Matt, and then he sat down in a chair to pull from his own. The cold, clean liquid helped clear the sticky taste from his mouth. "What did you want to talk about?" he asked at last.

Matt drank slowly, his eyes going lidded as he tipped his head back. "Last night for starters," he said when he was done. "About that chick you said was going to work out for us."

"About that...," Parker said. "I think there's still a chance we can get her. I talked to her again today, and she knows the deal now."

"But?"

"Well, I think she wants more money."

"Don't we all."

"I'm saying that she's taking a pretty big risk, what with it being her boat and all. It's a long way to Cuba and back, and a lot can go wrong. She deserves a little extra."

Matt laughed a little and drank some more. "I should have known it was all about the cash. She put on that whole act last night, but it was just a chick thing. They tell you one thing, but they mean something else. Only problem is, if she gets more money then there's less to go around to the rest of us."

"Yeah, I know, but—"

"But nothing. Do *you* want her to get a bigger cut?"

"I think it's fair."

"Fine," Matt said.

Parker stopped with the bottle halfway to his mouth. He lowered it. "Fine?"

"Sure. Fine. Only the extra comes out of your end, not everybody else's."

"Hey, I'm not getting that much already."

"So? You said it was fair that she get more, so you ought to pay. *I'm* not gonna pay. The deal is for ten grand and that's it. Whatever else is from your pocket. End of story."

Parker drank. His stomach was unsettled. He had eaten no lunch, and he was now pouring beer on top of nothing. It was hot in the house. "I'll try to talk her down," he said.

"Ah, see? When it's your money it's different, right? And tell her this, too: if I don't get a yes or no in two days, we're moving on to somebody else. She's out."

"I'll tell her."

Matt drained the bottle and put it on the floor by his feet. He rose from the couch. "And now I got to go. Get that bitch on board, all right? No more delays."

"Okay, Matt. It'll be all good. She likes me."

"It'd be better if she liked ten thousand bucks. See you around, bro."

Parker stayed in his seat, and Matt let himself out. He finished his beer, though he had no taste for it, and then he collected Matt's empty. He put both in the recycling bin in the kitchen.

"Dad?"

Lauren appeared at the door and leaned against the frame. She played with her hair the way she did when she was nervous. Parker went to her and hugged her. "Are you okay?" he asked.

"I shouldn't have let him in."

"It's all right. He didn't . . . do anything, did he?"

"No! Nothing. He's just a creep."

Parker stroked her hair. "Yeah, he's a creep. I know. But he's gone now."

CHAPTER ELEVEN

IGNACIO MONTELLANO APPRAISED the sandwich before him. It was pressed and still hot, layers of ham and roasted pork and cheese and pickles all laid in precisely as they should be. The thing was big, a two-handed affair if it hadn't been sliced down the middle, and he was prepared to wash it down with a large Diet Coke.

He sat in the detective's bullpen, his desk among a broad gathering of other desks. Most were empty for the lunch hour, but there were a few holdouts that took their meals in front of their computers, catching up on work or simply fooling around on the Internet. Ignacio was not a workaholic, so he did not touch his caseload during the appointed sixty minutes, but he felt more comfortable in the A/C in his own chair than he did eating behind the wheel of his idling car.

The first bite was perfection, flavors blending into flavors, the sour pickle kick-starting a new flow of saliva. He chewed thoughtfully, in no hurry to see the moment pass, before finally swallowing. A hit from the straw in his Coke cleansed his palate for the next mouthful.

He saw Pool coming with a plastic bag from Subway. Pool caught his eye and angled his way. "Hey, Nacho," Pool said. "How's it going?"

"Fine," Ignacio said. "How about you?"

"Good, good. You know, if you keep eating stuff like that, you're gonna pop."

"I have a good healthy weight."

"Yeah. Okay. Listen, I didn't catch you this morning before I had to head out on that robbery-homicide with Elmore. I had something I wanted to tell you."

"What?" Ignacio asked.

"You'll never guess who I saw yesterday when I was on my way home."

"Who?"

"Matt Clifford."

Ignacio put the sandwich down. "Are you sure it was him?"

"Oh, definitely. I saw him walking out of a 7-Eleven with a Slurpee. He could use the sugar, too, because he's as thin as he always was. Hasn't put on a pound as far as I could tell."

"Whereabouts did you see him?"

"I can write down the address for you."

"Yeah, would you do that?"

"No problem."

Pool left him, and Ignacio turned to his computer. He plugged in CLIFFORD, MATTHEW, and after a second he was looking at the booking photo of the man himself. Matt stared out of the screen as if he was challenging the camera, and maybe he was. He was that kind of guy.

A string of charges and convictions stretched out beneath his vitals. Ignacio scanned these, less interested in the closed cases than in the one left open. He found it and clicked the folder open. Immediately details leaped to mind, though they were four years out of date. The pawnshop and the three dead men inside: Joel Berlanga, Gerard Castanada, and Julián Moscoso. Berlanga was the one found by the open and empty safe, a single bullet in the back of his skull. Moscoso had been bludgeoned to death with a heavy object, probably a baseball bat. And Castanada had been shot through the heart. Three gone and no witnesses. Even the security cameras' tapes had been taken.

Pool returned with an address scribbled on a Post-it. Ignacio looked at it. "This is way out in Hollywood," he said.

"Yeah, I know."

"Now I have to get them involved."

"Not if you're only asking around. Besides, I have one better."

"What?"

Pool produced a second Post-it. "This is Clifford's address, fresh from the DMV. He registered a 1970 Dodge Charger and listed this as his place of residence. I don't know where a guy like him gets the money to buy a classic like that, but I can guess. You want it?"

"Of course I want it," Ignacio said. "Give it to me."

Pool held the paper out of Ignacio's reach. "I want you to pick up a shift for me on the weekend. It's my nephew's birthday, and I want to be there for a change. You'll have to pull a double."

Ignacio scowled. "You want to skip out for a kiddie party?"

"I told you: it's my nephew. He's nine."

"Okay, fine. Give it here."

The Post-it swapped hands, and Ignacio looked it over. "This isn't anywhere near Hollywood. What's he doing at a 7-Eleven over that way?"

"I heard Jackson Dewey has a place there. Clifford might be putting the old gang back together. Worth checking out."

"Yeah," Ignacio said absently. He folded the Post-its in half and put them in his breast pocket. "Thanks, Brady."

"Anything for Nacho. Enjoy the sandwich, pal."

"Right."

When Pool left, Ignacio turned back to his meal, but his eyes drifted away to the computer monitor, where Matt Clifford kept on staring. Ignacio made a gun with his thumb and forefinger and mimed shooting the man in the face. Click-click. Boom.

The sandwich tasted that much better when he took another bite.

CHAPTER TWELVE

SHE DID NOT have any charters that day, so Camaro slept in before going for her workout. When she was done, she looked out over the lawn and made up her mind to see to it. After changing into work clothes, she hauled out the old gas-powered lawnmower the landlord included with the house and pulled the starter cord a dozen times before the engine caught. The mower was junk when she found it, and it was hardly better now, but time with a tool kit had coaxed it into some semblance of life. Camaro started in the back and then, in a fit of ambition, mowed the front yard, too.

When she was finished, Camaro went inside and stood in front of the air-conditioning unit in the window until she stopped sweating. After that she went to the little room she'd made an office and sat at her computer. It was locked with a password and she punched it in before navigating to the Internet. A search turned up a long list of sites that did background checks. She chose the top hit and clicked through.

It was as simple as inputting the name *Parker Story* in the search box and weeding out the ones that clearly weren't right. There was only one Parker Story in Miami. The site promised her a photograph and a full report on the subject if she paid twenty-five dollars. Camaro arranged for a debit from her bank account, and then she was in.

His full name was Parker David Story and he was thirty-four as he said. His former spouse was Melanie Artis Story and the grounds for their divorce had been abandonment. There was only the one child, Lauren Victoria Story, and she was fourteen.

The site went on to list Parker's convictions, up to and including his time for motor vehicle theft. It even provided the locations where he'd been incarcerated. His current address was listed, as were the registration of his beater of a pickup truck and his employment record, which was patchwork.

Camaro leaned back in her chair and looked at Parker's driver's license photo once again. He looked disheveled and half-awake. There was no photo for Lauren because she was a minor, so there was no telling what the little girl on the beach had grown into.

After a while she got up and paced the small office, pausing only to nudge the mouse when the computer went to a screen saver. She looked at Parker's image from all angles before sitting down once more and reading through all the information the site provided, including every address where he'd lived for the past fifteen years. He never stayed in one place for long. He had been sued for back rent in civil court ten times.

"Goddamn it," Camaro said out loud.

She closed the browser and left the house with the keys to her bike in her hand. Out on the road with the wind in her face she could think a little better, away from the stuffiness and the closed walls of the office. Maybe she would go out on the boat, though the day was already more than halfway gone.

Parker tagged along in the back of her mind, with the sad, sorry tale of his life drifting out behind him.

CHAPTER THIRTEEN

"Be sure you eat all those green beans," Parker told Lauren.

Lauren poked at the French-cut green beans on her plate, and her expression was doubtful. "Why are they so *crunchy?*"

"It's because they're fresh," Parker said. "I didn't get them out of a can this time."

"I like them out of the can."

"There's too much salt in that. This is healthier. Eat. And don't forget your meatloaf, either. I gave you the end-piece special."

"Okay."

They had spent the day trapped in the house, with nowhere to go and nothing to do. Parker considered the beach because he always enjoyed the beach, but Lauren had shut herself up with her journal and said she wasn't interested in getting skin cancer. That had been enough conversation.

He escaped only once, to walk to the local convenience store and get the day's paper. He spread the classifieds out on the table and pored over them with a ballpoint pen, looking for likely listings and circling them, no matter what they might be. Only when he was done with that did he turn to the rest of the paper and read the actual news. None of it pertained to people like him, and even sports news did not excite him the way it used to. He read only to have something to do and not because it held any real meaning.

Eventually, he told Lauren he would be back, and he went to the grocery store. He bought the little bit he could afford with cash and his allowance from SNAP. In a moment of something like responsibility, he chose the green beans Lauren would later complain about and got a cheap metal steamer to prepare them in. The ground beef for the meatloaf was going to expire that day, so the store had it marked down. It was good enough for him.

The smells of food lured Lauren out of her room at last, but there was little talking at the table. Parker knew she wanted to ask him about jobs, and he knew he didn't want to talk about it. Tomorrow he would make all the calls, drive to all the places, fill out all the applications. Whatever it took. Today he wanted time.

"Did Uncle Matt call?" Lauren asked him.

"No," Parker said.

"Good."

There was nothing else to be said about it. Lauren finished the rest of her green beans with reluctance and cleared her plate of the meatloaf. She went to the kitchen and put her dishes in the sink, then went to the front room to watch television. Parker was alone at the table. He did not want to eat the last of his green beans, either, but he did it anyway.

He rinsed the dishes and dried them and put them away. His phone vibrated in his pocket and then rang. It was not Matt. He answered and Camaro spoke. He felt a sudden lightness at the sound of her voice, and he tried not to let it seep into his. "I wasn't sure you'd call," he said.

"I'm calling," Camaro said.

"Did you give any thought to what I said?"

"I did."

"And what do you say?"

"How much do you love your daughter?" Camaro asked him.

Parker walked to the kitchen door. From here he could just see the television, but not Lauren on the couch. "More than anything," he said. "She's my life."

"Then what are you doing? Do you *want* to go back to prison?"

"I'm not going back," Parker said. "Never."

"You act like you get a choice," Camaro said.

"Right now the choice is yours. Are you going to help me or aren't you?" A long silence carried over the phone. Parker checked to see if they were still connected. "Hello?"

"I'm here."

"I have to know," Parker said.

"I'm going to do it," Camaro said.

"Thank you, I just—"

"I'm not finished. I know you're in a spot. I've been in a spot before, so I know what that's like. But that's not why I'm going to help you. I'm helping you out because of your daughter. That's all. I'm not a part of your crew or whatever you have going on. I do this and then I'm out. I don't want to know anything about what happens after that, and I don't want to hear from you again."

"You're saving my life," Parker said.

"You need new friends," Camaro told him. "The ones you have are going to bring you down. If you love your daughter as much as you say you do, you're not going to let that happen."

"Never," Parker said.

"I'm going to hang up now. You call me when you have a date and a time. If you make me wait too long, I'm out. You try to add anything new to the job, I'm out. I take you to Cuba and back, you give me ten thousand dollars. Understand?"

"Yes, I understand."

"Good-bye, Parker."

"Good-bye, Camaro," Parker said, but she had hung up already.

CHAPTER FOURTEEN

IGNACIO SET UP on Matt Clifford's address early in the morning, when the sun was only a blister over the Atlantic. Clifford lived in a three-story apartment building shaped like a U, open into the center, where an overgrown forest of tropical plants ruled. The apartment was in the back corner on the second floor but was still visible from the street.

Ignacio was technically off the clock, but morning was the best time for catching bad guys. They stayed up late and rose late, so a cop could always tell where a suspect was likely to be: sprawled out in bed sleeping off the night before.

He decided to wait until eight o'clock to knock on Clifford's door and put on the radio to Mega 94.9 without cranking up the volume. A slow thread of traffic proceeded down the street, at first washing Ignacio with their headlights and then simply passing as the day brightened. Finally, the streetlights went out, and it was nearly time.

Matt Clifford's door opened at ten minutes to eight, and Ignacio sat up in his seat.

The man was not Clifford, but Ignacio knew who he was. He recognized the short, broad figure and the rolling gait of the man, even though his features were indistinct. Ignacio took a legal pad from the seat next to him and scribbled down a notation: *Sandro Soto—7:50am—leaving.*

In his mind he brought up Soto's sheet. It was long and detailed, covering a whole panoply of criminal activity, starting at Soto's eighteenth birthday and extending into his thirties. There were more crimes in his juvenile years, but those were officially sealed when Soto became an adult. Ignacio was not supposed to be able to see them, but there were ways.

Soto went down the steps to the ground floor, and Ignacio lost him in the leaves and branches of the courtyard. When Soto reappeared, he was walking quickly, dressed in jeans and a salmon-colored wife-beater with a beach scene printed on the back and front. He went to a car parked on the street, and the headlights flashed as he used the key fob to unlock the doors. Ignacio scribbled more on his pad: make and model and the license plate number.

He let Soto go. The man drove by within ten feet of him and saw nothing, his own radio cranked so loud that it boomed on the quiet morning street. Ignacio made a face at the racket and switched off his own radio.

A few minutes passed, and Matt Clifford did not emerge. Ignacio let his watch tick over to eight o'clock, and then he got out of the car with his legal pad tucked under his arm. He left his car unlocked. If someone stole it, the insurance was worth more than the vehicle.

The whole apartment building was still as Ignacio mounted the steps to the second floor. The air seemed pent up, a held breath, and it released only when Ignacio pounded on Clifford's door with his fist. "Police!" Ignacio announced. "Police! Open the door!"

No one came right away, so Ignacio used his keys to rap on the apartment's front window. The curtains were closed, and he could not see in. He went back to the door and pounded again, harder this time, until he heard the lock turn.

Clifford opened the door and squinted out at Ignacio. The sun angled directly into his face, and Ignacio saw his lids were red-rimmed and his skin was slightly pallid and blotchy. A hard night had passed into unforgiving morning. "What the hell, man?" he asked.

Ignacio smiled the largest smile he could muster. "Matt! It *is* you! You know, they told me you were back in town, but I didn't believe them. But here you are, and here I am talking to you! I didn't wake you up, did I?"

"Of course you woke me up, asshole," Clifford said. "Go away."

"Hey, now, let's not call each other names," Ignacio said.

"Okay. Just go away, then."

Clifford moved to close the door, but Ignacio blocked it with his foot. He put his hand on the door's face and pushed until it had opened wide enough to reveal Clifford's shirtless body and his long, gangly legs bare beneath the tight swaddling of white cotton briefs. There were some new tattoos on his belly and chest. "I think you and I need to have a little talk," Ignacio said. "So how about it?"

"Fine. Come in. Whatever."

The man stepped aside, and Ignacio moved into the front room. Cheap furniture that likely came with the apartment was scattered around, old and plaid. The television was a new flat screen, and Clifford owned a game console. Ignacio swept his gaze around the room, picking up the plastic wrapper on the coffee table that might have held a little crystal, the discarded fast-food bags around the couch, and the wall clock that was stopped at three thirty. The air was stagnant and smelled of smoke. There was a bare pillow on one end of the couch and an indifferently folded sheet. "Really great place you have," Ignacio said. "I like it."

Clifford only mumbled and stumbled off to the bedroom. Ignacio circled the room, peering into the dining nook at the table scattered with gun and car magazines, a layer of newspaper, and a half-completed model of a Ford Fairlane. The kitchen was spotless, as if it were never used, though the trash can overflowed with beer bottles.

After a few minutes Clifford returned with clothes thrown over his body, though he was barefoot on the carpet. "This is harassment, man," he said.

"It isn't harassment yet," Ignacio said. "Give it time."

The man flopped down on the couch. He gathered up a pack of cigarettes from between the cushion and the back of the couch and lit a smoke with a lighter from his pocket. "I didn't think I'd ever see you again," he said.

"I didn't think so, either. You left town in a big hurry and didn't leave a forwarding address," Ignacio said. "Mind if I sit down?"

"Do what you want."

"You know, we never did clear that case," Ignacio said. "The pawnshop. It's still open."

"That's too bad."

"Yeah, it is. Because I have to start looking into it again now that my prime suspect's decided to show his face in Miami. You *do* know you're my prime suspect, right?"

Clifford nodded and took a drag. He exhaled through his nose. "I kind of figured."

"There are still a whole lot of questions. In fact, here's one: what are you doing for money? Because I did some checking, and you haven't filed for income taxes in all the time you were out of town. Which means you never had a legit job. Of course, with what you took from that safe, you could live for four years easy, assuming you didn't spend it all in one place."

"I didn't take anything from anybody's safe. And I do construction for cash. It pays the bills."

Ignacio snorted. "Construction? Matt, you weigh a buck fifty soaking wet. I don't see you swinging a hammer for a living."

"What can I say? I also got a little money from my great-uncle. He died and left me something."

"Got any record of that?"

Clifford waved vaguely. "I'll ask my secretary to check the files."

Ignacio wrote on his pad. He felt Clifford watching. "So you're going with the 'I came into some money' thing, huh?"

"It's the truth. What are you writing?"

"Don't worry about it. Hey, have you seen Sandro or Jackson lately? I've missed those guys. They kind of dropped off the earth, too."

"Can't say that I have."

"See, now that's too bad," Ignacio said.

"What is?"

"I can take you lying to me, Matt, but not about stuff I can check. Like Sandro coming out of your place this morning. Sleeping on your couch. Maybe smoking a little crank with you."

"I don't smoke crystal anymore."

"Good for you." Ignacio poised his pen above the paper. "So let's cut the bullshit and get real, okay? I'm going to ask you questions, and you're going to give me answers. Maybe we can clear up some of what we missed out on four years ago."

Clifford watched Ignacio through a trickle of smoke. "You can ask," he said.

"Okay. Let's start."

CHAPTER FIFTEEN

CAMARO SPENT THREE days running charters in and out of the marina and tried to put Parker and his friend out of her mind. There were other things to do, and she refused to worry, and so the time passed and she was satisfied.

On the fourth day, Parker called to tell her that it was on. "Matt wants to have a meeting first. Everybody on the boat. You can meet us, and we can meet you."

"Okay. When?"

"Tomorrow night. After dark."

"When are we going out for the real thing?" Camaro asked.

"Friday night. Is that too soon?"

"It isn't for me if it isn't for you."

"Good. I'll see you, Camaro."

She stayed on the boat all of the next day, taking her meals in the cabin. When the sun began to fall, she checked herself. In one boot she kept a karambit, but in the other she holstered a Glock 38. It was a compact pistol chambered in .45 GAP, and it held a single stack of eight rounds. With the leg of her pants down over it, the bulge could barely be seen. If she needed it, it was there.

Behind a panel just inside the cabin was a large first aid kit stocked for serious injury, but there was room enough for more. Here she placed a Mossberg 590 Cruiser, a 12-gauge shotgun with a pistol grip that could be laid diagonally in the space with the panel secured over it. She loaded it with five rounds of double-ought buckshot. Boxes of ammo for pistol and shotgun were located in a compartment below one of the galley seats.

It was not long after dark when she heard the Charger's engine. She took up her spot on the flybridge and saw Parker with his truck beside the yellow-jacket Dodge. Two men got out of the Charger with Matt Clifford. One was built low to the ground, like a piece of earthmoving equipment, and the other was simply big. Matt moved with smooth confidence, chest out and shoulders back. He led the others with his body, trailing them in his wake in eddies.

She waited until they were close before she spoke. "Come on aboard," she said.

They stepped over the side and onto the back deck. Camaro surveyed them from where she was. The short one was Latino and dark, the big one a ruddy-faced strawberry blond. Parker was with them and apart from them, and she saw in his eyes a needful look she found she did not want to deny.

"You coming down from there?" Matt asked.

Camaro descended to the deck and stood before them. Of the men, only the Latino was eye level with her. Matt stood taller than her by six inches or more, and so did the other. Both tall men leaned in to make themselves larger. She did not step back. "Who are your friends?" she asked.

Matt pointed to the Latino. "Sandro. And this is Jackson."

"You're all coming along?"

"Yeah. Is that a problem?"

"The boat can handle ten," Camaro said.

"Good."

"Parker tells me that you're carrying one man."

"That's right. One guy."

"I won't bring this boat into any port," Camaro said. "That's closer than I'll go."

"Don't worry about it. The Cubans are going to bring this guy out to us. You won't have to go closer than ten or twelve miles offshore."

"Where?"

"You have charts?"

"Yeah."

"Let's see them."

Camaro and Matt went into the cabin, and Camaro brought charts that marked the coastline of Cuba. She spread them on the galley counter and switched on the overhead lights to shine directly down upon them. Their heads cast shadows as Matt traced his fingers along the land. Camaro glanced away once and saw Parker watching from the outside. She gave him a black look, and he moved off.

"It's here," Matt said finally. "Right here."

He showed her a spot about one hundred fifty miles east of Havana, off the place called the Baños de Elguea. There were many little islands off the coast there, but open seas beyond. Camaro marked the distance from shore to the waters beyond. Twelve miles kept her safely clear of the bay. "They can bring him out that far?" she asked.

"Yeah. It's all going to happen out there. They come to us, make the exchange, and we each go our merry ways. Done and done."

"What about Cuban patrols?"

"The Cubans say they won't be around. They're bribed off the spot for the night."

"And if they're not?"

"You're an American. What are they going to do except tell you to get the hell out of their waters?" Matt asked. "It's not like they're gonna haul you in."

Camaro looked at him. "You don't know what they'll do. They could force us to dock in Cuba, they could board us . . . there are lots of options. If the government in Cuba really doesn't want this guy leaving the country, this could still easily turn into something fast."

"Well, let's hope that doesn't happen, okay?"

"You hope. I want guarantees."

Matt straightened up sharply and nearly clipped his head on the ceiling. He ducked and glared and tried to lean into her again. Camaro put up a hand, and he stepped back. "What do you want?" he asked. "They wouldn't be paying us this kind of money if it was a cakewalk! You're getting paid good money to play taxicab, so don't be giving me any static. We go in, we pick the guy up, and we *leave*. No one's going to be boarding anybody."

Camaro did not raise her voice. "Let's get one thing straight right now: I'm skipper. Not one of your crew. And if you treat me like I am, I'll park this boat halfway to Cuba and push you over the side. Without this boat, you can't go anywhere or do anything. You know it, and *I* know it. So can the shit."

She could see the retort spinning around inside of him, wanting to be given voice, but Matt's lips merely quivered. In the end he smiled and raised his hands for peace. "Okay, okay. I'm sorry I got a little carried away. It's the stress, you know?"

"Let me talk to Parker."

"He doesn't—"

Camaro cut him off with a look. The corner of Matt's mouth curled, but he turned away and climbed up to the aft deck. She heard him speaking in low tones to the others, and then Parker descended. "What's up?" he asked.

"Close it," Camaro said.

Parker shut the wooden door. When he looked at her again, she saw fear. "What is it?" he asked her.

"How solid is this?" Camaro asked. "Is this guy blowing smoke, or is there really going to be a boat out there to meet us?"

"It's going to be there," Parker said. "Absolutely. This is a done deal."

"Who are we picking up?"

Parker peeked out through the window in the door. No one was watching. He moved to the counter and spread his hands across the charts. The shadow of his fingers fell on the rendezvous point off the Cuban coast. "I don't know a whole lot. From what Matt tells me, he's some kind of big deal. Maybe he's a Cuban official, maybe he's some rich guy...I don't know. All I *do* know is that these people in Miami are willing to pay top dollar to bring him here. And that's all that matters, right? What the client pays for? Isn't that how you work?"

Camaro stood opposite him. "I keep things together by not letting them get out of hand," she said. "When I can't handle something, I step back. I get the feeling your friend Matt would step into a nest of rattlesnakes if he thought there was a buck in it. And he'd take all the rest of you with him."

"It's a good deal," Parker said, and his voice turned pleading. "Matt says it's easy money, and so far that's true. They gave us fifty grand up front just to sign on. If you want, I can get you the ten thousand right now. Whatever it takes to keep you on board."

"I'm going to tell you, and I want you to tell your friend," Camaro said. "Are you listening?"

"Yeah, I'm listening. Whatever you want."

"As long as you people are on my boat, you do what I say. If I feel like we're going too far, I'll turn around and head back to port. There are a lot of miles between here and Cuba, and that water is full of ships and helicopters and planes and drones and who knows what the hell else. I don't want the money up front. I don't want any money at all if this goes sideways. I'd rather have my boat and my business than your ten thousand."

"I understand completely."

"Good. Now go make your friends understand."

"I will," Parker said. He reached out and took her hand, but when he saw her face he dropped it. "Sorry."

"Don't be sorry. Be smart," Camaro said, and she looked to the charts. "Tell your buddies to leave. I'll be ready when it's time."

CHAPTER SIXTEEN

On that Friday Camaro had a charter for seven, and the fish came in steadily all morning and into the early afternoon, when it was time to turn back. They were a well-behaved group and enthusiastically took pictures of everything in sight, from one another to the boat to Camaro herself. She would have declined the shots they snapped of her, but they were polite about it, and she decided it would do no harm. By this time tomorrow she might be on Facebook, but that was the risk she took by living a public life.

She brought the group ashore and took the boat for refueling. The trip to Cuba was a long one, and it would not do to let the tanks run dry. Then they would be adrift, and the Coast Guard would have to be called in, and there would be questions and more questions, none of which they would be able to answer truthfully.

Tonight there would be no sleep, so she napped in the bed in the bow. It was only the sound of Parker's voice that stirred her awake. She sat bolt upright, alert to the closed cabin around her.

"Hello?" Parker called again. "Anybody on board?"

Camaro checked her watch and saw that it was only three thirty. They were not set to be underway until five o'clock. She got up and peered through the window on the pier side. Parker was there alone.

On the deck again, she saw that Parker had a rod and a tackle box. In his sunglasses and with his tan, he might have been any one of the people in her morning charter. There was no subterfuge about him.

"Hey," he said.

"You're early," Camaro said.

"I couldn't wait anymore. I have nerves, I guess. Do you mind?"

"No. Come aboard."

Parker did, and he set his rod in one of the side holders. He tucked his tackle box in the corner near the bait locker. Afterward, he stood awkwardly in front of Camaro, anxious with his hands. "I brought my stuff," he said unnecessarily.

Camaro inspected his rod. It was good for sea fishing and seemed like it had seen use. "Nice one," she said. "You didn't tell me you did much deep-water fishing."

"I don't," Parker said. "I got that one used from the classifieds. Only cost me a hundred bucks. It's good, huh?"

"You got a deal," Camaro said.

"Awesome. It's too bad I won't get a chance to use it."

Camaro nodded, but said nothing. She crouched down beside Parker's tackle box and opened it, rummaging through the lures and hooks. Unlike the rod, most of these weren't what he'd need, but if someone wasn't paying much attention, it would seem like everything was in order. That would have to be good enough.

"You're real thorough," Parker said.

"I try to be."

Parker tried to find a place out of the sun. He leaned against the slick white side of the cabin and played a finger along the darkened glass of the window. "Think we can go below?" he asked.

"It's the wrong time to ask for that," Camaro said.

"No, I didn't mean it like that. It's just hot out here. I could use something cold if you've got it."

"There are water bottles in the fridge."

"Perfect."

They went below, and Camaro fetched out a half-liter plastic bottle of water. Cracking the cap, Parker guzzled half of it all at once, then wiped his mouth with the back of his hand. His forehead was speckled with sweat.

The couch beside the galley counter was open, and Parker took a spot. Camaro sat down with him, and they watched each other for a while, saying nothing. It was Camaro who spoke. "Are you worried about something in particular?" she asked.

"No, nothing in particular. Only everything," Parker said, and he tried a smile that quickly died. "You know."

"How'd you even get involved in this?" Camaro asked. "It's not your thing."

Parker shook his head slowly. He uncapped the water and pulled on the bottle. "I don't know," he said. "I kind of got sucked into it. Matt's like that. He's got gravity, like a black hole or something. You get in with him, and he carries you the rest of the way."

"How much time did you serve together?"

He finished his bottle and crushed it in his hand. "We served a year and a half together in the South Bay Correctional Facility. He was in for armed robbery, and I was doing my stretch for the car theft. They put us in a cell together and, I don't know, we got along. We kept in touch after we got out."

"How many jobs have you pulled together?"

"That's the funny thing," Parker said. "This is the first time we've ever done it. Sandro, you met him, he's Matt's go-to guy. Jackson, too. They were all together on some stuff before I even came into the picture. Matt had to skip town a few years ago in front of some trouble, and they all scattered. But I guess you can't stay gone forever."

"Why bring you in at all?" Camaro asked.

"Because I'm the trustworthy one," Parker said. "Sandro and Jackson might be tight with Matt, but he doesn't trust them more than he has to. He knew I would hold the money and wouldn't run with it. So he gave it to me, and I did what he said."

"Sometimes the guy holding the money is the first one to get hurt," Camaro said.

Camaro heard footsteps on the pier outside, and a glance through the window showed Matt, Sandro, and Jackson. They, too, came bearing rods for fishing they weren't prepared to do, but they did not wait for permission to come aboard. She watched them mill around on the aft deck, putting away their rods. They'd brought a brilliant yellow cooler and set it down heavily.

Out on the deck, Camaro looked them over. They were dressed right, like Parker, and Matt wore a cap that kept his unruly hair in place. Their rods were brand new and cheap, the kind that could break if a hundred-pound swordfish got on the line.

"Captain," Matt said, "your crew is here."

"You're my charter, not my crew," Camaro said. "I'm the crew."

"Whatever. We're here. Anytime you want to cast off, we're ready."

She took time to examine each man in turn, and they looked back at her. Finally she nodded. "Okay. Let's go. You know how to handle the lines?"

"I think I can figure it out."

"Cast us off."

On the flybridge she waited until the boat was free of the dock, and then she sparked the engine. A tremor ran through the length of the vessel, vibrating the deck beneath Camaro's feet. The pulsation quickened as she gave the boat some throttle and edged them away.

CHAPTER SEVENTEEN

AFTER THEY HAD been on the blue water for four hours, the sun settled low on the horizon and bled into the sea. They were well clear of land in every direction. Camaro had the radar switched on all the way, tracking the movement of ships beyond the skyline. There was no way to tell if they were pleasure boats or commercial craft or vessels of the Coast Guard or DEA or Border Patrol. Only if they angled near enough to be spotted would Camaro be able to distinguish the difference, and once the sunlight was gone even that would be lost.

Matt and the others passed in and out of the cabin, sometimes lounging in the fighting chair or against the sides of the boat, chatting over the continuous roar of the engine. The *Annabel* could cruise at forty knots, which was fast enough for what they had to do. Camaro would not push the boat further, and she was not asked to.

She heard someone climbing up to the flybridge and saw Matt's head appear. He stood up beside her, looking out at the purpling blackness ahead and breathed deeply. The air smelled of salt. In his hands he held bottles of beer. He pushed one in her direction. "Here," he said. "Take the edge off."

"No, thanks," Camaro said.

"You don't drink?"

"I'm your designated driver."

Matt chuckled at that. He tucked one bottle in his armpit and twisted the cap off the other. The cap went into the sea. He drank. "I only drink when I'm already relaxed," he told her.

"So you don't have any worries, huh?" Camaro asked.

"Nope. I see this going smooth all the way down the line."

Camaro was quiet.

"You know," Matt said, "I haven't had a chance to say so before, but you are a fine-looking woman. You have some Cuban blood?"

Camaro stared straight ahead. "No," she said.

"Huh. I figured you for a little Latina fire, you know? The way you stand up for yourself. I may not look like it, but I appreciate a lady who can hold her own."

"That's nice," Camaro said.

"You misunderstand me."

"No, I think I understand you just fine," Camaro said.

"Alls I'm saying is that once this is over with, I wouldn't mind getting to know you a little better. I'll have some spending money, and we can hit the clubs. Do a little dancing. Get a little freaky. You know what I'm saying?"

Camaro favored him with a glance. He was partially lit by the instruments, the ends of his hair peeking out from beneath his cap. His thin face was turned into a smile, and for the first time she saw that one of the teeth deeper in his mouth was capped with gold. It winked out from beneath his lip like a warning light. She looked away again. "You've got a pretty big set of balls," she said.

"The biggest. So are we on or what?"

"Or what," Camaro said. "I'm not on the market."

"Wait, you're not a lesbo or something, are you?"

Camaro breathed in through her nose and out through her mouth. She did it three times before she answered him. "I don't have to be gay if I'm not interested," she said.

"So what's the problem?"

Now she turned to him and let him see her face to face. "I don't date outside my species," she said.

A perplexed expression passed across Matt's face, and then there was anger. His lip curled, and she glimpsed the gold tooth again. "Hey," he said. "I'm trying to be sociable here."

"Be sociable somewhere else."

"I wouldn't screw you with a borrowed dick!"

Camaro sighed and turned away. The sun was gone completely, and the moon was on the rise. "You're not screwing me with anybody's dick. Now go drink your beers somewhere else and let me concentrate."

"Bitch!" Matt spat at her.

She raised a middle finger to him. He stayed only a moment longer and then climbed down from the flybridge. Camaro could not tell what he mumbled. It didn't matter to her anyway.

On the radar she saw a vessel ahead. She swung the boat wide a few degrees to cut an arc around it. If that vessel also had radar, they would know the *Annabel* was there, but they would never be close enough to see the *Annabel*'s running lights. And when the *Annabel* was close to Cuba, there would be no running lights at all.

On the deck, Matt complained to one of the others, his voice swallowed up by the sound of their passage and sunk beneath the waves of her indifference.

CHAPTER EIGHTEEN

AT TWENTY MILES out she killed the lights. The boat still churned the water, but it was oily black, marked only by the brief white of disturbance in the wake. The landmasses that enclosed the bay were visible on her screens. Camaro would come close to them, near enough to swim for it if the *Annabel* went down, and then stop. From there the Cubans were meant to do the rest.

No vessels had appeared on her radar for the last hour. The sea was empty. Camaro found herself glancing down every few seconds, expecting a blip to appear at the edge of her range, and further expecting that blip to close on their position rapidly, locked in and predatory. But nothing came, and she wasted her imagination on phantoms.

Finally, she shut the engine down. Where there had been constant noise for hours, there was now silence. Camaro heard the footfalls of the men on the deck and the gentle lapping of water against the hull. There was nothing for a full five minutes, but Matt broke the hush. "Is that it?" he asked.

Camaro stood over them on the flybridge, looking down on the tops of their heads in the weak illumination of stars and moon. Everything was limned in silver, the color sapped from shirts and shorts and flesh so that things were only light or dark. "That's it," she said. "Now it's up to your Cuban friends."

"You sure we're in the right spot?"

"This is where you wanted to go," Camaro said.

"What time is it?"

Camaro checked her watch. The dial luminesced in the dark. "A little past midnight."

"We wait until two o'clock," Matt said.

"That's a long time from now."

"We just *wait!*" Matt exclaimed. "Okay? You're getting paid, so do what I tell you! If they haven't showed by two o'clock, we turn around and go home."

Camaro let his words hang without responding. In the corner of the aft deck, Parker stood looking up at her, his face swept of its tan in the darkness and left pallid. All of them were pale and ghostly save for Soto, who seemed as black as a piece of stone.

She sat in her chair and turned her back on them. She allowed her attention to be taken up totally by her instruments. On a whim she switched on the fish-finder to see what was going on in the waters below. There was a little activity, but mostly it was like the surface: calm and clear.

The first hour passed without incident, and occasionally Camaro started the engine to maintain their spot. In the second hour, she saw the boat on her radar. It came directly from the farther shore and headed toward them at a steady twenty knots. The vessel had to skip around the natural obstacles that bordered the bay, but it circled around carefully to reach them, and before long she heard the thin sound of its engine carrying over the surface of the water, pushed along by the breath of a warm and humid breeze.

Light reflected off something on the approaching boat, and Camaro gauged the distance. The pitch of the other boat's engine dropped as it shed speed, until it was only coasting on its momentum. After that the pilot at the controls gave little bursts that oriented the boats parallel to each other. They edged closer until their sides were aligned. Camaro started her own engine and joined the dance, bringing the vessels nearly to contact before both slipped into silence.

On the deck of the Cuban boat there were three men. They cast over lines, and Camaro climbed down to help them lash the vessels together. Not a word was spoken.

A fourth man appeared from inside the cabin. It was difficult to tell the figures apart in so much shadow, but finally one switched on a flashlight and pointed it at the deck. In the reflected light she saw them. Two were young and two were much older. The first three were dressed in ratty shorts and worn T-shirts, but the fourth man wore an ironed short-sleeved shirt, slacks, and boat shoes.

"Señor Chapado?" Matt asked. Pieces of the quiet crashed to the water around them.

"*Sí*. You are Señor Clifford?"

"That's right. Come on aboard, sir."

Soto helped the man named Chapado navigate the gap between boats. Chapado thanked Soto and then brushed at his shirt as if the exertion had dirtied him. He looked around at all the faces on the deck. "Who is the captain?" he asked.

"I'm the captain," Camaro said.

"Señorita, *gracias*. You are doing a brave thing."

"We shouldn't stay long," Camaro said.

"I agree." He turned to the Cubans. *"Es hora de irse, mis amigos."*

"Vaya con Dios, Señor Chapado," said one.

"Gracias. Adiós."

Camaro cast off the lines that held both boats together. "There are places to sit or sleep in the cabin," she told Chapado. "There's water in the refrigerator. It's a long way back to Miami."

Chapado moved to take her hand, but she stepped away from him. She could not read his expression in the dark. "My gratitude, señorita. Thank you again."

"Thank me when it's over," Camaro said.

The Cubans started their boat, and they churned water as they gently pulled away. Camaro climbed to the flybridge and pressed the ignition, stirring the *Annabel* to life. Down below she heard Chapado enter the cabin. He would find it cooler there and the ride more comfortable. Maybe Matt would offer the man one of his beers.

She touched the throttle and turned the wheel to bring the boat about. On the radar, the Cubans' vessel was headed away, faster going back than coming in. Camaro found her heading and eased the throttle higher.

CHAPTER NINETEEN

SHE DROVE THE boat on through the rest of the night, until the sky began to pink with predawn. The hour and the sameness of the invisible horizon served to blend the minutes together, and Camaro did not realize at first that a new vessel had appeared on her radar. She cursed herself and throttled down instinctively. The vessel was headed their way without deviation. They were less than twenty minutes apart.

Parker was on the deck. "What's wrong?" he called up. "Why are we slowing down?"

"Someone's coming," Camaro said.

"Who?"

"I won't know until they're here," Camaro said. "Get everybody out on deck. Bait your lines and get them in the water."

"Chapado, too?"

"Him, too. Everybody."

Parker rushed to do her bidding. Camaro throttled down still further until they were almost drifting. They were some twenty-two miles offshore and fully in the grip of the Gulf Stream. Finally, she killed the engine altogether. Matt and the rest bustled on the aft deck as she switched on all the lights.

"What's going on?" Matt asked.

"We've been spotted. Someone's closing in on us."

"Can you outrun them?"

"If it's one of the Border Patrol's fast boats we'll never make it,"

Camaro said. "I need everybody fishing right now. We've been fishing all night. You understand?"

He did not answer her, but set about fetching his rod. Camaro directed them to the bait box, then came down to be sure they were doing it right. Chapado seemed confused by the borrowed rod and dropped his bait three times. She wanted to shout at him.

The sun was rising when she saw the Coast Guard vessel. It was an interceptor, coming in at about thirty-six feet and moving fast, cutting the water smoothly with twin engines in the rear. Camaro checked the men again to be certain they were positioned correctly and their lines were set, and then she climbed up to the flybridge and the radio. "This is the *Annabel* calling Coast Guard interceptor," she said. "Come in Coast Guard."

"*Annabel,* this is Coast Guard. Cut your engines and prepare for inspection."

"We're already drifting, Coast Guard. Be careful: we have lines in the water."

The interceptor closed on them. It was designed for long-range work, launched off the back of a Coast Guard cutter that itself would not have the speed or maneuverability to catch the go-fast boats that worked the waters off Miami. The Border Patrol had even quicker vessels.

Once it was within a hundred yards, the interceptor slowed noticeably and cruised in at low power. Like the Cubans before it, the interceptor slotted in alongside them. Two men stood on the after deck in the clear morning sun. Camaro waved to them, and they waved in return.

The crew of the interceptor tossed lines across, and they were bound together with another vessel again. Camaro came down from the flybridge and stood on the deck among the men, looking into the dawn. "What can we do for you, gentlemen?"

"Fishing?" asked one of the men from the Coast Guard.

"Looking for swordfish," Camaro said. "We've been out all night."

She felt Matt and the others shifting around her. She willed them to be still.

"How long you been in this spot?"

"Not long. I've been moving her around, looking for some good water."

"We tracked you coming in from way offshore. Pretty deep water for swordfishing."

Camaro elbowed past Matt and Soto so she could be face to face with the officer across the water. She read his name: Phillips. "I figured it was worth a shot," she said. "Sometimes I get lucky out there."

"Well, it caught our captain's attention," Phillips said. "So now you know why we're here."

"We've got nothing to hide," Camaro said. "I was going to give it another hour and then we'd head in. It's been a long night."

There was movement beside her, and Camaro glanced down. Matt still held his rod in one hand, but his right had slipped behind him. He lifted the back of his loose-fitting shirt, uncovering the butt of an automatic pistol. She caught his eye and shook her head slightly. He smiled.

"Mind if we come aboard?" Phillips asked.

"If you want," Camaro said.

They used gaff hooks to bring the boats hull to hull, and then Phillips climbed over. He had his own gun, a pistol holstered at his hip. The other man was armed, too, but he did not board. Camaro did not know how many were still inside the wheelhouse.

Phillips checked the bait box first. "You been chartering long?"

"About a year."

"How's it treating you?"

"I'm doing all right."

"Good, good," Phillips said, and he opened the transom fish box. He looked back at her. "No catch?"

"I'm catch-and-release."

"Gotcha."

The men watched Phillips as he stalked the aft deck, checking inside Parker's tackle box. Matt still had his hand behind his back. Camaro grabbed his wrist and pulled his arm to his side. Matt made a hissing sound, but did not speak up. None of them spoke.

Phillips pointed at Chapado, and the whole group of them froze in place. "You, sir," he said. "What's your name?"

"Sergio Chapado."

"Catch anything tonight?"

Camaro waited long seconds for the answer, aware of the thoughts clicking in Chapado's head. She made fists and screamed inside.

"Two mackerel," Chapado said.

"Good size?"

"Yes, I think so."

"Take pictures?"

"Yes."

"You want me to get the camera?" Camaro asked.

"Not right now," Phillips said. He continued with Chapado. "What's that accent you have?"

"Cubano."

"Where do you live?"

"Miami."

"For how long?"

"Twenty years."

Phillips paused. "I'm going to have a look inside," he said.

"I'll show you around," Camaro replied.

They went inside together, and Phillips bypassed the panel that covered the first aid kit and the hidden shotgun. Camaro breathed again. He looked in the cabinets and the tiny refrigerator and then in the stateroom and washroom. On his way out again, he stopped at the galley counter and fixed Camaro with his gaze. "Question," he said.

"What is it?"

"If I check the IDs of all your charter clients out there, are they going to be legit? American citizens?"

Camaro nodded. "Of course."

"Just checking, because so far everything's turned out all right. My captain thought you might be running dope in."

"Not me," Camaro said.

He thought. Camaro waited. "All right," he said. "Thanks for your cooperation."

"Anytime."

Phillips returned to the interceptor, and the ropes binding the two boats were undone. He waved once from the deck as the interceptor turned away, and the men all raised their hands in unison. Camaro watched him go.

"Very smooth," Matt said to her.

"Get your lines out of the water. Let's get this over with."

They cruised the last miles among boats coming out for morning charters or simple trips on the open water, and soon they were in the marina again. The men were all gathered on the aft deck as Camaro brought them in and Parker tied them off. One by one they bled onto the pier.

"Hey, Matt," Camaro called down when he had stepped off.

"What?"

"Where's my money?"

"You get it now. Parker?"

"I'm going." Parker left the others. Camaro watched him make the walk back to the old pickup in the lot. For a moment he vanished inside, and then he was out again, moving quickly with an orange envelope in his hand. She came down to meet him. He put it in her hand. "Here," he said.

"That's everything," Matt told her.

Camaro didn't count it. "Then we're all done," she said.

"We sure as hell are. I hope I don't see you around."

"You won't."

They walked away, only Parker looking back. He lifted his hand slightly, but she did not do the same. She climbed back aboard the *Annabel* and took the envelope inside.

CHAPTER TWENTY

ONLY MATT KNEW where the handoff would take place, so Parker followed. He was tired, and the road danced in the edges of his vision. When this was over he would sleep for twelve hours, but there was this last distance to go.

They drove for thirty minutes in quiet Saturday-morning traffic until they reached a fenced-in compound of bright-orange storage units. Parker's phone rang, and he saw Matt's number. He answered. "What's going on?" he asked.

"This is the place. Park out on the street, okay? I'll let you in at the gate."

Parker did as he was told. Matt punched in a code at the automatic gate and drove in. The gate was not quite closed again when Parker reached it, so he slipped through as it shut completely. The Charger squatted just a few yards beyond, its engine idling. Matt waved him over.

Through the driver's-side window Parker could see Chapado stuffed in the backseat with Soto. The man was sweating from the closeness and the morning humidity, and his shirt was stained at the pits. Matt snapped his fingers to focus Parker's attention. "We want unit 501," he said. "It's way back in the corner. We'll meet you there."

"Sure, sure," Parker said.

The Charger rolled away and picked up speed until it reached the far end of the row and right-handed out of sight. Parker started walking. It was much cooler out on the water, even with the sun. He wished he were on the water now.

Unit 501 was in the extreme right-hand corner of the complex, rows back from the street and hemmed in on two sides by a high cinderblock wall topped with razor wire. By the time Parker got there, Matt and Jackson were already out of the car, though Soto and Chapado remained in their seats. The day would be punishing. The shadowed interior of the car allowed some respite.

Matt pointed his finger at Parker. "That bitch," he said. "That bitch that *you* hired."

"What did she do?"

"She has *attitude,* bro. Did you see me trying to make nice with her? She might as well have spit right in my face. She got paid *good* for what she did. I deserve a little gratitude for cutting her in at all."

Parker did not know what to say. Matt was inflamed, pacing in front of the Charger. He took a pack of cigarettes from his pocket and shook one out. Parker watched him light up and drag deeply. "I'm sorry," Parker offered finally.

"You're sorry. You *are* sorry. A thousand charter-boat captains around and you have to pick the one who doesn't know her ass from a hole in the ground. Ten thousand is good money. It's *good money.*"

"Yeah, I know. I don't know why she did what she did."

Matt smoked angrily, spitting clouds. "She better hope I never run across her again, because I'll push her face in, bro. I'll give her a *beat down*. You know what I'm saying?"

"I know what you're saying," Parker said.

"And then she let the Coast Guard on the boat. Right on the boat! We could have been screwed then."

"Yeah," Soto agreed. "That was too close, man. Too close. She shouldn't have let them."

"How could she keep them off the boat?" Parker asked. "They

were coming on board no matter what. At least she kept her head. You were ready to start shooting."

Matt smiled thinly. "Oh, you saw that, huh?"

"Yeah, I saw it. I thought we were doing this with no guns."

"I make exceptions for my own safety," Matt said.

"If you had shot those guys or resisted them at all, we'd never have made it to shore," Parker said. "She did the right thing."

Matt regarded him through a miasma of smoke. "You got a little love affair going on with her?"

"What the hell's that supposed to mean?"

"I'm just asking because you seem real interested in sticking up for her. Well, I got news for you, bro: she's not interested in your dick. So don't go thinking you're gonna be setting up house with her later on. She's an ice queen."

Parker shuffled closer. He was more tired than before. "All I want is to get this done," he said.

"We'll get it done. I made a call. Chapado's people are on their way right now. All we have to do is sit tight, and fifty grand will come right to us."

Parker leaned against the Charger. Matt gave him a poisonous look. He took his hand from the car. "It's going to be all right," he said, mostly to himself.

"Hells yeah," Matt said. "*More* than all right."

CHAPTER TWENTY-ONE

IT WAS NEARLY forty-five minutes of waiting before Matt's phone rang. He dropped his latest cigarette and ground it under his toe before exhaling a billowing pall that lingered around him, stinking of ash. "Yeah, this is Matt," he said when he answered. "Yeah, you're in the right place. The code's 4837. Come all the way to the back. Unit 501. Yeah, he's with me. All right."

Matt thumped a fist twice on the hood and Soto opened the Charger's door. He clambered out, and then caught Chapado by the arm, dragging him into the light. Chapado was sweatier than before, though from nerves or the weather, Parker did not know. He was perspiring himself, the moisture crawling down from his pits and along his sides.

A few moments later they saw the SUV. It was white and gleamed in the steadily rising sun. It cruised slowly up the row, creeping past the storage units, until it was ten yards away. The driver did not turn off the engine but let it idle as two Latino men stepped out onto the asphalt. One was young and carried an attaché case identical to the one Parker kept hidden in his home behind the wainscoting. The other was much older and empty-handed.

"Hola," Matt greeted them. *"¿Cómo va todo?"*

The man who carried nothing looked through Matt and past him to Chapado. His brow had been furrowed, but when he saw Chapado, his forehead smoothed. He had deep lines on his face that did not go away. Parker could tell he did not smile often. "Señor Chapado," the man called, "are you all right?"

"Estoy bien."

Now the older man acknowledged Matt, squinting at him through the glare of the early morning. "I have brought your money as you requested," he said. "Fifty thousand dollars in used bills."

Matt smiled. "All right, all right, all right. That's what I'm talking about. You give us the money, and you can have your guy."

The older man signaled to the younger. "Go," he said.

The money was brought forward. Matt did not move from his spot by the Charger, half seated on the nose of the car. The younger man held the case out like a talisman, and it was only when he was within a few paces that Matt extended a hand to take it. "Thanks so much, *amigo,*" he said.

Parker did not see Matt draw the pistol from the small of his back. Suddenly it was in Matt's other hand, brandished in the face of the younger man. Both of them had their hands on the attaché's handle. The younger man let go only when Matt shot him in the eye.

It was a moment of perfect clarity. Everything around Parker snapped into focus, from the glint of the sun off the yellow paint of the Charger to the droplets of blood that remained suspended in the air when the younger man's head snapped back from the impact of the bullet. Parker saw the dead man's fingers slip free of the case and then the whole body collapse backward as every muscle released at once and the tension vanished from every joint.

The older man grabbed at his chest at the moment Matt shot him in the leg. The driver's-side door of the SUV swung wide, and a burly Latino in a suit bulled out. Matt stepped forward with the pistol and fired three rounds. Two drilled through the side window and into the driver, while the third ricocheted off the windshield and left a divot surrounded by sharp white cracks.

Chapado called to the dead men in Spanish, but Parker could not find his own voice. His mouth worked on empty air, struggling to form some sound, but there was only Matt laughing and the older man on the ground bleeding heavily from his wounded leg. Soto and Jackson said nothing and did nothing.

Matt stood over the wounded man and leveled the gun at his head. "Hurt?" he asked.

"I'm having a heart attack, I think."

"That's too bad. Maybe you'll bleed to death first."

"Why are you doing this? What have you done?"

"The price just doubled. You wanted to pay a hundred grand for this asshole, but now you're going to pay two hundred. If you want to see him alive again after today, you'll have the money together in *twenty-four hours*. I'll call you with the details. Don't try to call me. You understand? *¿Entiendes?*"

The man nodded, his face warped with pain. "I will tell them."

"You do that."

Matt turned back toward the Charger and flipped the attaché case over his shoulder, holding it loosely by two fingers. He smiled again, but only for Parker and the others.

Parker spoke. "Matt...what the hell?"

"Your cut just went up, my friend," Matt said. "Sandro, get that asshole back in the car. We've got to split before the cops show up."

"We didn't talk about this," Parker said. "You didn't say anything."

The smile became a frown. "Are you turning into a little bitch or something, bro? Is that what I'm hearing?"

"No, but—"

"Relax," Matt said. He put the gun away and clapped Parker on the shoulder. "I've got it all under control. You just worry about your end."

"What's my end?"

"Getting the front money. It's time for us to divvy up. I'll call you with the spot, okay? In the meantime, maybe you ought to get the hell out of here, huh? You don't want to be around here when the cops find this mess. Oh, and something else: *I'm* going to hang on to this fifty grand, okay?"

Parker struggled for more words, but he was breathless. He watched Matt get into the Charger and turn the ignition. The car peeled away, driving past the dead body of the younger man and leaving the older man in a pool of his own blood. Parker stood frozen for a whole minute, and then he ran. He ran and he ran and he did not stop until he was safe in his truck and headed for someplace far away.

CHAPTER TWENTY-TWO

CAMARO RESTED AFTER they were gone, sleeping away hours in the bed in the bow. She awoke feeling achy, and with the air conditioning off in the cabin, the air had grown uncomfortably sticky. The boat had a tiny washroom with a freshwater shower and sink, and she splashed cool water on her face and let some run down the back of her neck.

The envelope Parker delivered to her was underneath a pillow. She brought it out now. It was held shut with a red string that she unwound before opening the flap and dumping the contents on the bed.

Ten little bundles of fifty-dollar bills fell into a scatter. Camaro sorted them out, then took the rubber bands off them so she could count the money out. There were two hundred bank notes. Fifty times two hundred made ten thousand exactly.

There had been times when she'd handled more money than this. A lot more money. She had paid cash for this boat. And even at a bargain price—the seller anxious to get it off his hands—it had been a lot of cash. They had made the exchange much like this: bills in an envelope. But they had counted out the money in the galley.

"Are you running dope?" the man had asked her when the deal was done.

"No," Camaro had said. "I just want to fish."

She put all the money in a single stack and wound one of the rubber bands around it. After that she stuffed it into her back pocket.

The deck needed to be cleaned off and the boat rubbed back to a shine, but Camaro didn't feel like doing that now. Tomorrow she had no charters, so she could do it then, but the bait box couldn't wait. Camaro got a large plastic bucket and drained the melted ice from the box, then threw the unused bait overboard. A waste, but if there had been nothing in there to pass inspection, the game would have been over.

Thinking of Phillips, the Coast Guard officer, turned her thoughts to Matt Clifford and the gun he carried. She felt foolish now for not insisting everyone go unarmed. It was only when the pistol was revealed that she had realized everything could turn into bloody carnage with one poor decision. If he had turned the gun on her, she might have been able to get him with her karambit if he was close enough, or maybe even the shotgun if she was quick enough. But those were long odds, and she did not like the idea of playing against them.

A man who deceived was a man who could never be trusted with anything. That much Camaro knew. As she disembarked from the *Annabel,* she considered the position the others were in, Parker included. Parker had told her that Soto and Jackson were close to Matt. They had to worry less. But Parker was the outside man, nearly as dispensable as someone like Camaro, only he could not get away. Matt truly was a center of gravity, and everyone orbited around him.

She got to her bike and swung a leg, but she did not start the engine. She thought, and she turned over in her mind the events of those fourteen hours, and then she brought out her phone. Parker's number was in the memory, but she did not need the phone to remind her of it.

He answered quickly, but his voice was low. Camaro heard a television in the background. "Hello? Who is it?" he asked.

"It's Camaro."

"Camaro," Parker said, as if the name was new to him. "Why are you calling me?"

"I wanted to hear how things went. After."

The sound of the TV faded. Parker was moving to another room. The sound of the TV was cut off completely, and Camaro knew he'd closed a door. "Can I meet you?" he asked.

"Why? What's wrong?"

"I don't want to talk about it on the phone. Is there somewhere we can go?"

"There's the diner," Camaro said. "Is that too public?"

"No, that'll work. I don't think it's a good idea for me to come by the marina, just in case they spot my truck. I have to be careful. I need help."

"What can I do for you?" Camaro asked. "I'm out, remember?"

"Nobody's out," Parker said, and his voice was hollow. "I'll meet you at the diner in a couple of hours. Is that all right? A couple of hours? I can't just run out on my kid."

"I'll be there," Camaro said.

"Thank you."

"Take care of yourself, Parker."

The call ended. Camaro weighed the phone in her hand a long moment before putting it away. A feeling of desperation lingered, palpable as the sensation of the bright Florida sun on her body. He did not have to speak the words for her to know that things were wrong and set to worsen.

She could get out. She could close the book on Parker now. She did not. Instead, she started her bike and rolled out, knowing in two hours everything would be on the table.

CHAPTER TWENTY-THREE

IGNACIO MONTELLANO DROVE by Matt Clifford's apartment building twice. First he went by quickly, simply another car passing on the street. The second time he slowed and examined all the cars along the curb out front and the still face of the building itself. No one moved, and the Dodge Charger was not there.

The Charger interested him because it said things about where Clifford had gone and why. When he had returned to the station after the meeting with Clifford in his apartment, he did some research and found that a Charger of that vintage could run thirty thousand dollars or more if fully restored. Ignacio regretted not getting a look inside the vehicle, but he was willing to guess that the interior was all original and as mint as the bodywork.

They had never learned what was inside the safe at the pawnshop. The three victims had been the only three employees with access to the safe, but two part-timers had speculated there might have been as much as a hundred thousand inside. Not all in cash, but some in gold and valuables. Things that could be moved without being tracked. Things that bought expensive classics with all the trimmings.

On his third pass, Ignacio found a place to park and walked to the apartment building. He mounted the stairs one at a time. His heart was beating a little quickly by the time he reached the top, so he caught his breath before knocking on the apartment door.

An answer wasn't expected and there was none. Ignacio repeated the procedure three times to no avail before moving to the next door over. This one was answered by a small Latina in a cleaner's smock. He had caught her before her afternoon work, and behind her two small children wreaked havoc in a room filled with toys. *"Señora, estoy con la policía,"* he told her, and showed his identification. "Do you speak English?"

"Yes," the woman said.

Spanish was not an issue for Ignacio, but he also knew that speaking English was a point of pride for many, especially immigrants. He did not want to turn her away from him. "Do you know the man who lives next door to you?" he asked. "His name is Matt."

The woman thought and shook her head slowly. "I have only see him."

"Have you seen him today?"

"No. But sometimes I no see him for a long time. Days."

"Gracias por su ayuda, señora."

"De nada."

She closed her door, and Ignacio returned to Clifford's apartment. From inside his jacket he produced a folded leather case the size of a paperback book. He flipped it open, revealing a set of lock-picking tools. He crouched down in front of the door and eyeballed the lock before selecting his instruments.

The lock was cheap and loose and took less than a minute to open. Ignacio put the tools away and opened the door slightly, peering in through the crack. With the front curtains drawn, the room beyond was bathed in shadow, but he could still make out the things he'd seen on his last visit.

He opened the door all the way. "Police," he announced. "Your door is unlocked. I'm coming in."

Once inside, he shut the door again, but he drew the curtains to bring in light. The air conditioner in the window was turned off. Ignacio switched it on to its highest setting, and soon cool air circulated where stale heat had been before.

The television and the game console were gone, but the sheet and pillow were still on the couch, messier than before, left unfolded. On the coffee table was a wrinkled bit of plastic wrap. Ignacio took a handkerchief from his pocket and picked up the wrap by the edge, examining it closely. It was a makeshift bundle for crystal, put together by a dealer too cheap for baggies, and a little meth residue was still inside.

He put the wrap down and went into the kitchen. In the refrigerator was a pizza box with two slices of pepperoni inside, a six-pack of beer, and a jar of mayonnaise. Clifford's bread was stale, and what little flatware he had was all piled in the sink, left dirty and soaking in an inch of stagnant water. The cabinets were almost completely empty.

From the kitchen he went farther in, passing through to the bedroom. Clifford's bed was a mattress on the floor, his sheets black. An overflowing ashtray rested near the head by the wall, and there were several empty beer bottles scattered around it. A box of condoms was open there. Ignacio did not count how many were left inside.

There was a single closet, big enough to walk into, and it was entirely bare. A single wire hanger dangled from a rod, but none of the built-in shelves held so much as a pair of underwear. In the attached bathroom he saw that Clifford had elected to leave behind his toothbrush and a half-used tube of Crest. The room smelled faintly of mildew, and Ignacio saw that some was growing on the lower edge of the shower curtain.

Ignacio went back to the front room and stood in front of the air conditioner, letting it blow against him. He called out on his phone. Pool answered. "Hey, Brady, it's Nacho. I need you to put a BOLO out for Matt Clifford."

"What's up?"

"I'm in his apartment, and it looks like he skipped out again. Circulate a bulletin around to the other departments, and maybe we can catch him in the suburbs. Wherever. I have the tag number for his car. You ready?"

"Shoot."

Ignacio recited the license plate number from memory. "It's a 1970 Dodge Charger 440. Yellow and black. You can't miss it."

"I'm all over it," Pool said.

"Thanks, man."

"Do you think he's up to something crooked?" Pool asked.

"I *know* it," Ignacio said. "Let's find him before we end up with three more bodies."

CHAPTER TWENTY-FOUR

Camaro saw Parker's truck in the parking lot of the diner when she arrived, squatted in its space, low on its shocks, looking as if it were one step removed from the junkyard.

She spotted Parker sitting in the same booth where they'd last sat. His hands rested on a large glass of iced tea with two wedges of lemon perched on its lip. Even from where she sat on the Harley in the parking lot she could see his apprehension. He looked back and forth around the interior of the diner, and when the entrance opened to admit someone, he visibly jumped. She went in.

The look of relief on his face when he saw her was total, but it only served to expose the layer of desperation underneath. He was pale beneath his tan. When she slotted into the booth opposite him, he smiled in a way that was not reassuring at all. "Hi," he said. "Hi, hi."

"Hi," Camaro said.

A waitress came immediately and offered menus. Camaro took one and looked it over. She had not eaten and did not know when she'd eat that night. Better to have food in her stomach than continue on empty. She asked for a tea of her own.

Parker waited until the woman was gone. He leaned forward conspiratorially and spoke quietly, though there was no one close enough to hear. "Everything's gone to shit," he said.

"Matt?" Camaro asked.

"How did you know?"

"Who else would it be? He's an asshole and he's reckless. He's going to screw up anything he touches."

"I didn't think it would go like this," Parker said.

"What has he done?"

"He didn't do the deal. He backed out of the deal. And he...he killed two people."

"Where did this go down?"

"Up in Hollywood. He just gunned them down, Camaro. Took the money and gunned them down."

Parker took up his iced tea and drank, but his hand was unsteady. Even his lips trembled. He put the glass down too hard, and it made a loud bang that caught the attention of an old couple a few booths down. Camaro wanted to tell him to calm down but knew it would do no good. "Where's the guy? Where's Chapado?"

"He took him with him. He and Jackson and Soto took off together to somewhere. They're going to call me later with the address. I have no idea where it is. Maybe it's around here, maybe not. I don't know."

Camaro was slow to speak. Her tea came. She squeezed the lemon into the glass, dropped the lemon wedge in, and stirred the ice around with a spoon. The crushed lemon ended up at the very bottom. "I'm going to ask you something, and I want the truth," she said. "You understand?"

"Yes."

"Did you have any idea Matt was going to kill somebody today?"

Parker shook his head violently. "No, no! This was supposed to be totally clean. Nobody gets hurt, everybody gets paid. If I thought people were going to die, I would have said no right out of the gate. I owe Matt, but I don't owe him that much."

"What do you mean you owe him?"

Now she saw shame in Parker's face, drowning in the other emotions that gripped him. Despite herself, her heart echoed something in return. The sensation made her angry. "When we were inside, there were a couple of guys who wanted to... you know. They wanted to go to town on me. Matt kept them off. I'm still not sure how. These were big guys, and they were in for life, so they didn't have anything to lose. But Matt stopped them. He stopped them for me."

"He kept you safe," Camaro said.

"Yeah. He did."

"But now he's putting you in danger. You don't owe him anymore."

Parker flung his hands up in surrender. "I'm stuck in it, though. Matt didn't kill all the Cubans, so they've seen my face. They might even know my name. And there's something else, too."

"Wait a minute," Camaro said. "Cubans?"

"Yeah, Miami Cubans. They have some kind of thing going on. I don't really understand it, but they have money. It has to do with Chapado and what he was doing back in the home country. Matt never really explained it. But that's not important. What's important is the money."

"The money you're holding," Camaro said.

"He wants it now. Like *right now*. But it's the only leverage I have. As long as I'm the only one who knows where it is, he's out forty thousand. He has more money coming, but he's going to want that cash."

"He has more money coming? From where?"

"The Cubans have to pay double now. That's another hundred grand. But he's not going to let go of the first payment. He's gonna lean on me."

"Do you think he'd kill you?" Camaro asked.

Parker's face was misery. "I don't know. I can't risk it."

"So what are you going to do?"

"I need you."

"How?" Camaro asked.

"I'm going to try and hold Matt off. I'm going to tell him that I'm having a hard time getting my hands on the money. Because it's locked away somewhere that's tough to get to, or something. I'll hold on to it as long as I have to for him to finish off what he's doing, and then I'll get lost. I'll give him the money and get lost."

"That doesn't have anything to do with me," Camaro said.

"If something happens to me, I need you to get Lauren out."

A memory of Lauren in the photograph flashed through Camaro's mind again, flickering with the elements of life, but not quite, frozen in that moment. Now she was a fourteen-year-old girl whose father Camaro knew only a little but who had no one else to cling to. "I don't know, Parker," she said.

"*Please*. The money is hidden at my place. There's a loose board in the back of my closet. You pull it out, and you'll find the case. There's forty thousand bucks in it. Take some of it for yourself. Take *all* of it, I don't care. Just make sure no one can get to Lauren."

"What am I supposed to do with your kid?" Camaro said. "Take her on my boat and raise her?"

"My brother. He lives out in Texas. You can get in touch with him, make him come out and take her. I just know you won't let anything happen to her."

"You don't know me at all," Camaro said.

"I know you were a soldier. That has to count for something. You're not the kind of person who'd let a little girl get hurt. Tell me I'm wrong."

The waitress came in their direction. Camaro motioned her away. "No, you're not wrong," she said.

"You're not in love with me or anything," Parker said. "And I know I'm asking for something big. But don't think about me. Think about her."

He scrabbled for his pocket and brought out his battered wallet. Inside was the photograph. Parker folded the wallet open to the photo and put it on the table in front of Camaro. There they were again. Parker and his little girl on the beach, blonde hair long and face tanned from the sun. They smiled happy, unburdened smiles.

Camaro closed the wallet. "No more," she said.

"Please don't go," Parker said. "Not until I'm finished."

"You are finished," Camaro said.

"Listen, I don't have anywhere else to go!"

"I'll do it," Camaro said, more sharply than she intended.

"You will?"

"I will. If something happens to you, I'll be there for her. But you have to keep me in the loop. Whatever goes on, I need to know. I can't go into this blind."

"Done." Parker snatched up a napkin. "Let me give you the address."

Camaro watched him write, and a wall of dark anticipation rose up within her.

CHAPTER TWENTY-FIVE

ALEJANDRO GALDARRES OF the Intelligence Directorate was given access to an official car with the services of a driver, but he rarely used the privilege. Fuel was a precious and expensive commodity in the Republic of Cuba, even with the relaxation in American sanctions. The government was starved for money, and old allies could no longer help. In the mornings he left his Havana apartment in an old and cozy neighborhood and rode a steel-framed bicycle all the way to the directorate's headquarters. He would chain the bicycle to a lamppost, take his briefcase from the bicycle's basket, and go inside, where air conditioning awaited to wick away the sweat of his journey.

On this morning much was the same, though the day might have been hotter and his linen suit a bit more uncomfortable. Going in through the entrance and showing his identification to security before having his briefcase x-rayed, he reveled in the cool air. It was another almost unheard-of luxury in Cuba outside the resort hotels, but he enjoyed it nonetheless.

He gave his service weapon to one of the men operating the security choke point and passed through the metal detector. His pistol was returned on the other side. His briefcase emerged from the x-ray machine. Galdarres bid both men a good morning and went to his office.

Behind his desk he followed his routine, putting his lunch into the deepest drawer and then sorting through the overnight briefing documents. He found the one he sought immediately and read it thoroughly. It was only two pages, and it told him exactly what he expected to learn.

He left his office and went down the hall to another, larger one broken into two chambers. Galdarres gave his name to the secretary and asked to see the director. She bade him sit, and he did so with the briefing document across his knees. An air-conditioning vent was directly overhead, strings of tinsel hanging from the metal grille. They danced as the frigid air pumped into the room. Galdarres felt cold for the first time that day.

It was a fifteen-minute wait. A pair of men emerged from the interior office. Galdarres heard the director's voice following them out. He waited until the secretary indicated it was time for him to enter and he did, glad to be out from beneath the frosty vent.

The office of the director was well appointed, with heavy, leather-upholstered furniture. The walls showed pictures of the director with Fidel and Raúl Castro, along with many other luminaries from home and abroad. Several medals were framed and on prominent display.

The director himself was a short man, going to fat, with thinning gray hair. He wore large, owlish glasses, which made him look even older than he was. But Galdarres knew that despite appearances the director was a reasonably healthy man in his early sixties who enjoyed swimming and baseball, the latter, admittedly, with a league made up of seniors.

"Alejandro," the director said when Galdarres entered. "I was wondering when I was going to see you. You're right on time. Please, sit down."

"Director Celades, it's good to see you," Galdarres said.

The director smiled pleasantly, a professional expression and not personal. "And you. I can see you got the report about last night's arrests."

"I did, señor. It's what we anticipated it would be."

"Just so. Twenty-seven taken up in the sweep, but no sign of Sergio Chapado."

"So our information was correct," Galdarres said. "He has been spirited out of the country."

"Yes, but not so long ago. We missed him by less than twenty-four hours. I have the latest reports from the interrogations happening as we speak, and they've been revelatory. The escape plan has been in place for months, masterminded by the exiles. If only we'd moved a little bit quicker, we would have had their entire apparatus in Havana, Chapado included."

Galdarres nodded regretfully. "It's a shame, señor. But we had no idea. They were very good about covering their tracks. Even our source in the United States wasn't aware of what was happening until recently. They're growing more paranoid about leaks because of the travel happening back and forth. Anyone could be an informant. Everything is compartmentalized now."

"Do you feel your American source is reliable enough to continue doing his work?" Director Celades asked.

"Yes, señor, I do. They've taken him into their confidence, so he's privy to all the latest information about what they are doing and what their plans for the future might be. It's a breakthrough for us."

The director shook his head slowly and then rubbed his chin. He sighed. "You would think we'd be past this by now. It's been fifty-six years, and even the American government no longer cares to continue their sanctions. For them the Cold War is over. The old guard are dying out or are too decrepit to do anything. And the young ones follow their government's lead: they don't seem to care at all."

"Except for those who do," Galdarres said.

"Yes. Except for those who do."

Galdarres straightened in his chair. "The question now becomes what we are to do next. Do I continue my work turning over stones in our own backyard, or is there something else I can accomplish?"

The director's dark eyes glittered. "You have read my mind, Alejandro."

"I'm sure it's just coincidence, señor."

"No. We are of the same mind on this. Our problem does not end with crushing their operation in Cuba. We must reach out and destroy Chapado, as well. So long as he's alive, he's a potent symbol, and that cannot be allowed. They'll parade him around functions and have him give speeches, and before you know it we'll be wading hip-deep in conspirators again. We have to make the Americans believe we are good friends and that nothing happens on our island that would ever cause them to question us. But the revolution continues. Nothing has changed. No, I want this put to an end. I want it seen to immediately."

"What would you have me do, señor?"

The director stood up suddenly and paced the office. He paused before the window and looked out on the street beyond. The building was old, but the windows had all been replaced with ballistic glass, though from the outside it was impossible to notice the difference. "I want you to go to Miami," the director said. "You have the Venezuelan passport you were issued? It's up to date?"

"Yes, of course, señor."

"That's what you'll use. Travel today if you can, but no later than tomorrow. I want you in the United States as quickly as you can manage it. Once you're there, you'll be provided with the means to finance your operation and manpower to help you complete the mission."

Galdarres looked at Director Celades' back. "Do I need to ask what my mission is?" he asked.

"You needn't, but I will tell you anyway: find Chapado and execute him. If any of his coconspirators happen to get in your way, you have my permission to eliminate them, as well. There will be no more tolerance for this. I want to go to the president and tell him myself that the flies that have buzzed around the corpse of the Bay of Pigs have finally been eradicated. Nothing will stand in the way of our new friendship with the United States. And you will ensure that this happens. Won't you, Alejandro?"

Galdarres rose from his chair and stood at attention. "Yes, señor. Without question, señor. It will be done exactly as you instruct."

The director turned from the window, and there again was the professional smile that failed to reach his eyes. "This is the time to show what you're made of, Alejandro. A test. After this will be a promotion for certain. You'll have a larger office. A staff. Perhaps one day you'll even rise to my position. Not yet, but soon."

"I'm flattered that you think so, señor," Galdarres said.

"Go now. See to your travel. Before you leave the building, you'll be given contact phone numbers and the names of our resources in Miami. You'll have plenty of money. Everything you need to ensure Chapado's elimination."

"Thank you, señor. I won't let you down."

Galdarres left the office. The briefing document from the night before still fluttered in his hand, and he stopped in the outer office to feed it into the secretary's shredder, where it was turned into confetti. He walked briskly back to his office and unlocked the lap drawer with a key on his chain. The red booklet of his Venezuelan passport waited, its biometric data in place and a few visa stamps inside to give the illusion of travel. Galdarres had never used it.

He tucked the passport inside his jacket and sat down. He had calls to make and little time to make them. There was much to do.

CHAPTER TWENTY-SIX

THE SMALL CLUSTER of warehouses was poised at the edge of a swamp that extended away for mile upon mile upon mile. They were built on a man-made stretch of flat, dry ground, and it was only the broken-down hurricane fencing around the place that kept the gators out. Old, painted logos remained on the corrugated tin siding of the warehouses themselves, but the colors had been scoured off by sun and time. The place itself had been locked up for years before Matt picked it out. It was a long way from anywhere. It was perfect.

Making their way from Hollywood all the way down to within miles of the end of the state took an hour. Matt drove the Charger with the windows down, so the wind blasted in and chased away the worst of the heat. Halfway to his destination he put on the radio and listened to Big 105.9, Miami's classic rock station. They played a string of tunes from Skynyrd, the Stones, Kansas, and Creedence that had him singing along, totally ignoring the others in the car, especially Chapado.

From time to time he'd check in the mirror to see what Chapado was doing. The man sweated heavily, and his hair was in disarray. Doubtless his perfectly ironed clothing would be badly wrinkled by the time they got to where they were going. The thought of his crumbling façade of gentility made Matt smile.

At last they were there, out where no one could hear or see. Matt gave a key to Jackson and dispatched him to open the padlock that held the gate's chain. After he drove through and Jackson came back, Matt asked, "Did you lock it up again?"

"Yeah."

"Good. I don't want visitors until I want visitors."

There were five warehouses altogether, and the largest was in the back, completely hidden from view. Matt parked the Charger alongside it and then got out to stretch. The others hustled Chapado out of the car and stood waiting.

Wordlessly, Matt led them to a small door on the westward face of the building. There was a larger, sliding door that could open wide enough and high enough to admit a semitrailer, but Matt chose an entrance for a regular-sized human being that provided access to a small office space that still had a desk, a lamp, a chair, and a filing cabinet, though all were thick with dust.

In the open space of the warehouse itself, pillars came down from the ceiling at regular intervals and held the high roof up. Whoever had last used the place had abandoned some or all of what they stored there. There were still stacks of wooden crates and rotting cardboard boxes lashed to pallets with plastic ties or coated in wrap. The main lights were out, the power cut off from the building long ago. But in the center of the warehouse where a large natural clearing was formed, Matt had put two battery-operated floodlights and a chair with sturdy arms and a straight back. For now, sunlight filtered in through plastic panels in the ceiling and the windows spaced here and there around the walls.

A roll of duct tape lay on the chair. Matt pointed them out. "Strap him down," he said. "Make sure the loops are tight."

Jackson and Soto hurried to do Matt's bidding. He wandered away from the chair to where he'd left two folding cots and a pair of sleeping bags. There was an electric lantern sitting by them. He tested it. It worked.

When Chapado was secured, Matt came to him. The man's eyes rolled in their sockets, full of fear and confusion in equal measure. The pits of his shirt were dark with perspiration. "Here we are," Matt told him.

"Please don't hurt me," Chapado said. His voice was shaky and hesitant.

Matt laughed out loud, and Jackson and Soto did, too. Matt laughed until he had tears in the corners of his eyes. He wiped them away. "You know, that's exactly what I thought you'd say," he remarked. "You Cubans are so goddamned predictable. Castro this, Castro that . . . please don't hurt me."

"Anything you want," Chapado said.

"Sure. Anything I want. What I *want* is another one hundred grand. Now, I know you don't have it, but you better hope like hell that your friends have it, otherwise things are going to go real bad for you."

Soto cleared his throat. "Hey, Matt? I need to take a leak, bro."

"Do it outside."

"Okay."

Matt turned his attention back to Chapado. "You can piss your pants," he said.

He saw Chapado stiffen and the man raised his chin. "I won't."

"You won't? Well, you don't have any *choice,* because you're gonna be in that chair for the next day. You don't get up to stretch, you don't get up to take a shit, you don't get up for anything."

"There's no need for this."

"No?"

"No. We can be civilized."

This made Matt smile again. He reached into his pocket and his hand closed around the folded knife there. He brought it out. "Civilized, huh?" he said. "Are you saying I'm not civilized?"

"I only meant—"

"Shut the hell up!"

Matt brandished the knife and flicked open the blade. It was just over five inches long and gently curved. The finish was like a mirror. He paused only long enough for Chapado to see it before he dug the tip into the back of Chapado's arm.

Chapado screamed as the long gouge came out of his skin and the flesh underneath. Matt ignored him and cut across the first line once and then twice. Blood welled up and spilled onto the floor. Chapado jerked against the tape and shook the chair, but he could not move any way that Matt's knife could not follow. *"Please!"* Chapado howled.

"I was drawing a Christmas tree," Matt said.

Chapado's forearm oozed a steady crimson. Matt heard Soto rushing in from outside, his footfalls on the concrete. "What's going on?" Soto asked.

"Nothing," Matt said. "Just showing our friend who's civilized and who's not."

He caught Jackson's eye, and they chuckled together. He wiped the knife on Chapado's shoulder and then snicked it shut. It slipped into his pocket.

"Is he gonna bleed to death?" Soto asked.

"From that? No way. I barely cut into him."

Chapado sniveled, and Matt walked away. He took his cigarettes from his pocket. He'd smoke outside under the sun where he didn't have to smell the urine soaking Chapado's underwear.

CHAPTER TWENTY-SEVEN

Camaro returned home long enough to get behind the wheel of her truck and head out again. The street was completely still in the heat of the day. No one liked to move around in the humidity if they could avoid it.

She used the GPS stuck to her windshield to find Parker's house and drove by when she saw his truck parked on the curb out front. A part of her had hoped for Matt's Charger, but the yellow-and-black muscle car was nowhere to be seen. Reflecting further, Camaro thought that might have been a good thing.

An empty parking space two houses down and across the street provided a good view of the house. Camaro stopped there and put the windows down. Within minutes it was stiflingly hot. Sweat prickled at the back of her neck and between her shoulder blades.

Parker was at home for almost two hours. It occurred to Camaro he might not move at all that day, but finally he appeared from behind the front door and made his way down his little walk to the battered pickup. A visible cloud of pollution belched out of the tailpipe when he started up. Then he was on the move.

No one had ever taught Camaro how to tail a car. What she knew she'd learned from television and movies. In the end, she chose to hang back four car lengths, enough to let traffic intervene, but not so far back that she would lose him entirely. She didn't dare pull up directly behind him lest he spot her in his rearview mirror. This would have been much easier if he knew she was with him, but she did not trust he could keep the secret if pressed.

They drove a long while, the better part of an hour, headed south and farther south. In the end they passed through Homestead, the last finger of urbanity stretching out into the Everglades, and into the outskirts where only a few had settled in to live or run businesses. Camaro supposed land was cheap there, and so long as gas prices stayed low it wasn't a problem to drive a long way.

Eventually they were on a road alone, with no other cars for Camaro to hide behind. She fell back farther and farther, until Parker was at the limit of her vision. When she saw him come to a stop, it was so sudden that she almost forgot to pull off to the side of the road.

There were binoculars under the truck's seat. Camaro used them to look ahead through the flat glare of the day. She saw a small collection of buildings, warehouse or workshop spaces of various sizes, and a stretch of fence. As she watched, someone, maybe Jackson, came out to the gate and let Parker through.

She put the binoculars away and approached on foot. By the time she reached the fencing, Parker's truck was nowhere in sight, but she knew he hadn't left. Camaro studied the curling barbed wire blocking an easy climb over to the other side, and then she walked along the perimeter, checking all the way. Almost a hundred yards down she found what she was looking for: a place where the wire securing the chain link to the post had snapped from rust and age and the fencing could be rolled back.

Claws of metal caught at her shirt when she ducked through the hole. Then she was inside. She dashed to the nearest warehouse and walked quietly to the corner before peering around. There was nothing.

Venturing deeper into the little complex, she came upon Parker's truck first and then the Charger. Both were parked haphazardly in front of a large structure stained with corrosion. No one moved.

She went to the truck first, then crept to the Charger. When she heard nothing, she stole across the last few yards to the building itself and pressed her back against the hot aluminum. This close she could hear the murmurs of raised voices but not the words themselves.

There were three sets of windows on the long side of the warehouse, and they were wound open slightly to allow some breath of air inside. Camaro crept along the building until she was level with the first set, and she risked a peek inside.

Chapado was framed between twin stacks of wooden crates, fixed to his chair with duct tape. Matt was just visible, and his voice was the clearest. Camaro knew immediately that he was talking to Parker, and when Parker's replies carried to her she was proven right.

"I *told you* to get me that money! Where's the money?"

"I'll get it! I hid it somewhere that's closed today. I'll have it by tomorrow."

"This all happens tomorrow night, asshole," Matt said. "I'm not gonna be standing around with my dick in my hands waiting for *you* to cough up the rest of the cash! You better *get it,* and you better get it in a hurry!"

"It'll happen. I swear."

"I swear to God, I'll shoot you next time you bullshit me, Parker."

"It won't happen again."

Camaro heard the sound of metal grinding against metal. A door midway down the side of the warehouse jerked against its frame, someone trying to force it open. There was nothing but fifteen yards of open space in every direction.

She fled, arms pumping, making for the Charger. As the door came open, she slid on the gravel across the nose of the car, then scrambled out of sight as Jackson emerged into the sunlight and blinked, momentarily blinded. A thin cloud of dust slowly settled around Camaro.

Jackson brought out his penis and urinated against the side of the warehouse. It was a loud, rattling, metallic noise, and Jackson sighed audibly while he did it. When he was finished, he took one long look around before going back inside. He did not pull the door completely shut.

Camaro prepared to move, but then another, closer door opened, and she heard Matt speaking as he stepped outside. "You remember what I told you," he said.

"I remember," Parker said.

She peered underneath the Charger and saw their feet. Neither pair was pointed at the car. Parker's sandals crunched on the gravel.

"You can find your way to the spot?" Matt called after him.

"Yeah, I can do that. What time?"

"I told you: two o'clock in the morning. And you goddamned well better have that money."

"I promise, Matt."

"Screw your promises, okay? Just do it."

Parker got into his truck. Camaro heard his door open and then close.

"You could have saved yourself the drive and just called me with your excuses, bro."

"I'll call next time," Parker said.

"There's not gonna *be* a next time. Now get out of here."

Parker started his truck. Camaro watched the wheels turn on the gravel and then listened as the pickup drove away. She looked back toward Matt's feet, which stayed where they were. She and Matt were no more than twenty feet apart.

Matt spat on the ground and then went back inside.

CHAPTER TWENTY-EIGHT

HUGO ECHAVE WAS sixty-five years old. When he was nine, his parents took him from their house in Matanzas in Cuba and fled to the dock where his uncle's boat was waiting. He had not been allowed to bring his favorite toys, but only what could fit in a single suitcase. He had cried on the whole trip to Miami.

His parents had nothing in America. He had nothing. And it was all because of Fidel Castro and the 26th of July Movement. They had ruined his life.

That was 1959, and 1959 was a long time ago. Even so, Echave sometimes woke in the night expecting to be taken from his bed by his parents and whisked away to a country where no one wanted him and he did not speak the language. The sensation made him angry, and the anger simmered in him constantly. The name *Castro* in the wrong context could send him into a black mood that lasted for hours or even days. Things were different, better, for him now, but there was always the hatred. And now his government, the leaders of this land where he made a new home, had betrayed the old cause. They did not see the real face of Castro's Cuba, or they pretended not to. That was the worst thing of all.

They convened the meeting in his house in Hialeah. It had only one floor, but it was capacious and comfortable. He met with his people in the paneled sanctuary of his study, where the mementoes of lost Cuba were displayed among the record of his American experience.

There was Pablo Marquez, one of the young ones in the movement, and Álvaro Sotelo. Carlos Molina was his closest friend, the one who'd left Cuba at the same time as himself, and the one with whom he shared a birthday, though they were five years apart in age. The four of them together would make the necessary plans.

"How is Javier?" Echave asked Carlos when they were all seated with cold lemonade or tea in their glasses. The door was firmly shut.

"The wound is bad, but he will survive," Carlos told him. "The man, Clifford, he knew where to put the bullet."

"Or maybe he was simply lucky," Echave said. "The man is trash."

"I warned against using him," Carlos said. "You remember what I said."

Carlos was the eldest of their inner circle, seventy, his hair almost completely white. His mustache was thick and streaked with some remaining black, and his eyebrows gave him a perpetually grave look. Only now he *was* grave and his judgment obvious. Echave could not dismiss him. "He was available. He said he could deliver. There were not many options."

"There are always options," Carlos said.

"Perhaps sometimes, but not this time. If we hadn't gotten Chapado out when we did, he would be in prison at this very minute. Tortured. Maybe even executed. And the fools at the State Department would close their eyes to it. We had no choice."

"It's done now," Sotelo said in a conciliatory tone. "We must deal with the situation as it exists, not as we wish it did. This man has Chapado now, and he will not give him up unless we pay. Can we manage it?"

"It hurts, but it can be done," Echave said. "I've been in touch with some of our larger donors, and they've indicated that they can be relied upon. Only, I have no intention of paying this *cabrón* anything."

Carlos' eyebrows went up. "What? What are you talking about, Hugo?"

Echave looked to Marquez. "Tell him."

The young man cleared his throat. When he spoke, he spoke respectfully. He was a good boy and a former soldier, and he understood the way things were meant to be. "I've made arrangements to take Chapado from Clifford and his people by force. There will be four of us, all armed, and we'll stage an ambush at the exchange site."

"But why?" Carlos asked. "Chapado might be killed!"

"This man intends to kill Chapado anyway. And who's to say he won't simply try to double-cross us again? Ask for one hundred thousand *more?* Or two hundred thousand? It can't be risked. He's a dog, and he needs to be put down like a dog."

"This is risky," Carlos said.

"It must be done," Sotelo said.

"So you're in on this, too? Am I the only one who doesn't know?"

Echave put a hand on Carlos' arm. "It's all right. Pablo knows what he's doing. He was a Ranger, remember? We'll get Chapado, and we'll take this man's balls in the process. It's the best way."

CHAPTER TWENTY-NINE

PARKER CALLED AT close to eight o'clock with the news. "It's happening," he said.

"Where?" Camaro asked.

"Liberty City. I have the address."

He told her, and she wrote it down. "When?" she asked.

"Two o'clock."

"Tonight?"

"Tonight."

Camaro looked around her kitchen. All was still, though outside somewhere a person was using a gas-powered weed trimmer to edge their lawn. Soon they'd fire up a leaf blower, and the racket would be that much worse. "What's your plan?"

"I can't bring the money there," Parker said. "If I hand it over, I have nothing to hold over him. As soon as he gets it, he can do whatever he wants to me. I got to hold out for Lauren."

"He might kill you for that," Camaro said.

"No, he won't. It's too much money. He can't afford to lose it."

"You're playing right up on the edge," Camaro said. "Don't let him push you over."

"I won't. But if it... if things don't go right, you're still going to help?"

"I will."

"I hope everything works out and I can say thank you myself."

"I do, too. Take care of yourself, Parker."

They hung up, and Camaro was quiet. The buzzing of the weed trimmer was in her ear, bothering her like a particularly insistent mosquito. She wanted to smash the thing to pieces.

Camaro owned a gun locker. In the back of her bedroom's closet, it lurked blackly and was made of high-grade steel. Camaro went to it, dialed in the combination, and opened it up.

There weren't many guns inside. Only another, smaller .45 for when she wanted to carry something truly inconspicuous and a semi-automatic rifle chambered in .308. It was made by Colt, one of their civilian versions of an assault weapon, right down to the flash hider and the bayonet lug. Camaro brought the rifle out and laid it on the bed. She put two magazines on the mattress beside it, and then locked the safe again.

Afterward, she took the rifle to the dining room and stripped it down. She checked the components for dirt or grit and found none. When she put it back together again, she worked the action and found it smooth. Then she sat down in her living room with the rifle across her knees, listening to the noises of the gathering evening.

Around midnight she decided to eat something, even if it was only a sandwich and a glass of milk. Without turning on the lights in the carport, she stole outside with the rifle and its magazines, loading everything into her truck before backing out of the driveway and heading on.

Liberty City was north, and the city changed faces with practically every mile, nice blocks giving way to shady blocks giving way to grass-choked empty lots. Liberty City itself was poor and almost entirely black, and Camaro knew why Matt had chosen this place for the exchange. A gun could go off here, and no one would call the police.

She wound her way around the ugly blocks, passing apartments and convenience stores and clothing shops with bars on every window. Restaurants looked like they were prepared for a siege. Once she got within a quarter mile of the address, she pulled the truck over and parked in the lee of an abandoned building.

The Glock in her boot was loaded. She checked the chamber and found a round already in place. Now she fed the Colt rifle a magazine and put the spare in the back of her jeans. She got out of the truck in the dark, locking it tightly behind her and setting the alarm. There were thieves here, but she hoped they would go for easier pickings.

No traffic moved along the streets. Camaro jogged along the sidewalk with her weapon, making the rendezvous site within minutes. No one was there. It was one o'clock in the morning.

Matt had picked out an auto yard scattered with ailing cars. At one end of the yard, a wall of crushed vehicles rusted into dust. On both sides of the street there were square, bunker-like buildings with roller doors, marked out as metal shops and moving companies and other businesses that had a lot of in-and-out traffic of heavy trucks.

The crushed cars provided a natural firing position, but it was closer than she wanted to be. She searched across the street and behind the buildings. Each of the structures had a metal ladder to the roof. She slung the rifle over her back and climbed. On the flat top of the building, heat radiated from the black painted surface beneath her feet. Camaro crouch-walked to the raised rim at the edge of the roof and looked over. The spot offered her complete coverage of the rendezvous area. She'd have to fire at no more than thirty yards or so.

She checked her watch again and then settled in to wait. Whenever a car cruised down the lonely street, she tensed and peered out. But it was never Matt or Parker or anyone who seemed at all interested in the auto yard and what was meant to happen there.

It was fifteen to two when she heard the Charger's 440 grumbling through the night. Camaro raised her head only enough to see, and she watched the yellow-and-black shape clear the corner and roll down the street. Parker's truck was close behind, and together they moved cautiously along until they came to the auto yard.

Jackson got out of the Charger and opened the yard's gate to let the Charger through. Parker stayed on the street and came in on foot. One at a time the rest spilled out, Matt from behind the Charger's wheel and then Soto and Chapado. They stood in a loose group in the center of the yard's open space.

She saw Matt light a cigarette before he turned on Parker, shouting something she could not hear. Matt berated Parker for nearly five minutes, and Parker stood and took it. The others studiously minded their own business. Chapado looked around for salvation and found nothing.

Headlights drew Camaro's attention, and she turned away from the scene. A single black Mercedes cruised down the street from the opposite direction the others had come. It slowed as it approached the auto yard and then slowed some more, until it was barely at a crawl as it turned into the gate and stopped. The Mercedes blocked the only egress for the Charger.

Matt saw this, too, and he waved the Mercedes' driver on angrily, urging them farther into the yard. The driver obeyed unhurriedly, pulling forward until his car was parallel to the Charger but ten yards away from it. The car's quiet engine went silent.

These men, these two Cubans, were the opposite of Matt and Parker and the rest. They did not wear T-shirts or loose-fitting button-ups and shorts. They were in suits as black as their car, and they were well groomed. They seemed young, none of them older than thirty-five. Camaro had expected someone older, someone senior.

Matt went out to greet them. There was inaudible talk. Camaro watched them. She watched them so closely that when the movement came, she very nearly missed it.

The three gunmen crept along the fence line behind the wall of crushed cars. They were also in black, but this was combat gear and not tailored suits. Each of them carried a rifle. When they were nearly opposite Matt and the lead Cuban, they stopped and set up their fire arcs, using the honeycomb of the crushed cars as cover and opportunity.

A briefcase was taken from the Cubans' car, but wasn't handed over. There was more talk. Matt gestured broadly in anger, waving his cigarette around and drawing glowing lines in the dark with the orange coal.

Camaro looked to the gunmen. They were ready. One balanced his rifle on the lip of a compacted window and raised his free hand. The others steadied.

She brought up the Colt and took aim across the span of street and yard. Her thumb edged the safety off. In the red-dot sight on the rifle, she had the first gunman zeroed in. She pulled the trigger.

A .308 round crashed into the side of the gunman's head, and he went down. For a long moment there was nothing but the echo of the rifle's report, and everyone was frozen. Then they moved, and the gunfire began in earnest.

Matt and Jackson and Soto drew weapons, as did the Cubans in suits. Matt shot the man closest to him before a burst of rounds from the gunmen drove him back and into cover. Jackson was caught out in the open, and his chest burst apart before he could lose a single bullet.

The second Cuban dropped the briefcase and it burst open. Scraps of plain white paper exploded from within, scattering like heavy snowflakes in the dirt. He sought refuge around the back of his Mercedes, but he was exposed to Camaro on his flank. She shot him twice in the back, then shifted her aim to the gunmen, who laced the Charger with gunfire from their impregnable position.

Matt and Soto were still shooting, but Camaro could not see Parker. Pops and rips split the night. Camaro poured fire into the gunmen's position until the magazine went dry. She dropped the empty and swapped it out for the second.

She was firing again as Matt made it behind the wheel of the Charger and started the engine. The wheels spun as he geared into reverse and stomped the accelerator, then bit down. Matt shifted again and peeled out, swinging the car around in a rough circle, back tires burning in the dirt and kicking up a cloud of choking dust. Camaro could barely see as Soto hustled Chapado back into the car and boarded himself.

The Charger leaped forward, catching fire as it went. The two remaining gunmen moved out of hiding to pursue, shooting at the Charger as it fishtailed in the street. Its rear window turned white with holes and cracks. Camaro ignored the car and concentrated on the men, dropping one with three rounds to the chest and head and putting the other on the ground with a pair of bullets that ripped his shoulder.

Now she could see. The two suited Cubans were dead by their car. The gunmen were all dead or dying. Parker lay still on the ground.

Camaro gathered up the spent magazine, ran to the ladder, and descended fast. She dashed from between the buildings and across the street, into the yard where Parker remained.

His shirt was deeply stained from the wounds in his chest and stomach. He breathed only shallowly. Camaro ripped his outer shirt open and lifted the undershirt beneath. He'd taken one in the right lung, the hole sucking air, and another in the liver. The third entry point was two inches below his heart. He should have been dead.

She cradled his head. "Parker," Camaro said.

He could not focus his eyes, and when he tried to reach for her, his blood-sticky hand missed her face completely. More red was on his lips, bubbling up with every breath. The hideous sucking noise of the lung wound continued.

"I can't save you," Camaro told him. "You're going to die."

Parker found the energy to nod once. He closed his eyes. His body stopped.

CHAPTER THIRTY

THERE WAS A Texaco station not far from where it all happened, and Camaro stopped to use their restroom. Blood on her hands and arms swirled away into the dirty sink, though she thought she could still feel the stains. It was always the same.

When she was done, she filled up her truck's tank, the routine of the activity distracting her not at all from the thoughts whirling in her head. Police sirens called out in the night, overlapping and synchronizing with one another until it sounded like an army of cars was out there. And perhaps there were. Camaro would not go back to see for herself.

The rifle was hidden on the floor behind the front seats of her truck, a blanket over it, but she still had the Glock and her karambit on her. Once she was away from here completely, she would not have to worry so much about being stopped. And if she were stopped, she would claim that she had spent the evening at her boyfriend's in Hialeah. Close enough to Liberty City to make it possible she had been, but not so close that they'd want to take a look at her.

A part of her cursed and spat at the other part of her that had brought her to this place. It had been none of her concern, and she had not had to be there when it happened. But she had gone there, and she had done it anyway for reasons she could barely articulate to herself. She had not owed Parker. She had not loved him. He was almost a stranger. But he had been in need, and he asked her for her help.

She did not have to think long on the next step. The next thing to do was to leave this place and go to Parker's home, where a woman Lauren Story did not know would have to tell her that her father was dead. And Camaro would take her from there, along with the money Parker had hid, and she would make certain Lauren was safe until she could be sent far, far away and clear from all of this.

The gas nozzle's handle clicked, and Camaro put it back on the pump. She went to the cashier's window to get change from the two fifties she'd given the attendant. He barely paid her any mind, shoving the coins and bills into the little metal trough beneath the bulletproof glass without meeting her gaze or saying a word.

As Camaro walked back to her truck, another police unit came screaming down the street with its lights flashing and its siren alive. Camaro watched it go until it vanished from sight, then climbed into the truck and drove away.

While she went, she thought again about what she had done this night. The men she'd killed had not been the first. That honor went to an insurgent in Iraq just two weeks after her first deployment began in 2003. That man had rushed a position being guarded by her unit, his body laden with explosives, and she had been the first to fire. Afterward, they had told her she could have left it to the men, but she had said that it was her life in danger as much as theirs, so she did it herself because it had to be done. There had been looks after that and comments, but she ignored them all. Twice more during that tour she'd been involved in combat situations in the Sandbox. That's how she had killed her second man. A boy, really. Only eighteen.

There were others. People back in the world did not understand that a combat medic lived true to her title, and combat was where she went. One minute she could be fetching water for soldiers in her unit that needed it to stave off dehydration, and the next minute she could be taking fire. She saved lives, and she took lives. One may have been better than the other, but she was not afraid of either.

She drove south, out of Liberty City and away from Parker. In her mind she had an image of Lauren Story taken from the photograph in Parker's wallet, but that would not be the reality of it. Lauren was older now, and she would have to be shaken from sleep. When she heard the news, she would fall apart, and it would be up to Camaro to hold her together long enough to clear out of the little rented house. There was no time. Once the police identified Parker's body, they would come for Lauren. But they were not Camaro's first concern. Matt knew Parker, and perhaps the Cubans knew Parker, too. Either outcome was not a good one.

After New York she had promised herself no more, that she wouldn't stray. Tonight the promise was broken. Perhaps it had been broken all along.

CHAPTER THIRTY-ONE

WHEN THE PHONE first started ringing, Ignacio thought he was dreaming it and did nothing. It was only when the call went to voice mail, only to start ringing anew a few seconds later, that he stirred from sleep. He felt for the phone on the nightstand, found it, and put it to his ear. "Did somebody die?" he asked.

Pool was on the other end. "Somebody did die. A whole bunch of somebodies."

Ignacio sat up in bed and rubbed his eyes. It was dark and cool in his bedroom with the ceiling fan turning away above him to stir the air. "Who?"

"Right at this very moment I'm looking at Jackson Dewey."

"Jackson Dewey? Where? What happened?"

"I think you ought to come out here and see for yourself. It's a regular party in Liberty City tonight."

"Tell me where you are," Ignacio said. He turned on the bedside light.

Pool gave him the address and Ignacio memorized it. "I'll be there in . . . thirty minutes?"

"I'll keep everything fresh for you."

"Thanks. I'm moving now."

Ignacio tossed his phone on the bed and raided his closet for work clothes. He had the next two days off and was going to take his good outfits to the dry cleaner, so all that was left were things that were too small or not in fashion. In the end he dressed as if he were going out dancing and not to work, but at least everything fit.

He drummed his fingers on the steering wheel while he drove. A coffee would have been good, given the hour, but there was no time for that. Simple adrenaline would have to suffice to keep him going until sunrise. After that the sun would have to suffice.

Pool had not been wrong about the chaos at the scene. Police units blocked both ends of the street, and there were ambulances and more police beyond them. Colors were flashing everywhere, turning the dark into a stroboscopic nightmare. The CSIs had set up portable lamps in the auto yard, the plain white of their high-powered bulbs beating back the light bars. Every last grain of dirt in the yard was flushed in illumination.

The Mercedes drew his eye immediately, and the bodies next to it moments later. He saw the CSIs were working on the far side of the yard, behind some destroyed cars, so there must have been more that had happened there. Ignacio spotted Pool standing in an open space, and near him two more bodies. One of them was clearly Jackson Dewey. Ignacio knew him instantly.

"Welcome to the O.K. Corral," Pool said when Ignacio came close.

"What the hell happened here?" Ignacio asked.

"First guess: these fellows in the suits had a disagreement with Jackson and this other guy, and there were some heated words exchanged. Plus some bullets. We've got three corpses in nighttime camouflage, plus there's a dead man over there behind those crushed cars who looks like he might also have been backup. Took a rifle shot to the head. Those three in the military getups were also taken out with a rifle."

Ignacio looked, but only the dead men in black seemed armed. Jackson was the only one of the others brandishing a gun. A second man in a beach bum's uniform lay dead, with his outer shirt laid open and his undershirt pulled up to expose the bloody wounds beneath. The night picked out the reflective circles of the outer shirt's buttons in the dirt.

"We have a nice set of skid marks in the dirt here that shows there was a second vehicle, but it's long gone," Pool said.

"Who was shooting with the rifle? Jackson has a pistol. The dead guys all have assault weapons, but they didn't shoot each other."

Pool pointed across the street at the buildings opposite. There was a metalworking shop immediately facing them. The roofs of all the buildings were flat. "I'm thinking a sniper up there. I haven't sent anyone to look, though. Figured you'd want to give the order once you got here."

Ignacio went to the dead man with his shirt pulled up. A CSI took the corpse's picture. "What's this guy's story?"

"Story," Pool said, and he grunted a laugh. "That's his name. Parker Story. I don't know him by sight, but I'm willing to bet the database has his name in it. I've already asked them to run him. Looks like someone tried to do first aid on him, or at least they saw he couldn't be saved."

"This is all about Matt Clifford," Ignacio said. "I know it."

"We still have that BOLO out on his car, but no luck. You'd think it wouldn't be a problem spotting a car like his. I guess he's better at hiding than we thought."

Now Ignacio went to the Mercedes and crouched next to one of the dead men in suits. He looked over the scattering of plain white papers that spilled from an expensive leather briefcase. A case like that might have cost two hundred dollars easily. The Mercedes itself would run close to a hundred grand. The suits looked like they were top quality, perhaps even tailored and not off the rack. "What were you two doing out there with Matt Clifford?" Ignacio asked out loud.

"You figure all these other guys for Cubans?" Pool asked.

Ignacio went from body to body. One man in battle dress had clearly bled out from a pair of agonizing shoulder wounds. He wondered how long it would take for that to happen. "They could be," Ignacio said. "But they might not be. We can't just assume they are. Have we run the car's plates?"

"Stolen off a Hyundai. The VIN's still intact, though, so we'll be able to check that in the morning."

"Good. I know Jackson, and we'll figure out who this Story guy is, but these are the important ones. They're the reason everyone's here."

"What do you want to do next?" Pool asked.

"Check those buildings like you said. Have the CSIs take this whole scene apart. After that we'll see about pulling traffic camera footage, anything we can use."

"It's going to get crazy once the word gets out."

"I know it," Ignacio said. "I know it."

CHAPTER THIRTY-TWO

"MOTHERFUCKER!" MATT SCREAMED at the high ceiling of the old warehouse. "Motherfucker! Motherfucker! Motherfucker!"

Soto dragged Chapado to the straight-backed chair and taped him to the armrests again. Soto had been quiet the whole way back from the killing fields in Liberty City. He was quiet now. Matt was glad of his silence, because if Soto had opened his mouth to say the wrong thing, Matt might have put a bullet in it.

Matt turned to Chapado and drew his gun. He pressed the muzzle against the man's head. "I should kill you right now," he said. "I should *end* you!"

"Please don't," Chapado whispered.

"Huh? What?"

"I said, please don't," Chapado repeated more loudly.

"They don't care if you're alive," Matt said. "If they wanted you alive, they would have *paid the money* and you'd be on your way. But, no, they want to play games! They want to try and off me and Sandro and everybody else. You heard them shooting. Do you think they were worried about hitting you?"

"I don't know."

"You don't know. *I* know. I know what's up. Sandro knows what's up. You're the only one who thinks this is going to have a happy ending. God*damn* it, I hate liars."

Matt wheeled around with the pistol in his hand and stalked the open space in the center of the warehouse, moving in and out of the light, a thin shadow one moment and real the next. He muttered to himself and cursed out loud, but he did not go after Chapado again.

Soto finally spoke. "What do we do?"

"I need to sit. There's some folding chairs in a closet in the office. Bring out a couple."

He waited while Soto obeyed and regarded Chapado with blackness settled over his heart like a pall. His ears were still slightly stunned from the gunshots in Liberty City, though they no longer rang. The smell of gunpowder was on his clothes. He had a hole in the loose cloth of his shirt beneath his left armpit, where a bullet had passed between arm and body without striking either. Just a little more to the right and he would have been like Jackson, dead on the ground in a second.

Soto returned with the chairs and set them up. Matt dropped into one and let his gun rest on his knee. He glared at Chapado again until the man lowered his gaze to his lap and kept it there. Matt thought maybe Chapado would piss himself again. The odor of it had been strong in the Charger.

"What do we do?" Soto asked again.

"I have to think."

He thought and the broken pieces of the evening assembled themselves into something that might be considered a shape. The conclusion rose up slowly, rearing like a sea beast out of the ocean of his mind, as dark as his mood. "It was Parker," he said at last.

"Parker? How?"

"He must have cut a backdoor deal with them. That's why he didn't bring the forty grand to the meeting, because they told him he could keep it after they took us out. And I know exactly who put the idea in his head: it was that bitch."

"What bitch?"

"What do you mean, 'what bitch?' The *bitch*. The one with the boat. I *knew* something was going on between them. I'll bet you every nickel those assholes have that it was her on that roof across the way."

"But that means she was shooting them," Soto said.

"Huh?"

"If it was her up on that roof and she was working with Parker trying to take us out, why was she shooting the Cubans instead of shooting us? It doesn't make any sense, bro."

Matt muddled through this, and then he had it. "It was a double double cross," he said. "Brilliant."

"I don't get it."

He could not sit. He stood up with nervous energy and paced again. The shape that had formed before took on a new texture as the details accreted. The image of Camaro was the most vivid. Whatever else she might have been, she was a good shot, because she dropped the Cubans like they were nothing. If Matt had not been so quick, she would have gotten him, too. Or maybe it was not chance. "Here's the double cross," Matt explained to Soto. "First, Parker goes to the Cubans and tells them he wants to get out of my pocket and into business on his own. He cuts a deal to keep the $40,000 we got at the start, in exchange for Chapado and the rest of the money. But *then* he gets greedy. He puts his head together with the bitch, and they decide that if they shoot everybody at the meeting they can get the money Parker was holding, the money we got at the first exchange, *and* the money they brought for the final payoff. And here's the best part: if they leave me alive, the Cubans think *I'm* the one who cheated them again. It's why she didn't shoot me! Goddamn it, it all makes sense now."

Soto stared at him for a long time. "You were supposed to make it?" he asked.

"And you weren't. Nobody was. Only me, so I could take the fall!"

"That's crazy," Soto said.

"That's why they would never think of it. I'd be on the run, and the Cubans would be after me no matter where I went. And if they ever got me and I told them I was ripped off, they'd think I was just lying to cover my ass. They kill me and write the money off. The end."

"I still don't know what we should do now."

Matt noticed he was still gripping his gun. He stuffed it into his waistband. "The first thing we do is find the money Parker was keeping from us. We go to his place before the police have a chance to get there, and we turn it upside down."

"What if he didn't keep the money there?"

"Then we squeeze his little girl," Matt said. "She'll know. And if she doesn't...well, I guess that's just how it goes."

"When do you want to do this?" Soto asked.

"Right now."

CHAPTER THIRTY-THREE

IT HAD BEEN less than ninety minutes since the gunfire when Camaro brought her truck to a stop in front of Parker's house. There was no need to hide anymore, and no one to see her anyway. The whole neighborhood was as lifeless as the moon. Even the drunks disgorged at last call had either made it to their beds or were booked in by the cops for some time in a cell.

She went up the walk and paused at the door. On the way here she had turned over the possibilities of what she might say when the moment came, but none seemed adequate. Parker died with his head in her arms. That was not an image Camaro wanted to put in Lauren's mind.

In the end she knocked and she waited, and then she knocked again. A light went on in the front room, making the curtains glow, and Camaro sensed a presence on the other side of the door. "Who is it?" Lauren asked. She sounded younger than fourteen, and there was fear.

"Lauren, you don't know me, but I'm a friend of your father's," Camaro said.

"Where is he?"

"He can't be here right now. Listen, I need to talk to you. Can you open the door?"

Lauren waited for so long Camaro thought she'd gone away. Then the locks clicked and the door cracked open. A security chain extended across the open space. Lauren Story looked out at her. The same face as in the picture, only older and more tired. Her hair had darkened. "Who are you?" Lauren asked her. Again the fear.

"My name is Camaro. Something's happened, and I need you to trust me. Will you let me in?"

"Are you friends with Uncle Matt?"

Camaro thought for a moment. "No," she said.

Lauren shut the door.

Camaro leaned close. "Lauren, this is important. I need you to let me in."

Something metal rattled and the door opened again, more widely this time. The chain was disconnected. Lauren was in a pink-and-white nightshirt emblazoned with Hello Kitty. "I shouldn't do this," she said.

"It's okay. I'm not here to hurt you."

She stepped inside and saw the shabbiness of the place—the ground-in poverty of the furnishings and the few pictures on the walls, mostly posters in plastic frames. The drab yellow cast from the floor lamp in the front room made everything seem that much sadder.

"Where is my dad?" Lauren asked.

Camaro pushed the door closed. She looked at Lauren, and everything she had planned to say fled her mind until it was totally blank. They stared at each other.

"He's dead," Lauren said.

The words needed to be spoken. "Yes," Camaro said. "He is."

Lauren fled before the tears could spill from her eyes. She ran down the hallway that bisected the house and went into another room. The door slammed shut behind her. Camaro was left alone. "Lauren," she called after the girl. "I'm sorry."

There was no answer. Camaro passed into the shadow of the unlit hallway and stood before the closed door. She put her hand against it and listened, and she heard Lauren crying. The girl's breath came in huge, gasping sobs, then muted. Camaro knew she was pouring her grief into a pillow. Maybe a Hello Kitty pillow, so cheerful and bright and unlike this house.

"Lauren," Camaro said.

"Go away! Just get *out!*"

"I can't go away. It's important that I stay awhile. Long enough to get you out of here. You're not safe, Lauren. People are going to come, and you'll be in danger. I promised your dad I wouldn't let anything happen to you. So I'm not going without you."

Lauren said nothing and the crying went on. Camaro turned from the door and saw the back bedroom. She went in and found the mussed bed and the cheap particleboard dresser clad in wood veneer. The closet was already open, and she put on the bedside light to see by.

There were scratches on the vinyl flooring that showed where the wainscoting had been removed, and the wood was pulled back ever so slightly from the painted wall. Camaro dug her fingertips in and removed it, exposing the hollow behind.

She dragged out the attaché case and left the closet. In the light of the lamp, she opened it and looked inside. More bundles of fifties, just like the ones Parker had used to pay her for the Cuba trip. He had said there was forty thousand, and she had no choice but to believe him. There was no time for counting now.

"What is that?"

Camaro flinched and turned at the sound of Lauren's voice. She hadn't heard the girl stop crying or her door opening. Lauren stood in the doorway with her eyes swollen and red, wet splashes on her cheeks where the tears had not been wiped away. When she inhaled, her lungs hitched, the weeping only a hairsbreadth away.

"What is it?" Lauren asked again.

"It's money," Camaro said. "Your dad asked me to get it. For you."

"Did Uncle Matt kill my dad?"

"No, he didn't. But he's coming. And the people who hurt your father are going to come, too. We don't have much time. Get some things you need, and let's get out of here."

"How do I know I can trust you?"

Camaro shook her head. "You don't. You either will or you won't. But I'm telling you right now that you're coming with me no matter what. Even if I have to carry you out."

Lauren's breath hitched again. A fresh track of tears carved her cheek beneath her right eye. She swabbed at it with her fingers. "I'll go," she said.

"Hurry. Ten minutes. No more."

The girl vanished. Camaro checked the nightstand for a weapon. In Florida felons could not own one legally, but that didn't mean they didn't have them. Parker did not. She switched off the lamp and left the room.

Lauren was in her own room, and Camaro heard the skitter of hanger wires in a closet. She looked in and saw that she was right about the Hello Kitty pillow. The room also had a small desk and a red chest of drawers that looked like it might have been real wood. The girl had a suitcase on the bed and had it half-filled. Camaro willed her to be faster.

Camaro wandered the rest of the house, finding the nook where the washer and dryer were and seeing the small kitchen. She had returned to the front room when she heard the distinct sound of a Charger's 440 cutting through the night.

CHAPTER THIRTY-FOUR

Camaro extinguished the lamp in the front room and went to the window. She pulled back the curtain just enough to see out front and saw the Charger slotting in ahead of her truck. A few moments later the engine stilled and Matt and Soto got out. They did not have their weapons in their hands, but she knew they were armed.

She pulled the Glock out of her boot and considered simply gunning them down on the walk from the front door. She crossed the idea off in her head. Closeness was what she needed now, and Lauren had to be put out of danger.

Lauren was pushing on her suitcase, trying to get it to close enough that she could work the zipper. Camaro flipped off the lights in the room, and when Lauren looked to her Camaro put a finger to her lips. "Uncle Matt," she whispered. Lauren nodded, her eyes bright in the darkness.

They stole across the hallway down a short passage to the bathroom just as Soto kicked the front door in. The suitcase was left behind. The bathroom had no window and the shadows there were total. Camaro half-closed the door. Lauren clung to her.

Camaro glanced around the small room. The tub was old, built into the wall, and probably made of cast iron. She pointed to it. "Lie down in there."

Lauren looked as though she might not obey, but then she complied. Silently she stepped into the tub and lowered herself into a fetal position below the lip, completely shielded. Camaro returned her attention to the door.

"She's in here," Camaro heard Matt say. "That has to be her truck. I saw a light."

"I don't want to get ambushed again, bro," Soto said.

"Don't keep your head up your ass, then. Move it. I'll cover the front. You check the back. Parker's room is all the way on the end."

There was the scrape of an athletic shoe on the floor, and Camaro heard Soto come nearer. A moment later he passed the bathroom with his gun out, a dark shape against more dark. He paused at Lauren's room. "Hey, it looks like Parker's kid was packing," he said.

"Look under her bed."

Soto went into the bedroom. He was gone half a minute before he reappeared in the hallway. "No, she's not under there."

"Did you look in the closet?"

"Shit," Soto said, and he disappeared again.

Camaro had her hand on Lauren's shoulder. She felt the girl trembling. The tears were all gone. Now there was only adrenaline. "Don't make a sound," Camaro said into her ear.

Soto came out of the room. "Nothing in the closet."

"Go check Parker's room. Look all over."

She waited until he was gone before she eased the bathroom door open more widely and stepped through. When Lauren started to move, Camaro stilled her with a hand and touched her lips again. Lauren remained silent.

"I found it!" Soto yelled.

"The money?" Matt yelled back.

"No, but there's a hole in the wall. It must be where he was keeping it. That lady must have it now."

"She's around here somewhere," Matt said loudly. "You hear that, you bitch? We're gonna find you! And Lauren!"

Camaro advanced soundlessly until she was even with the hallway that split the house. She knew without having to look that Matt stood at one end. Parker's bedroom was on the other, only a few steps away. Camaro heard Soto rifling through the dresser anyway, just to be thorough.

"Lauren, honey!" Matt called out. "Can you hear me? It's Uncle Matt! Come over here! Nobody's gonna hurt you."

She did not spare a glance Lauren's way. The girl had not moved, would not move until Camaro gave the signal. Perhaps not even then, if fear overrode sense and she was paralyzed by it.

"Come on, Sandro," Matt said. "If it's not there, it's not there."

"Coming."

Camaro waited until he was exactly abreast of her before she struck. His weapon was at his side, and she seized his wrist, pushing in hard and rolling his forearm over even as she closed her other hand over the gun. Soto made a loud yelping sound. His body followed his arm, the shoulder joint turning and forcing him to tumble over Camaro's forward boot onto his back.

She heard Matt yell, and she crouched as his gun went off. Plaster dust burst into the narrow hallway as the bullets went wide, hitting nothing but wall. Camaro closed her finger over Soto's and triggered his weapon once and then a second and third time. The slugs did not land.

Matt reeled out the open front door, shooting wildly. Camaro wrenched the pistol backward in Soto's hand until she heard his finger break, and then she jerked it free of his grip. The gun passed into her right fist, and she emptied it after Matt, the muzzle flash strobing in the darkened hall. Matt was gone. The Charger's engine roared on the curb.

Soto struggled to make his feet, and Camaro dropped onto his back, turning until she clung to his back like a crab closing its legs.

One arm went beneath his chin, and she locked her wrists together to squeeze. Camaro felt and heard his breath rasping and the pressure of his pulse against her arm, and then he went limp. Outside, the Charger laid down rubber on the quiet street.

She put the empty gun back into his broken hand and pressed his fingers to it. "Lauren, come on," she said.

Lauren left the bathroom slowly. "Is he dead?"

"No, but he'll wake up soon. We have to go."

Camaro offered her hand, and Lauren stepped over Soto's motionless body. Camaro took the attaché case and they both rushed to the front door. Lights were coming on in houses all along the lane, and the silhouettes of the people inside were black against yellow windows. They ran for the truck. In less than a minute they were gone.

CHAPTER THIRTY-FIVE

"YEAH, I UNDERSTAND," Ignacio said into his phone. "I'm here now. I'll talk to you soon."

There were not so many police units on this scene as there had been at the killings in Liberty City. Three marked cars were on the curb in front of Parker Story's house, their light bars flickering, as the officers themselves collected on the tiny lawn. They straightened up when Ignacio got out of his car and they saw the shield dangling from its chain around his neck.

"Who was first on the scene?" Ignacio asked them.

"I was, Detective," said one. He was young, black, and could not have been in uniform for more than a year. "Officer Sapp."

"What's your first name, Sapp?"

"Quinn, sir."

"Okay. Walk me through it. Do we have any bodies?"

"No bodies, no. Lots of bullet casings."

"Let's go inside."

The front door was broken down and barely hung from its hinges. Ignacio made note of the shoe-print on the painted wood. "Someone needs to get a picture of that," he said.

"CSIs are on their way."

"What's taking so long?"

"You had them all up in Liberty City, sir."

Ignacio sighed. "Right."

There were a number of bullet casings scattered around inside and just outside the door. Ignacio counted eight altogether. He crouched down to look at them, careful not to disturb anything until photographs were taken. The rounds were 9 mm. Maybe a thousand stores in the Miami metropolitan area and beyond sold ammunition exactly like it.

"We have more in here," Sapp said.

All of the lights in the house had been turned on, so it was easy to see the bright, shining brass in the hallway. More 9 mm shell casings. This time there were at least a dozen. Ignacio saw the divots taken out of the wall where two bullets had landed. One slug was still embedded in the drywall. "Lots of shooting and no dead bodies," Ignacio said. "That's something, I guess. Show me more."

"The place has two bedrooms," Sapp explained. "One looks like it belonged to a little girl, and then there's the master bedroom. It looks like the girl was clearing out, because there's a suitcase full of her stuff. The master bedroom's been worked over pretty good."

"Let's see."

In the master bedroom the mattress on the bed had been pushed out of alignment, and all the drawers in the dresser were open. Ignacio stood by the open closet and almost didn't notice the hole in the wall. Sapp was there. "Somebody stripped off that wood there," he said.

Ignacio got down on his hands and knees. His keychain had an LED flashlight on it, and he shone the bright beam into the hole. It was dusty inside, but there were marks on the floor indicating that something had been pushed in and pulled out several times. He wondered what could fit in such a space. A case for a gun, maybe. Parker Story was a convicted felon, and if someone found a weapon in his house, it was a serious charge.

"Tell me about the cars," Ignacio said when he got up.

Sapp brought out a notepad. "According to the neighbors, there were two vehicles out front when the shooting started. There was a red crew-cab pickup and a yellow-and-black car. They said the car looked like it was for racing."

"It's a Dodge Charger," Ignacio said.

Sapp made a notation with a pen. "We didn't get a plate on the Charger, but we got a partial for the pickup. AUG. I called it in already. They're going to let us know when they come up with a match."

"That shouldn't take long," Ignacio said.

"No, sir."

"Did the neighbors see any *people?*"

"Yes. One unidentified white male and two white females, one about thirteen or fourteen. They said the girl lives here."

"She's Parker Story's daughter. What about the male? Have they seen him before?"

"No one said so, but they did say the car's been around before."

"But there's more, right?"

"Yes, sir. There's the guy."

"The guy? Who was the guy?"

"Latino male. A unit picked him up about a mile from here, running somewhere. They stopped and searched him and found he was packing an automatic. His trigger finger was busted up real bad, though."

"What was his name?"

"Sandro Luis Soto."

The flesh along Ignacio's spine tingled, and he nearly gasped out loud. "Why didn't someone tell me this in the first place?"

"Well, we heard you were interested in Parker Story, and this is his place."

"And Sandro Soto! Sandro Soto, too! Where is he?"

"Taken down to booking."

Ignacio left the bedroom and picked his way carefully through the hallway and its scattered brass. "I'm headed down to booking. Have someone call me when the CSIs get here, and tell them to call me if they find anything useful. Meanwhile, wake up all the neighbors again, and ask them the same questions all over. Somebody knows something they didn't say the first time."

"I'll take care of it."

"Good job, Quinn."

"Thanks, sir."

Ignacio went out of the house and instructed the other two uniforms what to do. He put Sapp in charge. "If anything weird happens, anything at all, I want to be told," he told them.

He hurried to his car. Sandro Soto was just an hour ahead of him.

CHAPTER THIRTY-SIX

Camaro drove until she found a motel in Coral Terrace that fit her needs. She wanted something with parking off the street and rooms to let by the week, and it had to be the sort of place that blended with the surrounding buildings. The place could not be shiny and scrubbed and part of a chain, but rather something that had melted into the neighborhood over years until it was all but invisible.

The night manager was asleep in the back office, but the buzzer woke him up. Camaro paid him with money from the attaché case and asked for a room on the third and highest floor, something that did not face the road. He complied. Their door was tucked down a short hallway where the stairs came up, down by the ice machine.

Inside there were two full-sized beds made up with simple but neat spreads. The carpeting was industrial and thinning in places, but it didn't matter. The television was old, not a flat screen, and was bolted to the ceiling in a steel frame. The phone, too, was affixed to the immobile nightstand with a metal bracket. It would have still been possible to steal the TV remote.

Camaro sat on one bed and Lauren on the other. Each said nothing to the other for a long time. A deep tiredness had sunk into Camaro's limbs, and she allowed herself to slump in place. Finally she said, "I'm going to take a shower. Will you be all right out here by yourself?"

"I'm not going anywhere."

"See if you can get a little rest. Turn off the lights if you want."

She let herself into the tiny room that held the toilet and the shower stall. First she took off her boots and put her knife and gun on top of the toilet tank. Afterward, she stripped out of her clothing and tried to make it neat on the toilet seat before getting under a lukewarm spray and scrubbing herself with the cheap, pink bar of soap the motel provided.

The towels were thin and barely dried her. She let her damp hair fall to her shoulders and dressed again. Her clothes smelled like sweat, but she had smelled far worse and gone without clean clothes for far longer.

When she came out of the bathroom the lights were out, but there was enough illumination from the open corner of the blinds to let Camaro find her bed. She lay down on top of the bedspread and rested her gun on the mattress beside her with her hand covering it.

Lauren was not asleep. Camaro heard her breathing, but it was not the sound of slumber. It did not surprise her when Lauren spoke. "I forgot your name," she said.

"It's Camaro."

"That's kind of funny."

"A little."

"You already know my name."

"I do."

"What else do you know about me?"

"Not a whole lot. That you're smart and pretty and you've had a tough time. And that your dad loved you very much."

Lauren stayed quiet, and Camaro heard her sniffle once. "Can you tell me what's happening?" Lauren asked.

"Your dad got into something he shouldn't have," Camaro said. "Some people turned out to be more dangerous than he thought. Things went wrong."

"Were you there when he died?"

Camaro weighed her answer. "I was."

"Did he die in pain?"

She flashed on the shuddering in his body and the sucking noise of his chest wound. The blood on his lips. Three terrible injuries, two of them inevitably mortal. "No. He never felt anything."

"How did you know him?"

"I was his friend."

"How come I never met you before tonight?"

"We weren't best friends," Camaro said.

A springing sound carried to Camaro from outside, and she tensed before she realized it was the compressor on the ice machine firing up. She let the sudden rush of nerves pass and listened to Lauren crying instead.

"Uncle Matt wanted to kill me," Lauren managed after a while.

"You don't know that."

"I do. He killed my dad, didn't he?"

"No," Camaro said. "But it was his fault. All of this is his fault."

"What can I do?"

"The first thing you can do is go to sleep," Camaro said. "Always sleep when you have the chance, even if you don't feel tired. You never know when you'll have to move, so you don't want to be ragged out. So close your eyes and try not to think about tonight. I know it's not going to be easy, but you have to try."

"Are you going to sleep?"

"I'm going to try."

"Will you be gone when I wake up?"

Camaro shook her head in the dark. "No. I won't be gone. But I'll have to go eventually. I'll need to get back to my house, pick up some things there. After that, we'll see how it goes."

"Just don't go right away, okay?"

"I said I wouldn't," Camaro said.

"All right. Good night...Camaro."

"Good night, Lauren."

She stayed awake until she was certain Lauren had finally drifted off. Only then did she allow sleep to come rising up through her body, to submerge her and carry her away in its currents.

CHAPTER THIRTY-SEVEN

IGNACIO LOOKED AT the clock on his phone. It was ten o'clock in the morning.

They had turned him away at central booking, insisting that he must wait until Sandro Soto was processed. Then they had turned him away because Soto had to see a doctor about his broken finger. After that was done he had been informed that there could be no questions until after Soto was put in front of a judge, at which point he could be sent downtown for an interview.

Ignacio spent the time eating. First, he attacked the vending machines at central booking, washing candy bars and pastries down with coffee. Then he stopped off at a place near headquarters to get a toasted bagel loaded with meat and cheese, a large orange juice, and still more coffee. No matter how much he ate, he still felt like he was spread too thin.

He was at his desk when the call came. Soto was there and in the interview room. He took a legal pad and a pair of pens with him.

Soto had not been changed into a uniform, but wore his street clothes. Immediately, Ignacio wished he had checked the charge sheet before coming in, but now it was too late. A quick appearance and a hasty exit would make him look stupid, and he could not afford that with a stack of bodies waiting for his attention.

The legal pad went on the plain metal table between them and the pens on top of that. The chairs in the interview room were made of hollow aluminum and barely weighed anything at all to keep them from being used as weapons. Ignacio was convinced they would fold under his weight every time he sat, but they held. Soto put his hands on the table. One of his hands was covered to the wrist with a cast, his index finger completely encased. He wore cuffs.

"Still have you hooked up, huh?" Ignacio asked.

"Can you help a guy out?"

Ignacio got out his keys and unlocked the cuffs. He left them in the center of the table where they would remain a presence but also an indicator of goodwill. Soto moved to rub his wrists, but one was covered and his right hand was in no condition for much of anything at all. "Thanks," he said.

"Hand's all messed up," Ignacio said.

"Yeah."

"How did that happen?"

"I just twisted it, is all."

"Must have twisted it pretty bad to get a cast like that. Did they have to cover up your whole hand?"

"That's what I told 'em, but they wouldn't listen. They said I couldn't have just a splint because the whole thing can't move. Gonna be weeks with this on."

"Can you pick anything up?"

"Yeah, kind of."

Ignacio nodded amiably. "Let me ask you something: do you remember me?"

Soto squinted at him. "Maybe."

"There was this crew going around knocking over pawnshops a few years back," Ignacio said. "They didn't kill anybody at first, but they were working their way up to it. Eventually, they managed to drop three people and make off with a serious haul. Antique gold coins. Jewelry. That kind of thing. The guys who died didn't like banks too much, so they kept everything in their safe, you know? Got themselves killed."

"That's too bad," Soto said. "Sad story."

"Anyway, I'm surprised you don't remember me, because I came around asking questions about that night. You told me you didn't know anything, and the very next day you picked up and moved out of town."

Soto made a show of screwing up his face in concentration. "Oh, yeah, I remember you now. You used to be thinner."

"Yeah, I was," Ignacio said. "You look about the same. Working out?"

"Always. Got to lift."

"Sure, sure. Anyway, Sandro, I have a problem: last night a whole bunch of people got killed in Liberty City, including your old friend Jackson Dewey. Now, I don't have proof yet that you were there, but I'm going to find it eventually. Plus, there's this whole other scene where a lot of shooting went on. And officers find you fleeing with an unlicensed handgun."

"I don't know nothing about it."

"Of course not," Ignacio said. "But let me tell it to you straight: I know this all has to do with Matt Clifford."

Soto hid it, but Ignacio saw the name register. The man rubbed the back of his cast with his good hand. A sign.

"I know Matt's back in town, I know you've been sleeping on his couch, and I know that whatever happened last night has to do with him. *Seven bodies* got pulled out of that auto yard in Liberty City. And I will bet my next mixto you were there. You were there both times. We have your gun, and we'll match it to the shell casings at the scenes. If we dig any bullets out of anywhere, we'll be able to tell if they were yours. I'll be able to lay it all down on *your* head."

Soto stared at him. He still rubbed the cast. "But you can't right now."

"No, no I can't. But I will."

"The judge said I could walk until my court date."

"I can hold you," Ignacio said.

"But you won't. Because you don't have anything. You think I'm gonna roll over just because you think you have some smart guy in a lab somewhere? You come to me when you got some proof, and then I'll talk."

"Sandro," Ignacio said. "Listen to me. I'll get you. I'll get Matt Clifford. And whichever one of you cuts the deal first is the one who doesn't go down for first-degree murder. It's just like that. So why don't you save you and me a whole bunch of headaches and tell me exactly what happened last night? Come on, bro! Confession is good for the soul!"

Soto was quiet. He leaned forward over the table. *"Vete a la mierda."*

"That's all you have to say?"

"That's all I have to say."

Ignacio got up and collected the legal pad, the pens, and the handcuffs. "I'll send someone to let you out," he said. "See you soon, Sandro."

He left the interview room and nearly walked into Pool. Like him, Pool was still dressed in his clothes from the early morning call and had a lined face fueled by coffee and sugar. "Hey, Nacho," Pool said. "I was looking for you."

"What is it?"

Pool presented him with a printout. "Something you'll like."

CHAPTER THIRTY-EIGHT

Jackson's blood was on the car. Matt stopped at a do-it-yourself carwash and pulled down the doors to get some privacy before feeding dollar bills into the machine and starting up the high-powered spray. He hosed down the Charger from nose to tail, careful to avoid the open window on the right-hand side. When it was done, he pulled out to the vacuums and paid more money to suction the floors and seats free of broken glass.

The passenger-side window had been completely blown out, and there were bullet tears in the cushions of the bucket seat on that side. The rear window was not broken totally but looked as though it had been pelted by heavy hail, some of which had punched through. It was impossible to see through the cracks and stars in the glass from the inside.

More upsetting were the holes in the bodywork. The Charger had taken a dozen rounds, the bullets puncturing neat holes in the metal skin. None had compromised the engine, which was a miracle all by itself, but anyone who happened to look the car over closely would see the marks of a gun battle and know immediately what had happened.

He knew the smartest thing to do would be to ditch the car. A 1970 Dodge Charger was conspicuous enough, but the yellow-and-black coloring stood out like a warning sign. As he drove, he found himself scouring the street ahead, looking to catch sight of cops before they caught sight of him.

In the parking lot of a grocery store, he got out his tools and stole a license plate off the back of an old Buick. He replaced the plate with the one from the Charger, despite the fact that it said it was a historic vehicle.

A switch like that wouldn't work miracles. Even as he drove away from the grocery store, he was aware that it was something he did only to ease his mind and not to truly hide from the police. Again he knew the Charger had to go. He could not do it.

When he had made the score four years before and left Miami with his portion of what they'd taken from the pawnshop owners, he was flush. He smoked a little of it. Maybe a lot of it. But a chunk of the rest he put into the Charger. It had been blue back then and had no interior left except the seats. Everything else had slipped away as he labored to bring the car back from the dead, scrubbing every bolt in the engine and checking every last part down to an original steering wheel. The pleasure of receiving his historic vehicle registration had been almost equal to a high.

The good move now would be to pull back to the warehouse and wait out the worst of what was to come. Down there, past the last bit of civilization, he could keep the Charger safe from suspicious eyes. But he wasn't ready to head back yet. Chapado could stew. Maybe he had shit his own pants. The thought of the man having to sit in his own filth was even more amusing than when Chapado wet himself.

He could use a high. Not a lot, but maybe a hit or two to take the edge off. He'd been using a bit more lately, but that wasn't unusual; he liked the amperage he got from smoking before a big job. Some said it made them feel fuzzy, but Matt felt jazzed. He would stay up all night and all day, and his mind would race through a thousand permutations of what was to come next. Smoking made him a human computer with a billion connections. That was nothing but good.

It was getting on in the morning when he pulled over to the side of the road and placed a call. He was pleased that it didn't take long for Echave to answer. The man had no time for greetings. "What have you done?" he asked Matt.

"What have *I* done? I can ask you the same question. This was a deal I made with you, and this time it was you guys who tried to screw *me*. But you missed, asshole. I don't have a scratch on me. Your guys were no good."

"Mr. Clifford," Echave said, "this must end. It's true that we tried to take Señor Chapado from you, but you must understand why we did it. We didn't know if we could trust you. Once already you betrayed us. How could we know if we could trust you this time?"

"I was gonna let you have him," Matt said. "If you came with the money. But you didn't come with the money. You brought a case full of paper. And then you tried to *kill me!*"

"I'm sorry," Echave said. "It was a miscalculation. Now we know where each of us stands. But I must know: is Señor Chapado still alive?"

Matt looked in the rearview mirror for cops, but the shattered back window blocked the angle. He adjusted the side mirror instead, turning it up the street so he could see the cars coming on. Nothing. "Yeah, he's still alive," he said.

"May I speak to him?"

"No, you *can't* speak to him. Maybe in twenty-four hours when I'm not feeling so pissed off, but not now. He's all mine."

"All right. What is it that you want?"

Matt smacked the steering wheel. "What do you *think* I want? I want the *money*. For reals this time, not some bullshit paper. I want one hundred thousand dollars, and I want it delivered to me at a place and a time of my choosing."

"Of course. Whatever you want. When will this be?"

"We'll do it in three days."

"Why not now? We have the money."

"I said *three days*. I want you to think about what you did, and I want you to think about this, too: if I don't have my hands on that money when I ask for it, I'm going to start cutting pieces off your guy and mailing them to you."

"I understand," Echave said.

"Good. I'll call back. Stay by the phone."

Matt ended the call and tossed the phone into the passenger seat. He turned the engine over and moved on.

CHAPTER THIRTY-NINE

It was past eleven in the morning and Lauren was still sleeping. Camaro understood that kind of rest. It was not the usual kind of slumber but a little coma that the body passed into after it had been shocked and the adrenaline finally faded. There had been times when Camaro slept for eighteen hours straight, the energy drained from her completely.

But now she was awake and listening to Lauren in the dark. All night she'd checked her watch periodically, watching the luminous hands tick through the minutes and then the hours. If she was going to do this, she had to do it now.

She rose from the bed. Immediately Lauren stirred. "What... what is it?" the girl asked.

"Shh. It's nothing. No one's here."

"What are you doing?"

Camaro put her foot up on the bed and tucked the Glock away in her boot. "I have to go for a while."

"What? Where?"

She spoke calmly to soothe the anxiety in Lauren's voice. "It's only for a little while. I have to go home and grab some things. I won't be gone more than an hour. I'll bring you food."

"What if Uncle Matt finds you?"

"Uncle Matt has bigger problems right now. Besides which, he doesn't know where I live. The worst he can do is go back to my boat, but I'm not going to be there. Not until this is all taken care of."

"When will that be?"

Camaro paused in the gloom. "I don't know."

"Take me with you."

"No. I want to be on my own for this. I'll move faster, and the fewer people who see us together, the better. By now the cops are going to be looking for you. We don't want to get tangled up in that."

"Why not just go to the police?"

Camaro sat on the bed and looked at Lauren's shadow in the dark. "I don't think the cops are going to be too happy with what happened last night with your dad. A lot of people died. I'd have to answer questions I don't want to answer. I don't know what they'd do with you."

Lauren was quiet. "They'd put me back in the system."

"The foster system?"

"Yeah. I don't want to go there."

"You won't have to. I already know what to do. But first I have to go."

She stood and Lauren made no move to stop her. Camaro went to the door, used the peephole first, and then cracked it open slowly to check the passage outside. There was no one. She looked back at Lauren, illuminated by the light coming in the doorway. Then she slipped out.

The truck waited. She got behind the wheel and turned up the air conditioner. The drive home from here was less than half an hour. She would be in and out before anyone knew she had been there at all.

Not a single police unit crossed her path on the way home. She parked in the carport and let herself in through the side door. The house was warm and quiet. She went to her bedroom, found a bag, and put it on the bed.

The first thing in was two changes of clothes. There was a photograph of her and her sister, taken when they were teenagers, next to the Dumbo ride at Disneyland. She took that and put it in. Next she went to the gun safe and dialed her way in.

The safe had a compartment for ammo. It was half-filled with boxes of .45 and .308 rounds. The other half was taken up with stacks of cash. She took these out.

There was not much left of what she'd come to Florida with. Together with the money Parker paid her and some she'd put aside, she had a little over thirty thousand. There was more, but it was locked away in a savings account, and she didn't want to touch that while there was a chance someone might be looking. For the most part, she lived her life paying for everything with cash or money orders. It had worked so far.

She stuffed the money into the bag and zipped it up. She left the bedroom and headed out to the carport. She had just pulled the side door shut when she saw the cop coming up the driveway.

He was not in uniform, but he wore a badge on a chain around his neck. Sunglasses hid his eyes, and he had a neat mustache. When he saw her, he lifted the badge up for her to see. "Hey, there," he said.

Camaro dropped the bag behind her bike. It had not been seen. "Hello," she said.

"This your truck?"

"Yes."

"So you're Camaro Espinoza?"

"Yes."

The cop stepped into the shade of the carport. "I'm Detective Ignacio Montellano. I'd like to ask you a few questions."

CHAPTER FORTY

THE DETECTIVE LOOKED very tired, and his clothes were wilted. As they faced each other, Ignacio removed the hat he wore and wiped his forehead with the back of his arm. He was going to fat and clearly got the sweats when temperatures rose.

"Is this a good time?" Ignacio asked her.

"Sure," Camaro said.

"Okay. You don't think we could go inside, do you? The heat is killing me."

"Come in," Camaro said, and she opened the side door.

He passed her bike and the bag without glancing at them, and Camaro hoped he'd paid at least the bag no notice. They went into the warm stillness of the kitchen, but when they came through into the living room, Camaro put on the air conditioner and cool air began to circulate.

"Thanks," Ignacio said. "It's this jacket. They say we have to wear one to look our best, but they're murder when it gets like this. Mind if I sit?"

"Go ahead."

Ignacio took a place on the couch. Camaro hesitated where she stood before taking a chair. She breathed and let calm spread through her.

"You're probably wondering why I'm here," Ignacio said.

"It crossed my mind."

"Let me ask you this: where were you between three and four o'clock this morning?"

"I was here," Camaro said.

Ignacio nodded and brought a small notebook out of his jacket. He used a pen to scribble something down. "I kind of figured you'd say that. There didn't happen to be anyone around who could vouch for you, was there? Boyfriend? Girlfriend?"

"No," Camaro said. "I was alone."

"Alone," Ignacio said as if to himself, and he made another notation. "That's too bad. Did you lend your truck to anybody last night? Somebody who might have driven it around after last call?"

"No."

"Right." Another note.

"Why are you asking me so many questions about my truck?" Camaro asked.

Ignacio studied her before answering. "I guess I can tell you. There was this shoot-out last night, and a fourteen-year-old girl disappeared from her house. A few witnesses said they saw a truck matching the description of yours at the scene."

"I'm sure a lot of trucks look like mine."

"Ah," Ignacio said, "that's true. *But* this truck *also* had three of the letters from your license plate on its license plate. Turns out there aren't any trucks in the whole state that look like yours *and* have those letters on their plates. So I have to ask: where were you *really* this morning?"

Camaro looked him in the face. "I was here."

He smiled a little and crossed his legs, leaning back into the couch. "Okay, that's fine. I'm going to go ahead and pretend that what you're telling me is true because I don't want us to get off on the wrong foot. It's not like anyone got killed in that shoot-out or anything. There's just the whole kidnapping angle if the girl didn't go willingly. That's pretty serious."

"I didn't have anything to do with it," Camaro said.

The smile did not go away. "Then tell me this: do you know a guy named Parker Story? And this time tell it to me straight. It's not a crime to know somebody."

She thought and then she decided. "I know him."

"Did you know he was killed last night?"

"I thought you said no one died."

"Oh, I meant there was a whole other shoot-out across the way in Liberty City where a whole bunch of people died. Parker was one of them. And the coincidental thing is that it was Parker's house and Parker's daughter I'm here about."

"I didn't know he was dead," Camaro said.

"Well, he is. Shot to death, along with six others. Looks like some kind of deal gone sideways, but I don't know what it could be. You don't have any ideas, do you?"

"None."

"How did you know Parker?"

"He came to me wanting to hire a boat for some night fishing."

"Oh, so you run charters?"

"Yes."

"Got a nice boat?"

"It's pretty good."

"Go on."

"There's not a whole lot to tell. He paid, but we never went out."

"Why's that?"

Ignacio was watching her, and Camaro knew he was gauging everything about her. If she moved, he would know why. If she lied, he would suspect. If she turned him away with nothing, he would only come back again and again.

"I asked you why that was," Ignacio said.

"You want the truth?"

"That would be a good start."

"Okay, here's the truth: Parker was fronting for a man named Matt. Parker told me he wanted a fishing charter, but Matt offered me ten thousand dollars to take him and his crew to Cuba and back overnight. I said no, and that was the end of it."

"I see. What did he want to do in Cuba that he couldn't do out in the open?"

"I didn't want to know, and I didn't ask," Camaro said. "I run a clean operation. I don't look for trouble."

"Is that why you have that gun in your boot?"

She resisted the urge to reach for the weapon and kept herself perfectly still. If there was something in her face, Ignacio did not react to it. She was stone.

"Do you have a concealed carry permit?" Ignacio asked.

"No," Camaro said.

"So I could arrest you right now for unlawfully carrying a concealed weapon," Ignacio said.

"Are you going to?"

He paused a long moment. "What kind of gun is it?"

"A Glock 38."

"I know that gun. Fires a special kind of .45 round, right?"

"Yeah."

"Then I'm not going to run you in for it," Ignacio said. "My shooters used 9 mm's. Of course, if I catch you some other time carrying that thing, I'm gonna have to do what I have to do. You can consider this a friendly warning."

"Thanks."

"No problem. If you knew how many people carried without a permit . . . it's a lot. We'd be busy all day long, and I'm more interested in finding out other things, like who killed Parker Story and why. And finding his daughter. Lauren's her name. Did you know that?"

"No."

"You wouldn't, would you? You plan on seeing Matt Clifford again?"

"Not if I can help it."

"Good idea. You might end up having to use that gun on him. He's not a good guy. But I think you figured that out already. Maybe that's why you didn't take him to Cuba."

"I just want to fish," Camaro said.

"Don't we all?" Ignacio said, and he got up. The notebook went into his jacket with the pen. "Listen, Ms. Espinoza, I know we agreed that you weren't at Parker Story's house last night and that you weren't the woman people saw running out of the place with his daughter, but I have a couple of requests."

Camaro stood. "What are they?"

"First of all, I don't want you leaving the Miami area. And the second thing is this: eventually, you need to tell me where Lauren Story is because the longer she's missing, the more the heat's gonna build. People are going to get involved that aren't as understanding as I am."

"If I see her, I'll tell you," Camaro said.

"I'm serious about staying close. If I think you've left town, I'll call the state police, and they'll track you down. If that happens, I can't be such a nice guy."

"I understand."

"Great. I'll let myself out. Thanks for the air conditioning."

Camaro stayed in the living room and listened to him leave. He went out by the side door, and a few moments later she saw him through the window, walking down the driveway in his withered jacket and slacks. She wondered how long he'd been awake and how much longer he would push.

She shut off the air conditioning and waited for him to drive away. It was time to go.

CHAPTER FORTY-ONE

Galdarres arrived in Miami in another of his white linen suits. At baggage claim he took a single suitcase and a garment bag with him. He removed his Panama hat like a supplicant when he reached the front of the customs line and smiled amiably at the woman in her uniform. "Where are you coming from?"

"My last stop was in Havana, but I come from Caracas."

"What's the purpose of your visit?"

"I've come to see relations."

"Will you put your luggage on the table, please?"

A black man with a stout chest barely contained by his uniform shirt went through Galdarres' things without a flicker of emotion on his face. He did not make a mess of the suitcase and made short work of the garment bag. When he was done, he nodded to the woman in the booth.

She stamped Galdarres' Venezuelan passport. "Welcome to the United States."

"Thank you so very much," Galdarres said. He put on his hat, took his things, and walked away.

A man in a short-sleeved shirt and slacks intercepted him near a small newsstand. The man was neat and clean and could have been anyone, but he approached Galdarres directly. "The men's room is closed," he said.

"I'll have to find another," Galdarres replied.

The man made to offer his hand before realizing that Galdarres' were full. He put his arms down straight at his sides. He had once been military, Galdarres noted. "I am Davíd Ocampo," he said.

"I am pleased to meet you, Davíd. I am Alejandro."

"I brought a car, sir," Davíd said.

"Very good. Let's go."

They walked through the terminal together, weaving through crowds of people that thronged like schools of eager fish. The airport was much newer and larger than José Martí International Airport in Havana, a triumph of American success. Galdarres guessed that more people traveled through this airport in a month than went through Havana in a year.

Davíd took them to short-term parking, where a bright yellow Volvo sedan awaited them. Galdarres put his things in the trunk and got in the passenger seat as Davíd started the engine and set the air to maximum. Even with the vents blowing full force it took a few minutes before the baking heat of the interior receded. They backed out of the space and went on their way.

"What can you tell me?" Galdarres asked.

"There has been a great deal of activity in the last twenty-four hours," Davíd replied.

"Begin at the beginning."

"You are aware that Echave and his people paid an outside man to retrieve Chapado from Cuba?"

"I had heard something of the kind. I don't understand why they didn't do it themselves."

"Echave insists on everything being very clean. That's what our informant tells us. Chapado could not leave Cuba legally, and smuggling aliens into the United States is still a federal crime, no matter who they are. He did not want to be caught violating federal law. He agreed to pay one hundred thousand dollars for someone else to take all the risks."

"So Chapado is here now?"

"Yes, but things have gone wrong. The man they hired demanded more money for Chapado's safe return. There was a terrible scramble to raise the funds before Echave gave the order to retrieve Chapado by any means necessary."

"Violence?" Galdarres asked.

They stopped at the ticket booth, and Davíd paid for parking. Once they were away from the lot and merged with traffic, Davíd continued. "He commanded that the man they hired be eliminated. No more money for him. Only, something has gone wrong. All of Echave's men were killed, and Chapado is still in the hands of this other man. Echave and his people are in a panic."

Galdarres turned over what he had been told. After his meeting with Director Celades, the outlines of the mission had seemed quite clear: isolate Chapado among Echave's people and eliminate him. But if Echave himself had no contact with Chapado, all else became impossible. "How secure is our informant?" he asked.

"He is very well placed."

"So any developments among Echave's people will be relayed to us immediately?"

"Yes. We have constantly monitored Echave and his inner circle for over a year now. If Echave or anyone around him suspects our man, they have given no indication of it."

"Where are we going now?"

"There is an office," Davíd said. "It's where I carry out my cover occupation. I've arranged for a meeting this afternoon with everyone."

"What is your cover?" Galdarres asked.

"I sell car insurance," Davíd answered. "We give excellent rates. Two of our people work under me, but the others have cover occupations of their own."

"How many do we have in the city?"

"Four, including myself."

"So few?"

"Times have changed, señor. There isn't the funding to support a large unit, and the number of people we're called upon to monitor grows smaller every year. Echave is not replacing his older membership with young people fast enough. In ten or twenty years there will be nothing left but a skeleton. Or a ghost."

Galdarres rapped the closed window beside him and chewed his lip. "Do we at least have access to weapons and gear? Are our men capable of handling an armed confrontation?"

"Yes, sir. Three of us have served in the United States military. I was a marine myself."

The irony of it did not escape Galdarres, but he made no comment on it. Galdarres had himself served in the Cuban Revolutionary Armed Forces as a young man.

"Would you care for something to eat? There is an excellent place near my office."

"I'm not interested in eating," Galdarres said. "I'm interested in moving forward."

"Of course. Of course."

Galdarres watched the city go by. So many cars and so many people. He hated it all.

CHAPTER FORTY-TWO

MATT STOPPED AT a food stand. It was a small, cheap place built into the side of a stucco structure painted brilliant pink. The shaded dining area consisted entirely of old wooden picnic tables, most of which were crowded with Cubans, light and dark, feasting on sandwiches and other things.

He ordered a *frita* and sat down on the end of a picnic table's bench to wait. It was only a few minutes, and then he had the sandwich in his hands. The Coke they gave him was the size of a bucket.

The *frita,* a Cuban hamburger with a patty of beef and chorizo sausage, was smothered with onion, tomato, lettuce, and shoestring potato sticks. Matt attacked it, not realizing until now how hungry he'd allowed himself to become, and took great, long swallows of the Coke between bites.

The Cubans spoke to each other solely in Spanish. This irked him. He understood little of the language and never cared to learn more. English was the language of the land. English was what people were meant to speak. Matt would take the Cuban food, but he did not have much use for anything else brought over from the island.

Once he was done he tossed away the *frita*'s paper wrapper and the empty Coke cup and headed back toward the Charger. He was nearly there when he saw the police unit emerge from beyond a corner two blocks farther down, shielded until the last second by the uprights of a small gas station.

Matt stopped in his tracks and reversed himself, heading back toward the food stand. He stepped into the shade and watched as the car moved up the street toward the Charger, then suddenly slowed as the driver noticed it was there.

The police unit came to a complete stop beside the Charger, and the officer got out. The man circled the car completely. Matt saw him make a note of the license plate number before getting back behind the wheel. A long couple of minutes passed as the officer consulted his computer, after which the unit pulled to the curb forward of the Charger and parked.

The cop was not going to leave. Matt left the food stand going the other direction, taking the first available turn. He was not certain of the neighborhood or the lay of the streets, but it did not matter so long as he put enough distance between himself and the cop by the curb.

His Charger was gone. That much he understood. The idea of it pained him, but it had been an inevitable thing. Even with the new plates, it was too striking a vehicle to escape notice. By now, police up and down the coast would have its description, along with Matt's. Had he been behind the wheel at the wrong moment, he would be in custody now.

A chime followed a vibration in his pocket. Matt brought out his phone and answered. "Sandro, where are you?" he asked.

"Fuck you, Matt," Soto said.

"What's up, bro? What did I do?"

"You left me, *bro!* You let me walk right into that bitch, and you let her break my hand, and then you *left!* You drove off and left me!"

"Calm down," Matt said. "Okay? There were reasons."

"Like what?"

"She was shooting at me, bro. I couldn't stick around. Besides, I knew she wouldn't kill you."

Soto did not sound convinced. "If she tried to kill you, then why wouldn't she try to kill me? You and me was together on this. She's got to know something. And she grabbed me around the throat and choked me out! I barely got out of there, man."

"If she choked you out, then she could have killed you," Matt said. "She didn't. That means I'm right. She's got a beef with me, but you're safe. And next time, she won't get the drop on us. We know she's coming."

"I'm so pissed with you right now," Soto said.

"I understand, bro. I totally get it. But we have to get past that. It's just you and me now, and there's a lot of money riding on what we do. You want to pull down some of that cash, right? So calm down a little bit."

He was now four blocks away from where he'd left the Charger. There was a little hardware store up the street from where he walked. Matt crossed the street to get to it. He could hear Soto breathing hard on the other end.

"Where are you?" Matt asked again.

"I'm downtown at the cop shop."

Matt stopped. "You're in with the cops?"

"No, man, I'm outside now. They put a weapons charge on me, but I got released on my own recognizance. Some detective tried to get me to talk about you and the Cubans, but I didn't tell them anything."

"They let you out because they want to see what you do," Matt said.

"What are you talking about?"

"They know you're in it with me. They want to nail both of us for what went down in Liberty City. You probably have a tail right now."

"I don't have no tail."

"You got cash?"

"Yeah."

"Take a cab. Then take a bus. Then take another cab. Watch your back, and see if anyone's following you. If they aren't, then you need to get back to the spot. Chapado's been by himself too long."

"I need a new gun. They took mine."

"I'll get you a new gun just as soon as I get a ride."

He was at the hardware store and went inside. It was sleepy and smelled of dust. It took him half a minute to find the tools he needed: a screwdriver and a pair of needle-nose pliers. An old man at the counter rang him out.

Soto was walking fast. His breath was not angry now, but rapid and shallow. Matt wanted to reach through the phone and tell him to chill out before he clued in every cop in the county. "I see a cab," Soto said.

"Take it."

"Where do I go?"

"Anywhere. It doesn't matter."

Money changed hands. The old man put the screwdriver and the pliers in a bag. Matt ignored his thank-you and went outside. His gaze traveled along the street he was on, picking out different cars parked under the unforgiving sun. He heard Soto tell the taxi driver where to go.

"Here's what you do," Matt said. "When we get off the phone, I want you to pitch yours out the window."

"What? This thing cost six hundred bucks!"

"These things can be tracked. I'm getting rid of mine, too. At the first 7-Eleven you see, go in and pick up a prepaid phone. Once you're sure you're not being followed, head to the spot, and I'll meet you there. We'll trade numbers."

"My phone—"

"Screw your phone! Get rid of it, okay? Now I got to go. Remember what I said: take a bus to anywhere, get off, find another cab.

Watch all the time."

"All right, man. But we're not finished talkin' about what you did."

"Later. Now go."

He hung up and dropped his phone on the ground. He stomped on it in the middle of the street, driving his heel into the plastic body until it was shattered under his sole. A hundred yards away was a green Kia Soul. When Matt got to it, he looked both ways and saw no one. He used his elbow to smash the driver's-side window.

Inside the car, he used the screwdriver to strip the plastic off the steering column. The needle-nose pliers were like a key in a lock. The car started. Even though the window was out, he ran the air conditioner.

Matt drove.

CHAPTER FORTY-THREE

SHE STRAPPED HER bag to the back of the Harley's pillion seat and set off on a lazy circle back toward the motel where Lauren still waited. Camaro needed time to think, and it was easier to do that when the wind was in her face and in her hair and she had the temporary illusion of freedom.

With her bike and her money she could head north or west and never look back. It would mean losing everything, and not for the first time in her life, but it would also mean she was shut of the whole situation. She could call the detective from the road and tell him where to find Lauren. Eventually, the girl would make it to her uncle. Maybe it would take a while, but they wouldn't keep her from family. Or maybe they would. Camaro did not know how these things worked.

There were countless miles of road between Miami and the state line. Enough that getting lost in them would not be so difficult a thing. The detective had promised to set the state police on her, but even they could not be everywhere at once. If she kept off the interstate highways and took obscure roads, she might travel more slowly, but she would be practically invisible.

Even as she thought all of these things, she knew she would not go. Thirty thousand dollars was money, but it was not money enough to make a new life. And the life she'd created for herself here would be lost irretrievably. She would never pilot the *Annabel* again.

The only true option was to get ahead of the situation somehow and make the chaos of Parker's death mean something. Keeping her promise was one thing, but it would not shield her from a man like the detective. It would not do away with the threat of Matt Clifford. All he had to do was speak and everything was shattered. Maybe he wouldn't, but maybe he would. The latter wasn't worth the risk, and she knew how the first could be guaranteed.

She glanced at her watch to see the time. Already she had been gone longer than she intended. Now she angled back toward Coral Terrace, blowing through a yellow light at the last moment and accelerating too quickly up a long straightaway. The possibility of a cop lighting her up occurred to her, but she was far away from that. What she saw in her mind were open waters and bright sun and escape at the end of a line.

CHAPTER FORTY-FOUR

THEY CAME TOGETHER after lunch in Hugo Echave's study. Carlos and Pablo and Álvaro were there, and Álvaro had brought his son, Ulises. Ulises was good and young and full of fire. Echave had considered him for the team meant to kill Matt Clifford but had decided at the last moment to hold him back. Given the way things had gone, he was glad of that choice.

This was the only thing that brought Echave relief. The rest was intolerable, and his mind had been afire with thoughts of it all day. Only now, with these men gathered around him, could he give voice to anger, but even then he tempered his words with control. He could not afford to be wild. "How could this happen?" he asked quietly.

"It's terrible," Carlos said.

"Yes. It is terrible. It is unspeakable. But *how* did it happen? Pablo, explain it to me."

Marquez cleared his throat. He was visibly uncomfortable in his skin. His gaze skipped from man to man in the intimate confines of the study, as if he expected one to lunge at him, catch him by the front of his shirt, and shake him until the answers spilled out onto the carpeting. "It's unclear. Because there were no survivors, we have no report from our own men. The only things I've been able to find out have been what the police have made available to the public. I called them posing as a journalist. They told me very little."

"What did they say?" Echave asked.

He cleared his throat again. "They said that it appeared two groups of men had opened fire on each other in a drug deal gone bad and that seven were left dead. They were willing to confirm that five of the men were Latino, but they were withholding names until they could notify the families."

"We know their names," Carlos said. "And we know exactly why they were there. Now you see why I was not in favor of this from the beginning. Drug deal! This is what we've been reduced to? Confused for Colombians or some other Latino trash. It's like the eighties all over again."

"Did they give any indication of how they died?" Echave asked.

"By gunshot. That was all I was told."

"He was ready for you," Carlos said. "Clifford was ready for this. He knew that we would try some sort of double cross, and he had men lying in wait for ours to show their faces."

"He lost two," Ulises Sotelo spoke up. "We drew blood."

"With respect, Álvaro," Carlos said to Sotelo, "your son wasn't even here at the planning of this thing. Why is he here at all?"

"Because he wants to be of help," Sotelo said sharply. "At a time like this, we need everyone we can muster. We don't have the numbers we used to, and many of us are too old for such things. If we are to succeed in our cause, we need young men like Ulises and Pablo to step forward and take responsibility. And right now. Not later. *Now.*"

Echave waved them all silent. "No one is more upset about this than I am. When I heard the news, I could barely see, I was so angry. Matt Clifford does not know what kind of fire he has lit in me. Or in all of us. He'll regret it."

"You can't seriously suggest going after him again," Carlos said. "Hasn't there been enough bloodshed? The whole purpose of this was to bring Sergio Chapado somewhere he could be safe and contribute to the cause. Raising another hit squad won't get us anywhere closer to that goal."

"We must fight," Ulises said.

"Álvaro, please tell your son to shut his mouth."

"No," Sotelo said. "I will not. He has a right to speak."

"Enough!" Echave said. "I won't have us bickering amongst ourselves! This is exactly what Clifford wants: for us to be in disarray and making mistakes. He can't be made to pay for what he's done to us unless we are of one mind. Rescuing Chapado from him is paramount, yes, but this does not end even if he falls into our hands tomorrow."

Carlos snorted. "How do you suggest we proceed?"

"We must pay," Marquez said.

"Never!" Ulises exclaimed.

"Now *I* will tell you to be silent," Echave said. "Pablo is right. We must pay. Or at least we must make it seem that we will pay. It is the only way to draw Clifford close to us. In the meanwhile, we use every resource at our disposal to locate him."

"What resources?" Carlos asked. "We lost five of our best men."

"The police," Echave said. "Some are sympathetic to our cause. We've received donations from a few of them. Let's find out if any of them are on this case or if they have access to the case's files. Who is the lead detective?"

"Ignacio Montellano."

"Is he Cuban?"

"I don't know. Perhaps."

"Find out. He may be partial to us and might be persuaded to give up information we can use to find Clifford."

"That's doubtful," Carlos said.

"You have other suggestions?" Echave demanded.

Carlos looked away. "No."

"The important thing is that we have the intelligence we need. There is much we can do with the right information. Álvaro, your son worked in the prosecutor's office, did he not?"

"Yes," Ulises said. "Before I went into private practice. I have friends in the district attorney's office still. Plus, there are a number of policemen with whom I remain friendly."

Echave turned his gaze on all of them in turn. "My friends, this began as a mission to save a comrade, but now it's something else. We've been attacked. People have died. It is an affront to everything we have striven for all of these years. Let us reach out now and close our fist around Matt Clifford. Let us crush the life out of him."

CHAPTER FORTY-FIVE

THE KEY TO the motel room rattled loosely in the lock as Camaro let herself in. She had two bags of food from McDonald's, but no drinks. Lauren was on her bed watching television. "Hi," she said.

"Hi," Camaro said. She put one of the bags beside Lauren. "I brought food."

"No soda?"

"I don't have cupholders on my bike."

"I'm thirsty."

"Drink water from the sink. There are glasses."

Lauren got up from the bed. She went to the sink, where two water glasses stood with paper wrappers over their mouths. She tore the wrapper off one and filled the glass, then returned. "I didn't think you were coming back."

"I had some things to do," Camaro said. She tore open her bag to lay it flat on the bedspread. She had a Double Quarter Pounder and a large fries. "Eat," she said.

Lauren was slow to her meal. She took small nibbles. "Where did you go?" she asked Camaro.

"My house."

"Is it far?"

"No."

They ate silently after that. Camaro finished off her burger and fries and went to the sink for the second glass. After a moment's consideration, she left the room with the ice bucket and returned with it filled. Plain water tasted better chilled. Camaro remembered long, hot days and drinking water the temperature of blood from a hydration pack.

It was only when Camaro balled up her trash and threw it away that Lauren spoke again. "What are you going to do with me?" she asked.

"What do you mean?"

"You can't keep me here forever. You said the police would be looking for me. And Uncle Matt is out there, too."

Camaro sat on the edge of her bed. "I think the first thing you need to do is stop calling him 'Uncle Matt.' He's not your uncle. You have a real uncle."

"That's what my dad told me. But I never met him, I don't think. Not since I was real little, anyway."

"You're going to meet him now. We're going to figure out where he is and contact him and get him here somehow. If he has you, the state won't try to take you away. Or maybe they might, but he's family, and family counts for something. It won't be like before."

Lauren thought about this. Her burger was half-eaten, but she showed no further interest in it. "My dad told you about what happened to me when he went to prison?"

"Yes."

"It wasn't good. They sent me to a house where they had bunk beds in all the rooms like we were in the army or a jail or something. The family was real strict about stuff like water and electricity. And then there was all the church. They were super churchy."

Camaro thought a moment. "That's not a life for a kid."

"So that's why you don't want me to go with the cops?"

"Yes. I said I'd look out for you. I don't think dumping you in some barracks qualifies. So it's your uncle or it's nothing."

"My uncle's name is Richard. Not Dick. Richard."

"Richard Story," Camaro said. "Out in Texas."

"I've never been to Texas."

"It's all right," Camaro said. "It's a lot like here. Hotter, maybe. Drier. I guess it depends on where he lives. There's some nice hill country, and the coast is pretty."

"When were you there?"

"Not too long ago. Finish your food."

Camaro waited while Lauren forced herself to eat. The television blathered. She would have preferred it off, but at least it put some sound between them when there was no talk. Camaro had not spoken to a fourteen-year-old girl in a long time.

"Can I ask you something?" Lauren said after she was done.

"Sure."

"Are you going to kill Unc—? Are you going to kill Matt?"

"Does that bother you?"

"No. He was always weird with me. Asking for hugs. Touching me."

"Did you tell your dad?"

Lauren shook her head. "Not about that."

"He might have done something about it," Camaro said.

"My dad would never go against Matt."

"You don't know what people will do when they find out about that," Camaro said. "I know."

"Did somebody touch you?"

"No. But if they did, I would have killed them. I had a friend, though. She wasn't so lucky."

"Did you kill the man who touched her?"

Camaro let a long breath out. "No, I didn't. But I wish I had."

"Have you killed a lot of people?"

"Yes."

"How many?"

Camaro got up from the bed and changed the channel on the television to a game show. “I think it’s better if we talked about something else,” she said. “Like what you’re going to say to your uncle about what’s happening here.”

“I’ll tell him the truth.”

“That might not be a great idea.”

“He has to know what happened.”

“He’ll find out what he needs to know to make you safe,” Camaro said. “Nothing else matters.”

“Should I tell him about Matt?”

Camaro looked at the TV. “Maybe someday. When Matt can’t hurt anybody anymore.”

CHAPTER FORTY-SIX

When he finally made it home, Ignacio fell into a long, black sleep while still wearing his clothes. He awoke feeling especially dirty and sweating under his collar, so he shed his clothes for a long shower that finally managed to throw off the last twenty-four hours. Afterward, he luxuriated by donning only boxers and a T-shirt and cooling from the hot water.

It was getting dark outside while he prepared himself a sandwich in the kitchen. He ate by the window, staring out at the varicolored sky as the sun went away. Afterward, he put real clothes on and holstered his gun at his side. It was a twenty-minute drive to the station in light traffic. He went straight to his desk.

Ignacio checked his voice mail and found a message from Pool. The man's desk was empty, and Chatman said Pool was out on a call. Ignacio called from his work phone, and Pool picked up right away. "Hey, Nacho," Pool said. "Up and at 'em again, huh?"

"Yeah, I needed the sleep. I was like the walking dead there at the end."

"We're getting old, man. Used to be I could pull forty-eight hours without blinking. Nowadays? No way."

"I was calling because you said you had something," Ignacio said.

"Yeah, I do. Have you checked your email?"

"No, not yet."

"Go now. I sent you some stuff I turned up this afternoon while you were playing Sleeping Beauty."

Ignacio opened his email. There were a dozen or more new messages, from department notices to reminders about the police softball tournament. There were two from Pool at the bottom. He clicked on the first one and left the second for now. "What am I looking at?" he asked.

"Those are the files for two of the dead guys in Liberty City. Turns out they're both Cubans, and they have a real interesting history. You ever heard of Alpha 66?"

"No. Should I have?"

"They're an anti-Castro group that formed up in the '60s. I put some information on them in the email."

"They still have anti-Castro groups?"

"Oh, yeah. As long as there are communists in charge of Cuba, the Cuban community isn't gonna let it go. Anyway, both of those guys, Pol Mendiola and Arnau Crusellas, are known associates of Alpha 66. And it gets better: both of them have weapons charges on their records. Nothing that put them in jail, but it's the kind of thing that rings my bells when I find guys shot to death in an auto yard."

Ignacio looked at the booking photos of both men. They were not exceptional in any way. If anything, they appeared to be ordinary people getting a snapshot taken for a passport photo and not for police records. One had been wearing a suit at the time of the Liberty City killings. The other had worn black combat clothing and was armed with a rifle modified to fire fully automatic. He browsed their sheets. "You think this Alpha 66 thing has anything to do with what happened?" he asked Pool.

"It's too good to just be a coincidence. Alpha 66's a paramilitary deal. Used to train out in the Everglades for an invasion of Cuba. I don't know if they still do that kind of thing after the president decided to make nice with the government over there, but now that we have a whole squad of them dead at the scene of a gun battle... there's fire to go with that smoke."

"Thanks for checking into this," Ignacio said.

"No problem. Keep me in the loop. I'm working a convenience-store shooting, but I'll lend a hand where I can."

"Okay. See you around, Brady."

"Not if I see you first."

They ended the call. Ignacio sent the files for Mendiola and Crusellas to the printer and went to pick them up. He spread them out on the desk, comparing known associates. A few names cross-indexed, and Ignacio looked them up in the system, too. Some were clean, with nothing so much as a traffic citation on their records, but a couple others had minor violations, like discharging a weapon illegally. These men, taken together as a whole, were not a hardened gang of criminal masterminds. They had families and mortgages, and there was nothing about them to suggest anything like what happened in Liberty City.

Ignacio read through the information Pool had sent about Alpha 66. Most of it read like history, stretching back to the sixties and the seventies and then going silent by the time the eighties and nineties rolled around. Two men associated with Alpha 66 had run for local political offices and won with heavy support from the Cuban community. Ignacio was not embarrassed to admit he'd never heard of them, or about Alpha 66 either.

The second man in a suit had been identified as José Valle, another Cuban American, but with no priors to his name. The men with the guns, with exception of Crusellas, were nameless, their fingerprints not in the system.

He made a note of the addresses of both the identified men, plus their known associates. It was too late to go around knocking on doors, which meant another long night waiting for an even longer morning and afternoon doing legwork. He'd start with the dead men first, then work his way around to the others systematically. There was no trick to it, only focus and determination.

There was still a single email from Pool that was left unread. Ignacio opened it and saw there were files attached. He read the message and sat back in his chair sharply. "Oh, boy," he said.

CHAPTER FORTY-SEVEN

Camaro was reluctant to head out with Lauren, but there was a place to get breakfast only a block away from the motel. They rose early. Camaro waited on Lauren to wash in the shower and put her old clothes back on. "We need to get you a change of clothes," Camaro said.

"And a toothbrush," Lauren replied.

"Okay. I also need to stop by a bike shop and find a helmet for you. If we need to move, you'll have to ride with me, and the last thing we need is some cop pulling us over because you're a minor without a helmet."

They went to the eatery and took a table far from the door, though Camaro sat where she could watch the whole dining room. Lauren chose pancakes and sausage and eggs for her breakfast. Camaro opted for an omelet with four eggs, cheese, and ham. She asked for coffee and it came quickly.

The other diners were mostly Latino and mostly older folks who slept little and needed somewhere to go early in the morning where they could read their newspapers or meet up with friends and chat. Camaro estimated she was younger than the next youngest patron by thirty years. Only Lauren carried fewer birthdays.

Service was prompt. They tucked into their meals. Camaro's omelet was good, and she ate it more quickly than she intended. Lauren smothered her stack of pancakes in blueberry syrup and washed all the sugar down with a glass of milk.

Lauren was the first to speak. "We need the Internet," she said.

"What for?"

"For my uncle. I don't know how else to find him."

"I don't know if there are any Internet cafés around," Camaro said.

"What about a library?"

The waitress came back to refresh Camaro's coffee. "Excuse me," Camaro said, "but do you know if there's a library around here?"

"In this neighborhood?" the waitress asked.

"Anywhere is good," Camaro said.

"I think there's one up by West End Park. Do you know where that is?"

"I can find it," Camaro said. "Thanks."

Lauren waited until the woman was gone and Camaro had tipped cream into her coffee. "They'll have computers you think?" she asked.

"Probably. I should go alone."

"No. I don't want to spend all day in that room again."

"It's not safe out here. I told you that."

"I want to *go,*" Lauren said.

Camaro stirred her coffee, the spoon ringing against the sides of the cup. "Okay, fine. We'll go together. But I need to get those things for you first. We'll head out around lunchtime when it's busy on the street. Is that all right with you?"

"It's fine."

They finished their meal, and Camaro paid before they made the quick trip back to the motel. Once Camaro was certain Lauren was comfortable, she headed off again, angling west out of Coral Terrace until she saw a Target. She parked in the lot and went inside where the icy cold made the small hairs on her arms stand up.

It had been a long time since Camaro was a teenager, and she didn't know what teenagers wore. She selected two blouses, some jeans that seemed all right, and some underwear. After she put a bag of socks in the cart, she went looking for toothbrushes for both of them and toothpaste, mouthwash, and sticks of deodorant.

She put everything she bought into one of the bike's saddlebags and then circled back toward her own neighborhood. There was a bike shop not far from her house, and by now it was open. She stayed only long enough to buy a helmet that would cover Lauren's face completely. Soon she was back at the motel.

Camaro dropped the Target bags on the bed. "I hope you like it," she said.

Lauren's face was unreadable as she sorted through the things, until finally she smiled and said, "Thank you."

The girl changed in the tiny bathroom, and then she and Camaro took turns brushing their teeth and freshening up with the deodorant. They did not have to look or smell like fugitives, though Camaro wondered if the slightly mildewed scent of the room clung to them when they left.

At noon exactly they went out. Camaro rode with Lauren tucked away on the pillion seat behind her, clinging to her waist through the turns. It was busy like Camaro had hoped, and they weren't the only motorcycle on the road.

They found the library on the same block as an animal hospital and a ratty strip mall filled with businesses catering to the Spanish-language community. The small parking lot was almost empty. Camaro took a space near the door. They went inside.

It was not a large place. Camaro feared that it was too small to have computers until they found the stations tucked away in the farthest corner behind shelves crammed to overflowing with books.

Lauren parked herself in front of an old CRT monitor. Camaro pulled up a chair. "Richard Story. Texas," Lauren said out loud.

It took less than a minute to find the information they were looking for. First they identified Richard Adam Story in Del Rio, Texas, and then they were able to use a white-pages lookup to get his telephone number. Or at least the last phone number he'd used. The library provided pads of paper by the computers, and Lauren took down his address and other information.

"I want to check some more things," Camaro said.

"What?"

"Look up the name Sergio Chapado. Add 'Cuba.'"

Lauren did as she was asked. There were many results. The girl chose the top one, and a site opened up. It was a blog called *Cuba Libre,* and it prominently displayed the Cuban flag. Some of the entries were in Spanish, but the one with Chapado's name in it was written in English. "What do you want to know?"

Camaro pointed. "Scroll down so I can see all of that."

The entry was short and featured a photograph of a group of people protesting with signs in Spanish. The protesters were identified as pro-democracy activists, and Sergio Chapado was mentioned as a "prominent voice." He was not in the picture, but he was quoted. "The world is freeing itself everywhere," he said. "And now it is time for our little island to do likewise."

"Who is Sergio Chapado?" Lauren asked.

"I don't really know," Camaro said. "Is there any way to search this thing for his name?"

"There's a search box."

"Do it."

Chapado's name appeared in four more entries, all dated within the last three years. In each, he was associated with the same pro-democracy groups. A Canadian reporter informed her newspaper Chapado feared no reprisals for speaking out. The times in Cuba were changing. But maybe not so much, even with the thawing of relations with the US.

"I need to know more," Camaro said.

"You can send a message to the blog owner."

"Okay. Send him my email address."

Camaro gave Lauren the address and watched as the girl input the note with Camaro's words. It was sent. "That's it," Lauren said.

"There's one more thing. Search the news for anything about a shooting in Liberty City. Maybe look on the *Herald's* site."

Lauren found the story quickly and Camaro read. There were no pictures and little information to share. No names had been released to the public, the police citing an ongoing investigation. Even the detail that some of the men had been armed with fully automatic weapons did not make it into the story. Camaro finished. "Let's get going."

"Can we have lunch?"

"Sure. Clear that browser. I don't want anybody seeing where we went."

CHAPTER FORTY-EIGHT

CAMARO CHOSE A small restaurant with a Spanish name, tucked between a hair salon and a Cuban grocery in a strip mall. The place had only six tables, and four of them were already filled with workmen in sweaty clothes, some of them smelling of road tar. Somewhere nearby there was street work going on.

They both ordered mixtos. Lauren had an iced tea. Camaro had a Coke. They waited for their food, and Camaro saw Lauren watching her from across the table. "What?" Camaro asked after a long while.

"What's going on?"

"I told you."

"You didn't tell me anything."

"I told you everything you needed to know."

"That shoot-out in Liberty City," Lauren said. "Was that where it happened? Where my dad... died?"

Camaro looked sidelong toward the table beside them. The four men eating there continued their conversation in Spanish and paid them no mind. No one but the waitress seemed to speak English at all, and even she talked to the customers in Spanish. Camaro could make herself understood in Spanish if she had to, but it was not easy. Following the rapid stream of talk around the dining room was nearly impossible for her. "It's where it happened," Camaro said. "But I don't think you should worry about that. There's plenty of time for you to find out everything. Think about yourself right now."

"What does Sergio Chapado have to do with it?"

"It's not important."

Lauren glared. "It *is* important! I want to *know!*"

One of the men at the table near theirs glanced over at the tone of Lauren's voice. Camaro smiled at him apologetically and then leaned forward to speak quietly. "Even I don't know it all," Camaro said.

"Just tell me. Please."

Camaro exhaled. "Your dad's friend Matt had something going on with a bunch of Cubans," she said. "I don't know what. They had me bring a man out of Cuba. His name was Sergio Chapado. Before today, I didn't have any idea who he was or where he came from except that he was coming into the country illegally. They paid me ten thousand dollars to do it."

"Why was my dad doing this?"

"Because Matt had his hooks into your dad. I think you know that."

Lauren sat back. Her lower lip trembled. Camaro feared she might cry. Everyone would notice them then. "My dad wasn't a bad guy. He was a good guy. When my mom left, he worked really hard to take care of us both. And when he went away... I always knew he would come back for me. They told me he never would, but he did. Then Matt came, and things went wrong again."

"Your dad seemed like one of the good ones," Camaro said.

"How long were you friends?" Lauren asked.

"Not very long. But I liked him. I get a feel for people, and he felt all right to me. And once I found out about you and how he took care of you, I knew I was right."

"He should never have gone out that night," Lauren said.

"No, he shouldn't have. But you can't blame him."

"I don't blame him," Lauren said. "I blame *Matt*."

"That's good."

"Who's going to stop Matt?"

"I don't know," Camaro said. "The cops maybe. Or the Cubans he crossed. It might take someone to put it all together, though. Matt seems like the kind of guy who slips out of things when he ought to go down for them. I've met his type before."

Lauren looked at her. "Can you stop him?"

Camaro looked back. "Maybe."

"Will you?"

"I don't know yet."

The food came. Camaro's mixto was enormous, swollen with meat. Lauren's was much smaller, on a petite bun. Once more they lapsed into silence as they ate, as if putting food into their bodies was the most important thing before them. They ate until they were both stuffed. Camaro paid.

Outside, Camaro swung onto the Harley and waited for Lauren to climb on behind her. The girl paused. "Are we going back to the motel?"

"For now."

Lauren seemed about to say something else when Camaro's phone rang. She answered it, and Ignacio Montellano's voice came down the line. "Ms. Espinoza," he said, "can we talk?"

CHAPTER FORTY-NINE

LAUREN OPENED HER mouth again, but Camaro waved for silence. The girl obeyed. "Now's not a really good time," Camaro said. "I'm kind of in the middle of something. How did you get my number?"

"It's on your website," Ignacio said. "Coral Sea Sport Charters. I notice you don't have any pictures of yourself on there."

"I didn't see the point," Camaro said.

"Sure. And I can think of other reasons, too. Like maybe you didn't want anybody to come snooping around after your name and find your face plastered all over some web page somewhere."

"I don't have anything to hide."

"Don't make me laugh, okay?"

"What do you want?" Camaro asked.

"I want to meet. Where you want to do it. Your place, the station... wherever."

Camaro was aware of Lauren watching her. She turned her face away. "I don't want to meet anywhere. We had our talk."

"We had *a* talk, but that was before some things came up that are really interesting. Do you want me to tell you all about it?"

"Could I stop you?"

Ignacio chuckled slightly. "One of my fellow detectives put your name through the system, and it turns out that you have some trouble in your past. Multiple homicides in Brooklyn, New York, where you're a person of interest, which is just the latest. *And* it turns out you have a bench warrant out for failure to appear, which means you're a fugitive up there."

"I don't know anything about any murders," Camaro said.

"Yeah. Just like you don't know anything about what happened in Liberty City. But you know, I called up there and talked to a detective named Hernandez, and he told me all sorts of things about how you breezed into town one day and got yourself tangled up in something bad. Next thing they know, they're picking up bodies in a pool hall that got shot to pieces, and you're in the wind. Detective Hernandez got *really* interested when I told him about our shoot-out, because it was pretty much the exact same thing: lots of dead guys and your name in the middle of it. Only this time you didn't disappear afterward."

"I'm not hiding from you," Camaro said. "I didn't leave the city."

"That's good. I appreciate it. Especially because Hernandez is really hot for me to pull your chain and maybe get you shipped up to his neck of the woods to answer questions about what happened up there."

"So why don't you?"

"Because I'm more interested in solving Miami cases than New York cases," Ignacio said. "Which is why I called. I wanted to know if you feel like telling me a little more truth than you laid on me yesterday."

"I told you everything I know."

"I'm starting to disbelieve you."

"Believe whatever you want," Camaro said. "I'm not involved in this. I told you my part in everything and that's it."

Ignacio paused, and then he said, "I really want to close this thing. You know what I'm saying? I've got a whole bunch of homicides and not a lot of time on my hands. This is a busy city. I've got a captain who's breathing down my neck and new homicides rolling in every day. So I'll take whatever you got. I'll even do it off the record. No one has to know it was you who talked, and you'll never hear from me again once it's all over. How about that? Is that a deal, or what?"

Camaro looked at Lauren. She looked away again. "I can't help you. Not now."

"When?"

"Soon. Maybe."

"Are you playing games with me?"

"No, I'm not."

"Good, because so far I've been real nice to you. I could have you in a cell right now and have someone hauling you out to sweat you every hour on the hour, around the clock. Who's going to look after little Lauren then?"

"I'll get back to you," Camaro said.

"Don't make me wait a long time, Ms. Espinoza."

"Call me Camaro," Camaro said, and she killed the call.

"What's happening?" Lauren asked. "Who was that?"

"Police. Get on."

"Are they coming to get you?" Lauren asked her.

"No, not yet. Come on, get on the bike. We need to move."

Lauren shook her head. "From here on out I want to know everything. If the cops come to get you, I need to know what's going on."

Camaro looked at her with hard eyes and then she sighed. "People saw me at your dad's house. They saw us leaving together. This detective, he knows I'm hiding you, but he isn't coming for me yet. He thinks I can help him."

"Can you?"

"I don't know. Until I find out more, I can't make a move."

"You're going to get killed," Lauren said. "Just like my dad. You're going to go away, and you're not going to come back."

"That's not going to happen."

"How do you know for sure?"

"I don't. But I'm not going to break my promise to your dad, and that's to keep you safe until we can get you to your uncle. I'll promise you, too."

Lauren shook her head. "Why do you even care?"

Camaro put her hands down on the warm gas tank of the Harley and willed a stillness into herself. Only when she felt it in her center did she speak again. "You know how you told me your dad was one of the good guys, even though he did bad things sometimes?"

"Yes."

"The same goes for me."

They stood looking at each other without speaking for a minute. "Okay," Lauren said, and put on the helmet.

Camaro waited until Lauren was settled in behind her before she started the bike. The engine spoke. She touched the throttle to make it exclaim. Then she let the clutch go.

They rolled.

CHAPTER FIFTY

IGNACIO PUT HIS phone in his pocket and looked down at the technician. The man's name was Liles. He was a gearhead like all the other gearheads, buried in a forest of electronics in the bowels of the station. On a broad flat-screen monitor was a grid map of the city, and on that map a red dot pulsed. "That's it," Ignacio said. "Did you find her?"

"Yeah," Liles said. "She's in Coral Terrace. I can get you everything right down to the street number. You want me to call out and mobilize a unit?"

"No," Ignacio said. "I just wanted to see where she was hanging out."

"What did she do?"

"According to her? Nothing."

"What do you *think* she did?"

Ignacio frowned at Liles. "Why are you geeks always so curious? Don't you have enough to do around here?"

"Sorry. I like knowing something about what I'm doing, that's all. Especially when I'm not technically allowed to do what I just did without a warrant."

"Okay, fine. If I wanted to, I could probably pin her with kidnapping and maybe false imprisonment. Obstruction of justice. All the good stuff."

"So why don't you?" Liles asked.

"That's a really good question."

"Is it?"

"Yeah. And I'm not gonna answer it. See you around, Liles."

Ignacio left the room and headed for the elevators. He got to the third floor and made his way back to his desk. He sat down. When he nudged his mouse, the screen saver on his computer clicked off, and he saw the article he'd been reading earlier. Nestled in the text were black-and-white pictures of Cuban exiles doing military-style exercises in the swamp. Men in crisp uniforms lining up for inspection. Men shooting on a makeshift firing range. Alpha 66 in the midsixties.

A new report was in his email in-box and he opened it up. The VIN of the abandoned Mercedes had been tracked back to a dealership owned by Álvaro Sotelo. Ignacio instigated a search for Sotelo's name in the system and came up with nothing. Another man without a criminal past, mixed up somehow with the shooting deaths of seven men.

He looked up the website for Sotelo's dealership and wrote down the number. His desk phone rang. He answered. "Detective Montellano."

"Nacho, it's Brady."

"Hey, Brady. What's happening?"

"I'm on my way in. Did you get much use out of what I sent you?"

"Yeah, lots. I spent the morning following up on the two we identified but didn't find anyone at home. I still have a whole list of names to go through. Known associates. That kind of thing."

"You think they're all in on this Alpha 66 business?"

Ignacio clicked back to the article. The pictures were grainy, almost antique looking. Another world. He had been three or maybe four when the photos were taken. "I don't know for sure, but it makes sense. I just can't figure out what a bunch of Cuban fossils have to do with these young guys. I'm looking at some of this stuff, and the original Alpha 66 members have to be in their seventies or eighties. Everybody we pulled out of that auto yard was under forty."

"You'll figure it out. How about the rest? The Espinoza woman."

"Camaro," Ignacio said. "She told me to call her Camaro."

"First names, huh? When's your date?"

"I don't think we're going to go out dancing anytime soon. She's a strange one. I can't figure if she's holding out on me or if she really doesn't know anything."

"She's wanted out of New York. Lay into her."

Ignacio puffed air at the thought. "It's misdemeanor bail jumping at best. Besides, if I squeeze her too hard, she might up and disappear on me. She has that boat, and all she has to do is get on it and it's *adiós*."

"Don't give her too much line," Pool said.

"I won't. I got one of the eggheads downstairs to ping her telephone for me, so I have a pretty solid idea where she's at. She didn't go too far from home. The guy says he can do it again even if she's not talking on it, just so long as it's switched on. Something about bouncing signals off cell towers. I don't get it."

"I'll see you in thirty," Pool said.

"I'll be here."

Ignacio hung up the phone and returned to the article. He scrolled down to the final paragraph and read a line that had been highlighted: *Despite all of this, Alpha 66 is still considered by the United States government to be a potential terrorist organization.*

"Terrorists," Ignacio said to himself.

He opened a side drawer in his desk and came up with a printed directory with a spiral binding. Ignacio paged through it until he found the section for federal agencies. The FBI was listed halfway down. He picked up the phone and tucked it into the crook of his neck as he dialed out.

A woman answered. "Federal Bureau of Investigation," she said. "How may I direct your call?"

"This is Detective Ignacio Montellano of the Miami Police Department. I'm calling to talk to somebody about terrorism."

"Terrorism in general, sir, or do you have something specific in mind?"

Ignacio wasn't sure if she was mocking him or not. "Don't you have some kind of antiterrorism guy I can talk to? I mean, that's what you guys do, right?"

"Maybe you'd be better off speaking with the Department of Homeland Security, Detective Montellano."

"Look, whatever. I'll talk to whatever agent you have. Give me anybody."

"One moment, please, sir."

The line beeped and was silent. After thirty seconds it beeped again. Ignacio waited.

Someone picked up. "This is Special Agent Mansfield," said a man.

"Agent Mansfield," Ignacio said, "I'm a detective with the Miami PD. I wanted to ask some questions about a group called Alpha 66."

CHAPTER FIFTY-ONE

THE FIVE OF them met in the garage of Davíd Ocampo's home. They sat on folding lawn chairs, and Davíd set up a flimsy card table on which he put a pitcher of fresh lemonade and enough plastic cups for all of them. Chunks of ice floated in the lemonade, and the pitcher sweated heavily.

Galdarres also sweated. The garage was not ventilated, and for secrecy's sake they had chosen to meet with the door closed to keep Davíd's neighbors from seeing the group together. Similarly, entrance and egress through the side door kept them out of the main house, where they'd be visible through the sheer drapes in the windows, and able to disappear into an alley if the doorbell was rung. They had all been careful to arrive singly and spaced out over two hours, parking as many as three blocks away.

Davíd had reserved a room at a serviceable hotel not far away from the beach. Galdarres was comfortable there, but it was no place for them to meet. Davíd's insurance office was also too high profile. Which left them this dirty, dusty-smelling garage that steamed in the unforgiving heat and humidity of the city.

One by one they took their turns getting lemonade, until they sat in a circle in their shorts and shirts looking like typical civilians with a day off from work. Maybe they would work on their lawns. Maybe they would relax watching television. Only Galdarres dressed formally, but even he had been forced to abandon his jacket in favor of shirtsleeves. Rolling up the cuffs helped only a little.

"I am glad we could meet today," Galdarres told the men. "It's important that we move quickly in relation to our problem. How many of you already know why you are here?"

None of the men raised their hands. Only David indicated that he knew. Galdarres sighed. "Would you like me to explain, señor?" Davíd asked.

"No. I will do it. The situation is very simple, gentlemen: there is a dangerous element loose in this city, one that could cause troubles for us at home. His name is Sergio Chapado."

"Who is he?" asked one of the men.

"What is your name?"

"Gerard Peyrera, sir."

"How long have you been a part of our organization?"

"Ten years, sir."

"How old are you?"

"Thirty-three."

"You're too young to have exile parents," Galdarres said.

"That's not so, sir," Peyrera said. "My parents came from Mariel in 1980."

"Why did they leave Cuba?"

Peyrera looked down and his voice dropped. "My father was charged with crimes. But my mother was an outstanding citizen. They exiled her anyway. She did not want to go. All of these years she's wanted to return."

"And your father?"

"He is dead, sir."

"But your mother still wishes to go back?"

"Very much. If the government will allow it."

"Then we shall have to see how we can arrange it," Galdarres said. "If you continue to serve the DI well, any barriers to your mother's reentry can be dispensed with. Even you could come back, if you wish it."

"Gerard was born here," Davíd interjected. "He served in the US Army."

Peyrera straightened up. "I would gladly give it up for Cuba," he said.

Galdarres smiled. "That is good to hear. And to answer your first question: Sergio Chapado is a militant. He has been a spokesman for the counterrevolutionary forces inside Cuba for several years, and we have searched long and hard for him. Just when we thought we had him trapped, he managed to secure passage to the United States, even as we swept up many in his organization. The group he represents is Alpha 66."

Glances were cast around the circle. Galdarres did not have to explain further.

"If he is gone from Cuba, what threat does he pose?" asked another of the men.

"What is your name?" Galdarres asked.

"Joel Icaza."

"The threat he poses is simply this: as a refugee from our country, he can speak out against our government, raise money for our enemies, funnel support to other militants on our shores. The United States has opened the door to Cuba, and we must keep it open. If they hear wild stories, then the sanctions might return. We can't have that. Chapado cannot be allowed to exploit any crack in our image."

"So we kill him," Peyrera said.

"Yes. But there is a problem. Alpha 66 does not have Chapado. They do not even know where he is."

"Where has he gone?" Peyrera asked.

"He was taken by the people tasked with bringing him to the United States and is being held for ransom. Our source inside Alpha 66 has informed us that they intend to pay this ransom in a matter of days, at which point Chapado will be under their protection and perhaps even under the protection of the United States government. They would love to have an outspoken exile after all this time. A new face to put in front of the cameras. It will start the troubles all over again."

"What is your plan, señor?" Davíd asked.

"It is very simple: we continue to receive information from our informant about where and when the exchange is to be made. When we know, we will intercept Chapado and kill him. We will kill the people who took him from Cuba, and we will kill the members of Alpha 66 dispatched to receive him."

Murmurs of satisfaction passed between the assembled men.

"But we do not have the manpower to ensure this is done completely," Galdarres said. "Therefore, it is my intention to poison the waters still further. If we do it correctly, these people may do half our work for us, leaving only the scraps to be cleared away."

"Tell us what to do," Peyrera said.

Galdarres looked to Davíd. "Find out from our man inside who exactly is involved in the Chapado business. We choose one of them for elimination now."

"Why now?" Davíd asked.

"Because I want these people at one another's throats even more than they are now. I want them salivating for the opportunity to kill. As I said, they will work for us, and they will never know who pulls their strings."

CHAPTER FIFTY-TWO

MATT COULD SMELL Chapado. The man had finally crapped his pants, and now he was sitting in it, unable to move because of the fresh bonds of duct tape that secured his hands and feet. Occasionally, Chapado would stir, as if testing the elasticity of the tape, but these moments did not last long. Chapado slept most of the time.

Soto had not come back yet, and Matt did not know where he was. He considered calling Soto to find out, but he didn't want the number of his new phone showing up in Soto's records. Once they had both switched out to burners it would be a different story, but for now they had to be extremely careful.

It was all the Cubans' fault. If they had played along like they were supposed to, this wouldn't be an issue at all. Sure, they were pissed about the change of plans, but this was a dangerous business they were in, and sometimes the situation didn't always go their way.

He found himself wishing that he'd had the time to pull Jackson's body out of the auto yard. That was the key to the whole thing. As soon as the police found Jackson, they knew that Matt was into something because Jackson did not make a move without Matt's say-so. That Detective Montellano would be all over his ass because of the pawnshop thing, and he wouldn't step off until he had something to pin on Matt, rightly or wrongly.

Thinking about all of this made Matt too angry. He looked to Chapado. "Hey, you," he said. "Hey, asshole. Wake up."

Chapado roused slowly, or perhaps he was only pretending. The wound on his arm was inflamed, puffy, and red around the edges of the cuts. It was probably infected already, but that wasn't Matt's concern. He considered carving up Chapado's other arm to make them match. That would be amusing for a little while.

The man said nothing to Matt. He only watched. "What are you dreaming about?" Matt asked him.

"No dreams," Chapado said.

"Bullshit. I bet you're dreaming about a nice soft bed and a clean pair of pants that don't have a pile of crap in the seat. I know that's what I'd be dreaming about."

Chapado was quiet.

"It won't be too long now. A couple of days. I might even give you something to drink. Of course, that means you're just gonna wet yourself again."

"Why are you doing this?" Chapado asked.

"For money, dumbass," Matt said.

"My people offered you money."

"They didn't offer me *enough*. As soon as I saw they were willing to pay out a hundred grand for you, I knew you were way more important to them than they let on. Anybody someone will pay a hundred grand for is worth twice that much, I figure. Turns out I was right. Minus a few complications."

Chapado slumped in the chair, as if the effort of holding his head up required more energy than he had. He said something under his breath.

"What's that you say?" Matt asked.

"It is nothing."

"You better not be calling me any names! I'll mess you up. Don't think I won't."

Chapado's eyes were weary when he looked at Matt again. "I know."

Matt took out his knife and cleaned under his fingernails with the point. He could feel Chapado watching the blade. "So why don't you tell me what it's all about? You some kind of big deal in Cuba? Government type or something?"

"No, not government. I was simply a business owner."

"That's a bunch of crap. Nobody pays two hundred thousand for a guy who runs the local bicycle shop. Stop jerking me off."

"My business was repairing small engines," Chapado said. "That was all. It was the other things I did that made me important."

Matt paused with the knife. "Like what?"

"I am a patriot for Cuba. I oppose the communists."

"Communists? You mean like the people who run the show down there?"

"Yes. The communists. The Castroites. They have been a poison in my country for fifty-six years. I fight them. I help others to fight them."

Matt whistled. "Fifty-six years is a long time, bro. Maybe it's time you gave it up and realized those communists ain't goin' anywhere. I mean, isn't Fidel Castro still alive?"

Chapado nodded.

"It's all the same to me," Matt said. He put away his knife. "Communists got to have money. Capitalists got to have money. Everybody's got to have money. I'm just a businessman who makes things happen. I don't know what your boys here in Miami are playing at, but it don't mean shit. I only care about the cold, hard *cash*."

"And you will have it," Chapado said.

Matt stood up and stalked around Chapado's chair. He saw the tension rise in Chapado's shoulders, the instinctive preparation for violence. But Matt would never break his hands on Chapado's face. That kind of thing only happened in movies, when the hero got tied up and the bad guys took turns punching him out. "Your little gang have a name? What do you guys call yourselves?"

"Alpha 66," Chapado said.

"Scary. What's it mean?"

"You wouldn't understand."

"I don't give a shit anyway," Matt said. "You could call each other the Cuban Butt Boys for all I care. Sit around and yank each other's dicks over a big map of Cuba. It's probably the only way you can get off."

Chapado said nothing for a long time. Eventually, Matt settled into his chair again. It was dull in here. Matt did not have so much as a magazine to read. He would have to go out again, take a room somewhere, get a good night's sleep, take a shower, watch some TV.

"Señor Matt," Chapado said finally.

"What?"

"I know you will not listen, but I beg you anyway: let me live. Let my brothers take me. Get your money and be happy. I will not resist you."

"If you resisted me, I'd cut your face off," Matt said. "Nobody'd recognize you then. Not even your mother."

They sat quietly after that.

CHAPTER FIFTY-THREE

Camaro had just started to doze when her phone chimed. She sat up on the hard motel-room bed and took the phone from the nightstand. An email waited. She read it.

Lauren watched her. "What is it?"

"The guy from the blog," Camaro said. "He wrote back."

"What does he say?"

"That he'll answer my questions."

She hit the reply button and then thumbed her way through a message to the blog's writer. Instead of asking her questions, she asked for a phone number where she could reach the man. She added her own number at the end. *Call me if you want,* she added, and then clicked Send.

An hour later the phone rang. The caller ID showed no number. Camaro answered. "Who is this?" she asked.

"I don't give people my name," said a woman's voice. She sounded young. Not a child or a teenager, but maybe in her early or midtwenties.

"So what do I call you?" Camaro asked.

"You can call me . . . Marta."

"Okay. Marta."

"You are Camaro?"

"I am."

"You read my blog. You know about Sergio Chapado."

"I don't really know anything," Camaro said. "He's some kind of radical, that's all. Mixed up in some rallies in Cuba. I don't get it."

"Why do you want to know more about him?"

"Because he's involved in something I'm trying to sort out. People have been killed. He's missing. I want to know what kind of situation I'm in."

"Are you Cuban?" Marta asked.

"No."

"How are you involved?"

"Does it matter?"

"It does if you want my help."

Camaro sighed, and then she started at the beginning. She left out the names because Marta did not need names. Camaro took her through the hire and the trip to Cuba and the things that had gone down since. When it came time to talk about the shoot-out in Liberty City, Camaro was careful not to mention that she'd been there or that she had put down some of the men herself. Of Lauren she said absolutely nothing at all.

"That's it," she said when she was done.

"Chapado is in the United States now," Marta said.

"Yeah."

"Do you know if he's still alive?"

"He was alive the last time I saw him. Who wants him, anyway? Who are these people?"

Marta was slow to speak, as if she was being as cagey about details as Camaro herself had been. "Sergio Chapado is not only a dissident in Cuba, but the main contact for a Cuban American group calling themselves Alpha 66. Have you ever heard of them?"

"Should I have?"

"Not many people know their name. They are a very small group now, but those who continue to work for them have resources behind them. For years Alpha 66 has sent money to Cuba to help Chapado finance popular defiance against the government. Protests. Vandalism. Thefts. Anything that could turn the people against the Castroites."

"Why is he here if he's doing all of that there?"

"The Intelligence Directorate in Cuba has been removing radicals and counterrevolutionaries for years. Putting some in prison and killing others. If they were close to Chapado, Alpha 66 would have tried to pull him out. Here in the United States he can be put in front of people with money to raise funds for the cause or talk on the radio or television. There are still many Cubans who want the communists out of Cuba and are very angry that the United States will not help them do this. To them, the president has betrayed the cause men and women have bled and died for over decades. It's a travesty."

Camaro digested this. Lauren watched her, and Camaro put her hand over the phone and said, "It's good."

"Okay," Lauren whispered.

"So they're pissed. Are these Alpha 66 guys willing to kill for Chapado?" Camaro asked.

"Alpha 66 began as a paramilitary organization. Their whole purpose was to train for the invasion of Cuba they hoped was coming. The original soldiers are all old or dead, but there are some who would still kill, yes. You've seen that. This man who took Chapado, he's in great danger, and not simply from Alpha 66."

"What do you mean?"

"The DI in Cuba has connections in the United States. We don't know how many, but there are DI operatives in Miami. They will want to silence Chapado before he has a chance to speak out for the cause. If Chapado is here now, the DI will also be looking for him. If Alpha 66 will kill, the DI will be twice as likely to do the same."

"Who are you?" Camaro asked. "How do you know all of this?"

"I'm a believer," Marta said. "I believe in a free Cuba. The Internet will help us overthrow the Castroites, and there will be democracy. I do whatever I can. People tell me things."

"People like Alpha 66?"

"And others. My grandparents were exiled from Cuba in 1959. I have never seen my own homeland, but I won't go so long as the Castroites are in power. There are thousands and thousands of others exactly like me, waiting for the moment when the communists are routed and Cuba is free. Going to Cuba now is putting money in the pockets of murderers and thieves. I receive over a thousand hits a day on my blog. Cuban Americans are hungry for Cuban freedom."

Camaro frowned. This didn't matter. None of it mattered. "I need to get in contact with the people in Alpha 66," she said. "They're some kind of secret group, right? How would I find out who I can talk to?"

"You want to talk to Alpha 66?" Marta asked.

"Yes."

"Then try their Facebook page," Marta said.

CHAPTER FIFTY-FOUR

THEY WAITED UNTIL ten o'clock. Galdarres rode in the black SUV with Davíd, Peyrera, Icaza, and the older man, Pedro. Davíd kept weapons in a locked safe in his garage, and now all of them were armed with pistols. Peyrera brought his own shotgun. Davíd had heavier guns at his disposal, but they would not need them tonight.

Pablo Marquez's house was a neat house on a row of the same. Each home had a perfect square of yard, a place to park a car alongside the comfortable-looking house, and brightly lit windows in the early darkness of evening. The sun had fled the sky only an hour before, and in the west there was still the faintest coloration of lingering light, nearly invisible to the eye.

"Now," Galdarres instructed Peyrera, and they rolled slowly up the street.

Once they were abreast of the house, they spilled out onto the sidewalk, careful not to display their guns. Peyrera could not hide his, but he held it to his side, concealing it with the line of his body as they advanced up the walk.

At the door, Galdarres signaled to Icaza, and the young man hit the porch light with the butt of his pistol, smashing the bulb and immediately plunging the front of the house into shadow. Galdarres opened the storm door. Davíd held it open as Galdarres knocked.

Footsteps sounded inside, and the tiny light from the peephole went out as someone peered through from the other side. The locks rattled and the door swung wide. It was Marquez's wife, Carolina. "May I help you?" she asked.

"Yes, señora," Galdarres said. "I am here to see your husband."

Carolina looked toward the broken porch light. The first inkling of trouble appeared in her eyes. "He's busy upstairs. It's late. Could you come back tomorrow?"

She tried to close the door on him, but Galdarres pushed against it. He stepped over the threshold, with the others behind him. Marquez's wife opened her mouth to scream, but Galdarres showed her his gun. "Silence, please," he said.

All five were in the house, and Pedro closed the door behind them. Carolina put a hand to the wall to steady herself. She trembled visibly. "What do you want?" she asked them. "We have no money in the house."

"Into the living room," Galdarres said.

They marched her into the house's welcoming living room. The curtains were drawn against the night. No one would see what happened here. At Galdarres' silent command, Carolina seated herself on the couch while the others spread themselves around the space.

"What is your husband doing upstairs?" Galdarres asked.

"He's taking a shower."

Galdarres listened and heard the faint rush of water in pipes. Even as he cocked his ear, the sound of the valves closing squeaked through the ceiling and the rushing stopped. In a moment Marquez would be naked and dripping on the bathmat. "Go and get him," Galdarres commanded his men. "Gerard. Joel. Do it now."

Peyrera and Icaza vanished from the room, and then their feet sounded on the stairs. Galdarres covered Carolina with his pistol casually. "Please, don't hurt us," Marquez's wife said.

"Why do you think I want to hurt you?" Galdarres asked.

"I don't..." Carolina began, and then her voice trailed away.

"If you are cooperative and do as I say, there will be no violence," Galdarres assured her. "Your husband will understand why we are here."

It did not take long for Marquez himself to appear. He was muscled into the living room by Icaza and Peyrera. Marquez was shirtless and wet, hastily dressed in a pair of gray sweatpants. Galdarres pointed to the couch, and his men forced Marquez to sit.

Galdarres looked at Marquez. The man had fear in his face, but he tempered it with anger. He was a fighter. If Peyrera and Icaza had not been armed like they were, he would have resisted every step of the way. He might still do something foolish simply to prove he was not a coward. It didn't matter. Soon the situation would be resolved.

"Do you know who I am?" Galdarres asked Marquez.

"No."

"My name is Alejandro Galdarres. I represent the Intelligence Directorate of the Republic of Cuba."

Fiery eyes settled into blackness. "I won't tell you anything," Marquez said.

"You will if I promise your wife will suffer," Galdarres said. "Every man cares for his wife. Even the vermin of Alpha 66."

He had hoped the mention of Alpha 66 would shake Marquez, but the man's demeanor didn't change. Of course, as soon as he knew where Galdarres had come from, he knew why he was here. The men of Alpha 66 were delusional, but they were not stupid. "If you hurt my wife, I'll kill you," Marquez said.

"Don't give me a reason," Galdarres said.

Marquez glared and said nothing.

"Where is Sergio Chapado?"

"I don't know."

"Hit her," Galdarres commanded. At his word, Pedro stepped forward and smashed his fist into Carolina's face, driving her against her husband with the yelp of a wounded animal. Marquez nearly erupted from the couch, but Peyrera struck him with the butt of his shotgun. The man reeled.

"Where is Sergio Chapado?" Galdarres asked.

Marquez put an arm around his wife. "I don't know! It's the truth! He's been taken!"

"Then you admit that Alpha 66 is responsible for Chapado's escape from Cuba."

"Yes. But we don't have him. You can't get him through us."

Galdarres smiled thinly. "I know. I only wanted to see how easily you could be made to talk. You're pathetic. Cut their throats."

Davíd and Pedro drew knives and closed on the couch. Marquez and his wife shouted, but there was no one to hear. Galdarres stepped back to avoid the worst of the mess.

"What now?" Davíd asked when it was done.

"Now, we—" Galdarres began. A movement drew his eye, and then all of them saw it. They turned to the living room door.

The girl looked to be three years old and no more. She wore pink pajamas. She looked at Galdarres and the men, looked to the bodies on the couch and the floor, then opened her mouth and screamed.

CHAPTER FIFTY-FIVE

Lauren was asleep. Camaro watched one of the late-night shows on television, keeping the sound low, whiling away the time until it was past midnight and the streets would be mostly still. Only then did she turn off the TV and gather up her Glock to venture out of the room, careful to close the door silently behind her.

She took the steps down to the parking lot two at a time and crossed to her Harley, which stood shining under the glare of the parking lot lights. Starting it probably woke anyone nearby, but she hoped the noise would not reach Lauren's ears.

She raised the kickstand and curved out of the lot onto the street, heading east toward the coast. As she'd hoped, the traffic was almost nonexistent. She ate up the miles hungrily with few cars on the road to keep her company.

She didn't stop at the marina right away. First she rode past and then returned at a slower clip. The lot was mostly empty. Though the piers and some of the boats were lit, it was dark and undisturbed. Only when she was certain no one was set up to watch the place did she ride in and park.

The cops did not have to have someone stationed there permanently. The units that patrolled through here could have been set to check out the marina on a regular basis, watching for her truck or her bike when they put in an appearance. She could not stay very long.

Camaro jogged down the pier to the *Annabel* and climbed aboard. She unlocked the door with her key and entered the dark cabin.

Without switching on the lights, she went to the panel over the medical kit and popped it open to reveal the shotgun inside. She brought it out.

The shotgun was black and ugly, but it was not meant for beauty. Camaro put the panel back in place and went to one of the galley seats. She lifted it and uncovered the two boxes of shotgun shells and the three boxes of .45 GAP ammo. She opened one box of shotgun shells and pulled five free. These she stuffed into her pocket. The rest she left alone and concealed again when she lowered the seat.

She went out of the cabin and locked the door behind her. A scan around the marina revealed no movement. Her phone began to buzz as she climbed out of the boat onto the pier. The ringer was alarmingly loud in the quiet.

"Hello?" Camaro answered.

"Camaro," Lauren said, "where are you?"

"How did you get my number?"

"You sent it to the blogger, remember? I remembered it."

"You're supposed to be asleep."

"I was, but then you were gone. Where did you go?"

"I had to pick up a couple of things," Camaro said. She walked up the pier quickly with the shotgun and kept her voice low. "You need to go back to sleep."

"Are you coming back?"

"Yes. Soon."

"When?"

"Before dawn."

"What did you have to get?" Lauren asked.

"You're too nosy for your own good," Camaro said. "I have to do something, and I have to do it alone. And that means *alone*. If I tell you what I'm doing, you're going to worry."

"I'm already worried."

"Don't be. I'm going to be all right."

"You don't have to lie to me."

Camaro stopped. "I'm not lying," she said. "I'll be okay. And I'll be back."

"I'll wait up."

"Sleep," Camaro said. "Remember what I told you. You need to be fresh so we can move. We're not staying at that hotel another day."

"Where will we go?"

"You'll find out when we get there. Now put down the phone, and let me do what I need to do."

"Okay," Lauren said reluctantly. "Be careful."

The parking lot was still deserted except for a scattering of cars and trucks. Camaro put her phone away and went to her bike. The shotgun was not long, especially since it had no stock, just the pistol grip. She was able to jam the whole length of it behind one of the saddlebags, in such a way that only the grip was exposed. A close eye would not miss it, but someone simply passing by would never notice it was there.

She left the marina quickly and vacated the neighborhood entirely in as little time as possible, the Harley's engine roaring into the night. After the oppressive heat of the day, it was maybe twenty degrees cooler. Not enough to raise goose bumps, but refreshing enough that it felt good in her face and on her body.

It took her twenty minutes to find the next place. She had not paid much attention to it when she saw it before. The building was set on its own lot, with a concrete parking area surprisingly populated given the hour and the area. Bright pink neon striped the front and sides of the building. The walls were painted a strange, blushing color that looked unappetizing in the daylight but seemed to glow under the lights now that night had fallen.

Camaro parked between a truck and a minivan to hide the bike from the street, then went to the entrance. The door was heavily grated with steel and was locked. She had to press a buzzer to alert the worker inside, who released the electric locks from where he sat behind the counter a yard or two beyond the way in.

The man was in his twenties, skinny, and wearing a Hawaiian Punch T-shirt. The thin rudiments of what was meant to be a goatee sprouted from his chin and upper lip. Random hairs poked out along his jawline and on his cheeks. He looked at Camaro as she came in, his eyes settling on her chest. "Evening," he said.

Every wall was lined with porn magazines. They were inches thick on the shelves, all wrapped in plastic envelopes and sorted into sections by kink. Bins occupied most of the floor space, these also packed with magazines. There were security cameras everywhere.

"Help you with anything?" the attendant asked her. "Mags up front, DVDs in the back. We have live booths and video peeps. Whatever you want."

"Sex toys," Camaro said.

The man's eyebrows went up. "Sure. Right down here."

He led her down the counter to where it transformed into a glass display case like the sort used to show off jewelry. There were no diamonds but many dildos and vibrators and rubber plugs and beads, all in different colors and made of different materials. Camaro ignored those things and traveled farther down until the selection gave way to kinkier fare. She pointed. "Those," she said.

"Okay. Popular item. Special man or special lady?"

"Just get them out."

The attendant unlocked the case and took the flat box out. "Thirty bucks," he said.

"Thirty bucks?" Camaro asked.

"They're double locking."

"Whatever," Camaro said, and she put a fifty on the counter.

The attendant took her money to the register and made the sale. He brought a plastic bag from beneath the counter.

"Forget the bag," Camaro said.

He handed them over. "Enjoy," he said.

Camaro ignored him. She went out of the porn shop and into the night.

CHAPTER FIFTY-SIX

Ignacio hardly felt as though he'd slept at all. His phone was ringing, and he was awake abruptly, switching on the bedside lamp and blinding himself. He answered. "Go away and die," he said.

"Detective Montellano?" asked a woman.

"Yes, this is Detective Montellano. Who is this?"

"I'm Sergeant Kathryn Stinson. I work out of Coral Way."

"Hello, Sergeant. What can I do for you at two o'clock in the morning?"

"I'm at a crime scene, sir, and a Detective Kirby from the Homicide Unit has instructed me to call you down here."

Ignacio sat up. "What's going on?"

"I think it's probably better if you come and see for yourself, sir. Let me give you the address."

"Wait a minute. I need to find something to write on."

He struggled with the sheets before escaping the bed and raided the jacket from the day before to find his notebook and pen. Sergeant Stinson repeated the address twice to make sure Ignacio had it. He thanked her and hung up.

There was no time for showering or shaving. Fresh clothes would have to do. He pulled himself together before making a cup of instant coffee and taking it with him in the car. He felt the caffeine picking him up by the time he arrived on the perfect little street in Coral Way, now marred by the presence of police units and a meat wagon from the medical examiner. The CSI van was already there, too.

Yellow crime-scene tape circled one of the lovely, restored houses. Uniforms kept back the curious, who even here managed to collect on the sidelines, hoping for a peek at the worst thing they'd ever seen. Ignacio showed his badge and let himself under the tape, advancing across the yard. A woman with sergeant's stripes waited on the darkened porch. "Stinson?" Ignacio asked.

She came to him and they shook hands. "Detective," she said. "Everybody's inside. It's pretty bad, sir."

He went up the steps and through the open front door. Plastic sheeting had been put down in the foyer. A couple of uniformed officers stood idly by the entrance to the living room as camera flashes burst inside. Ignacio entered.

The first and most striking thing in the room was the blood that seemed to have pooled and splattered everywhere. The couch was thick with it, dark with saturated gore. The coffee table and its magazines were splashed with gobbets of red. The walls were sprayed, and even the ceiling had managed to catch droplets. The dead man and the dead woman were soaked in their own vital fluids. And then there was the writing.

Nolan Kirby stood in one corner while the CSIs took pictures. He was an older man, graying into his sixties and ripe for retirement. When he spotted Ignacio, he waved him over to stand by the front window. "Nacho," he said. "Come on."

They clasped hands briefly, and then Kirby looked back to the mess. "Sorry to call you in like this, but I heard from Brady Pool that you were working an angle on another case with some Cuban group. It just so happens that I know this guy, and he's a big Cuban activist. Pablo Marquez. That's his wife, Carolina."

Ignacio read the writing again. A thought was dawning. "How did it go down?"

"No sign of forced entry, so either Pablo or Carolina let the killer or killers into the house. I already have uniforms canvassing the neighbors, but I haven't heard anything about strangers in the neighborhood or anything like that. We'll see how it pans out. In the meanwhile, I'm still waiting on Children's Services to send somebody out to talk to our witness."

"You have a witness?"

"Yeah: Pablo Marquez's daughter, Renata. She's three years old. We're not getting a whole lot from her. The kid barely knows how to talk, so asking for a statement is a little much."

"Where is she?" Ignacio asked.

"Upstairs with an officer."

"I'll want to talk to her."

"Give it time. Let Children's Services try to bring her down first. She saw it all happen, and she's not in any shape for an interrogation."

"It doesn't matter," Ignacio said. "I know who did it."

Kirby looked at him sharply. "Who?"

"Matt Clifford and Sandro Soto. Two tweakers I'm after. They have some kind of bad blood with a bunch of activist Cubans. Cutting throats isn't exactly Matt's style, but one of his crew killed a guy by caving his skull in with a baseball bat, so it's not like he's not capable of doing it. I'm surprised he let the kid live."

"We've got to get these guys' names out there," Kirby said.

"Already done. I've been looking for Clifford and Soto for days. They dropped off the map, but they're still doing business. A night ago, two of his boys got shot to death over in Liberty City, but they managed to take out five Cubans in the process. This is war we're talking about here."

"I guess that explains the writing," Kirby said.

"Yeah," Ignacio replied. He looked at the living room wall and the words painted in blood in foot-high letters.

I WANT THE MONEY.

CHAPTER FIFTY-SEVEN

CAMARO WAS HALFWAY there when she spotted a 7-Eleven and pulled in for something to eat. She bought a burrito and a Big Gulp and sucked on Coke while she waited for the microwave. Afterward, she took a prepaid phone from a display and put that with the rest of her purchases.

It took a couple of minutes for the burrito to cool down. Camaro ate it sitting on her bike, drinking Coke between bites. She balanced her cup on the tank when her phone rang. This number she knew. "Detective," she answered. "It's late."

"Does it matter? You're awake."

"I was just going to bed."

"Busy night?"

"Something like that."

"I'm standing in a house in Coral Way. You ever been to Coral Way?"

"I've gone through it a few times. Why?"

"Because there are two dead bodies here. A man and a woman with their throats cut. And the killer left a message about some money that's owed. I want you to tell me the truth: what do you know about it?"

Camaro took a bite. Chewed. Swallowed. "I don't know anything about it," she said.

"You ever heard the name Pablo Marquez?"

"No."

"Never?"

"I said no."

Ignacio exhaled. "There's a part of me that wants to take you in right now," he said. "Tell me why I shouldn't."

"Because I don't have anything to do with that."

"Both you and I know that's a crock of shit, pardon my language. You're tied up with Clifford in some way, and now he's gone and killed two more people. In front of their *kid*. I can't afford to play any more games. You have to be honest with me, otherwise I will find you, and I will arrest you."

Camaro balled up the burrito's wrapper and made a shot toward the trash can twenty feet away. It bounced off the rim and fell to the concrete. "You want me to be honest?" she asked.

"You have no idea. And listen, if you agree to spill on Matt, I will make sure that you get immunity. Anything you've done to help him, you'll be safe. I give you my word."

"I'm not working with Matt Clifford," Camaro said. "I'm not helping him."

"Camaro, listen—"

"No, *you* listen. When I told you I didn't have anything to do with whatever he's pulled, that's the truth. He's getting people killed. He's killing people himself. The man is rabid. He needs to go down."

"Who are you, anyway?" Ignacio asked quietly.

"You know who I am."

"Lady, you're a mystery to me. What did you do up in New York? Who did you kill?"

"I told you before: I didn't kill anybody. But I know some people died. They were bad guys, just like Matt Clifford, and I'm not sorry they're gone."

"That is cold. What did they do to you?"

"They didn't do anything to me," Camaro said. "But they did something. And if you want to know anything about me, then you should know I wouldn't kill anybody who didn't have it coming."

"So you're gonna kill Matt Clifford now?"

"I didn't say that."

"You don't have to. I think maybe I know you better already."

"Are you going to stop me?" Camaro asked.

"I should. Because killing Matt's not going to resolve whatever crazy shit is going on between him and these Cubans. It might slow things down a little, but people are dying left and right, and that doesn't clean up so easy. You sure you still want to be stuck in the middle of all that?"

Camaro drained the last of her Coke. "When I'm in the middle, I can see everything," she said.

"Except what's coming up behind you. I'm telling you sincerely, don't go down for this. Tell me where to find Parker Story's daughter. Tell me how I can get my hands on Matt. Tell me *anything*. Tell me something I can use, because right now I'm confused as hell."

"When it's all over, it'll make sense," Camaro said. "I promise I'll tell you everything. But I have to do this my way."

"Why?"

"Because I don't trust anybody else as much as I trust myself," Camaro said.

"That's no way to live."

"It's what I know."

"And what's your plan? You do whatever it is you're going to do, and then you just walk away from all of this?"

"Yeah. Something like that."

"That's a pretty lousy plan, if you don't mind my saying so. This kind of thing has a tendency to stick to people. Especially people with secrets."

"I don't have any secrets," Camaro said.

"Now you're lying again."

"Maybe. Good-bye, Detective."

"Good-bye, Camaro. And whatever you're doing... good luck."

CHAPTER FIFTY-EIGHT

THE QUIET WAS getting to him. Soto had at least brought some reading material, but there wasn't much to an issue of *Maxim,* and the pictures were not enough for Matt to get excited about. He wasn't even sure what a magazine like that was for. Without naked women, it seemed pointless.

Chapado was sleeping again. He made tinny whistling noises as he breathed. Matt thought he'd rather hear the man scream. But the time for that kind of thing was past. Soon Chapado would be transformed into a bag of money, and then the Cubans could do whatever they wanted with him.

"I'm going," Matt announced. He stood up and his back creaked. The chairs were terrible.

"Where?"

"I'm gonna get something to eat, and then I'm gonna bed down somewhere. I'll be back by noon."

Soto's voice pitched up. "What am I supposed to do?"

"Watch him!" Matt said. "Make sure he doesn't run off or nothing."

"He's stuck to a chair."

"Then make sure he doesn't get *un*stuck," Matt returned. "I'm going. You better be here when I get back."

"Goddamn it! This isn't fair!"

"You can talk about fair when you have your half of the money. Until then, you do what I say and shut the hell up."

He went out before Soto could say anything more. The night was alive with the sounds of frogs and night creatures. They were right on the edge of the Everglades here, well away from everything. Why anyone would build in this spot was a mystery. The land must have been cheap as hell.

The stolen Kia started with no problem with the pliers, and he made his way out, taking special care to lock up the gates behind him. He drove for half an hour until he saw a Waffle House and pulled into the parking lot. He made sure to put the Kia away from the few other cars waiting there because if someone happened to glance inside, they would see the stripped steering column and know the car was hot.

Inside, he took a booth and accepted the menu from the waitress. He had hoped for a lady who was young and hot and maybe interested in a little something, but this woman was old and heavyset and had a hairy mole on her chin. At least she took his order without trouble and left him alone. Nothing was worse than a chatty waitress without good looks.

Eventually, she brought him his waffles and bacon and hash browns. Matt put syrup on the waffles and the bacon, too. He liked the crispy salt and the sweet together. He ordered a Coke to go with it, but then changed his mind and asked for Sprite. Sprite had no caffeine.

He had cleared the hash browns and the bacon and was starting in on his waffles when his eyes strayed to the television bolted to the ceiling in the corner of the dining room. The sound was down, but the picture was clear enough. He saw a reporter doing a stand-up at a police line, a house lit up with floodlights behind her. Matt recognized the house and stopped in midchew.

When he had first taken the job from the Cubans, he'd managed to follow one of them home. He was one of the young ones, not an old guy like Echave, and he never noticed the Charger creeping along behind him as he went to his pretty little two-story in Coral Way. That day a little girl had been playing on the front lawn with plastic toys as her mother looked on. The Cuban man swept the little girl up in his arms and twirled her around. There were laughter and smiles. Matt drove straight on.

Now he looked at the text at the bottom of the screen. TWO SLAIN IN HOME INVASION, it read. Matt swallowed.

His new phone was deep in his pocket, and he clawed at it. It was very late, and dawn wouldn't be too far off, but he knew when he dialed Echave's number that the old man would be awake.

Echave answered before the phone had a chance to ring a second time. *"Bueno,"* he said.

"Echave," Matt said, "you know who this is?"

Matt heard a sharp intake of air on the other end. When Echave spoke again, his voice was tight. "You son of a bitch. You dishonorable bastard."

"What are you talking about?"

"You know exactly what I'm talking about. You wouldn't call otherwise. You've killed Pablo, and now you want to gloat. Well, you can go to hell, Mr. Clifford. To *hell!*"

There were only a few people in the dining room, but Matt kept his voice down. "Hey, now, you need to get a grip on yourself. I don't know what anybody is telling you, but I don't know anything about any murders. I don't even know who Pablo is. He the one who lives out in Coral Way? The one who got home-invaded?"

"Don't play stupid with me, Mr. Clifford," Echave said. "We *know* it was you. The message you left was unmistakable. What we don't understand is *why*. We already agreed to your terms. We were only waiting for you to tell us where to meet you and make the exchange. There was no reason to kill Pablo, and no reason to kill his wife.

You've left a child an orphan. But you don't care, do you? You're an animal. *An animal.*"

"I'll take the hit for the people I killed, but I didn't have nothing to do with your boy or his wife. That man's kid is a baby."

"Then you admit you know him!"

Matt smacked himself in the head and then again. He forced calm into his tone. "I know all kinds of things about you people, but that don't mean I killed that man. You gotta believe me. I want things to go real smooth from here on out."

"Oh, they will go smoothly," Echave said. "But know this: I will find you wherever our money takes you. I will ensure that you are killed slowly. Your last hours will be the most painful of your life."

"You watch what you're saying. I still have Chapado."

"And when will we see him?"

"Real soon. I'm working out a spot where we can do this privately."

"You told us three days!"

"I'll make the deadline!" Matt snapped back, more loudly than he intended. A man looked over at him. Matt ducked his head and cupped his hand over the phone. "It's all gonna go down the way I said. You give me the money, you get Chapado. End of story."

"You are a parasite," Echave said.

"Keep talking, old man. Maybe I change my mind and decide to off *you*."

"Fuck you!" Echave shouted down the line.

Matt ended the call and then turned off the phone. He still had food on his plate, but he had no appetite for it now.

CHAPTER FIFTY-NINE

CAMARO CREPT ALONG the fence line in the dark, picking her way through the scrub and grass by the faint light of the moon. She gripped the Mossberg, conscious of the package from the porn shop in her pocket and a can of spray paint tucked into the back of her jeans. Her boots seemed to make incredible noise no matter how slowly she went. In the end, she simply hurried along and stepped as lightly as she could until she reached the gap in the chain-link fence.

She ducked inside and jogged through the compound toward the big warehouse in the back. There was no guarantee that this place was still in use. Everything depended on good fortune. Camaro wished it were different.

Before she set off toward the warehouse complex, she had stopped at a motel in Florida City to prepare for the next step. It was worse even than the place where she kept Lauren but was fairly isolated on a little-used road headed out of town. An old kind of travelers' stop, it was a single story and had a string of rooms all in a row and a porch out front. Camaro asked for the very last unit and got it. The place was completely deserted. She left ammo behind in the top drawer of the dresser.

Now she was here, and the warehouses were all dark. Only when she turned the last corner did she see the light in one of the windows of the last structure and knew that Chapado was still there. A Nissan hatchback was parked nearby.

Camaro slowed up and walked the final distance. She edged along the long wall of the building in order to see from the same spot she had on her last visit. There was no sound of talking. No radio. No anything. Chapado sat in the chair, secured with tape, his chin resting on his chest.

Turning from the window, she stole backward to the side entrance. It was as Jackson had left it, barely closed and loose in the frame. Camaro one-handed the shotgun and put her fingers to the door, pulling it open gingerly.

The hinges protested but did not shriek. Rust ground against rust, but unless someone was alert to every sound, they would have missed it entirely. Camaro opened the door just enough for her to slip through it sideways and into the shadows. She eased the door closed behind her.

She was in among a collection of boxes, all stacked higher than her head. Crouched down in the midst of them she was invisible. Quietly she moved, keeping low, aware of the light shining on the other side of the stacks, careful never to rise where the illumination that cast through the gaps might reveal her.

It took two minutes for her to work her way into position. She was sidelong to Chapado and could see him between two towers of crates. One column was shorter than the other, and she raised herself up until she could barely peer over the top.

Soto was there, sitting in a chair reading a magazine. Camaro watched him for a while and saw him rub his eyes with his free hand, the other encased in a cast.

Ducking once more, she scuttled from cover to cover until she was behind Soto, her back to the little office through which Matt and Parker had come and gone. Out of his line of sight, she straightened and approached from the rear, the shotgun up, until she was ten feet from his chair.

"Don't move," Camaro said.

He jumped when she spoke, and the magazine tumbled from his fingers. "I'm not moving," Soto said.

"Put your hands in the air and get up slowly," Camaro told him.

Soto obeyed. "I knew we'd hear from you again," he said.

"Shut up. You only talk when I ask you questions. Turn around."

He turned and faced her. Behind him, Chapado was awake, his eyes wide in the glare of the portable lights. Camaro ignored the man. She addressed Soto. "Where's Matt?"

"Gone."

"Gone where?"

"I don't know. He didn't tell me."

"That's all right. It doesn't matter."

"You come to kill him?"

"I might have. If he was here," Camaro said. "Or maybe not."

"What are you gonna do with me?" Soto asked.

"I'm going to have to shoot you," Camaro said.

Soto had a gun in his waistband, and he reached for it with his left hand. His fingers closed around it at the same moment Camaro triggered the shotgun. The blast was deafening, captured and reflected by the metal walls and ceiling of the warehouse, brought crashing back against Camaro where she stood. Soto's chest split open red, and he flopped onto his back and was still.

Camaro stepped over with the shotgun ready. Soto was dead.

"Thank you," Chapado said. "Thank you for coming."

"Quiet," Camaro said. She could barely hear.

The shotgun went on Soto's empty chair. Camaro caught the corpse by both ankles and dragged it out of the light to leave a wide space in front of Chapado, marked with a smearing trail of blood. She took the spray can out and shook it before proceeding to write on the floor. The paint dried quickly, but Camaro was careful not to step in it. Then she put the paint away.

She drew the karambit from her left boot. It was a forward-curving blade, gripped in the fist in a reverse hold so a forearm slash brought the hook of the edge around like a spur. Camaro didn't use it on Chapado. Instead, she cut the tape binding his wrists and ankles. She saw the injury on his arm.

Chapado rubbed his wrists where adhesive still clung to the skin. He looked as though he was about to thank Camaro again, but she silenced him with a look. From her back pocket she brought out the flat package from the porn shop and opened it. A pair of matte-black handcuffs and two keys slipped out. "Get into these," she told Chapado. "Hands in front."

"I don't understand."

"You don't have to understand. Just do it."

He locked himself into the cuffs. Camaro helped him to his feet. He was unsteady, and he reeked of feces and urine. "Where are you taking me?" he asked.

"Somewhere safe."

CHAPTER SIXTY

CAMARO BROUGHT LAUREN to the remote motel only a little before dawn. The sky was already pink in the east. It seemed like it had been forever since she slept. Together they cleared out the saddlebags of their stuff and went inside. Lauren saw Chapado immediately.

He was handcuffed to a pipe beneath the sink in the room's small bathroom with his hands behind his back. A wad of washcloth had been stuffed into his mouth deep enough that it could not be spat out. The room was redolent with his smells.

"Oh, my God," Lauren said. "Who is that?"

"That's the man who got your dad killed. He's the reason we're hiding out," Camaro said.

"He killed my dad?"

"No, but he's why."

Camaro put her phones on the nightstand and tucked the shotgun between the bed and the wall in a way that she could get it if she needed it. She went to the bathroom and yanked the washcloth from Chapado's mouth. "You all right?" she asked. "You need water? Got to use the toilet?"

"Water, please," Chapado said.

This motel room did not supply glasses but gave their guests plastic cups in separate wrappers. Camaro tore one open and filled it from the tap. She saw Lauren watching them, frozen by the door, her eyes feral. "What is it?" Camaro asked.

"You should kill him," Lauren said.

"No," Camaro said. "Not him. Him we want alive. Your dad died because there are people who want this guy no matter who they have to kill. Matt played games with them. Now none of them have him. As long as we have this guy, we have power."

She helped Chapado drink. The man gulped at the water. When the cup was empty, he said, "You know who my people are. If it's money you want, they will give it to you. I'll tell them you saved me. They won't try to hurt you. I promise!"

Camaro crouched on the bathroom floor beside him. She held up the cup. "You want more?"

"Yes."

The cup was filled again and Chapado drank. Some escaped his lips and trickled down his chin onto his sweat-soaked and dirty shirt. Camaro noticed he had some of Soto's blood on him. "There's no reason to keep me," Chapado told her. "This can all be made right."

"I don't need your help to make things right," Camaro said. "I just need you alive for a couple of days. Let me see your arm."

Chapado twisted his wrists around so Camaro could examine his wound. It was deep, but not so deep that stitches were needed. The flesh was swollen and an angry red. Two flaps of skin were completely loose. "That man, he tortured me," Chapado said.

"These look like they might be getting infected," Camaro said. "They have to be cleaned out."

She left Chapado in the bathroom and went to the room's small desk. There was stationery in the drawer, along with a Bible and a pair of pencils, both sharp. She sat and scribbled a few things down. Lauren was still by the door. Camaro handed her the sheet of paper. "What's this?" Lauren asked.

"It's a list of supplies. There's not a whole lot I need. I saw a drugstore about a mile or so back up the main road. I want you to walk down there when they're open and pick this stuff up."

"I thought you didn't want people to see me."

"There's no one out here who'd recognize you. It'll be all right. I don't want to leave you here alone with him if I don't have to."

"Is he dangerous?"

"Not locked up, but I don't want to take the chance."

Lauren accepted the paper. She folded it in half twice and put it in her pocket. Finally, she left the door and went to sit on the bed. In this room there was only one. "Okay," she said. "I'll do it."

"Hey, you," Camaro said to Chapado. "You want to take a shower?"

"Very much."

Camaro went to the bathroom with the key to the cuffs. "I'll let you loose for five minutes. You try and get out of this room, I'll break your arm."

"My clothes... they're filthy."

"There's nothing I can do about that. Make sure you wash that arm with plenty of soap. We'll take care of it better later."

She unfastened the cuffs. Chapado stood slowly. "Thank you."

"Five minutes," Camaro said, and she closed the door.

CHAPTER SIXTY-ONE

Matt slept a few uneasy hours in an Econo Lodge in Homestead. The room was clean and nice, but all he could smell when he woke up was stale cigarette smoke and sweat. If he showered, he would just have to put on the same clothes again, which made the whole thing pointless. Instead, he washed his face and his hands and got his hair wet in the sink. Enough to feel a little fresher, but that was all.

He got back on the road earlier than he expected and made his way south out of town to the warehouse. Nothing was disturbed at the gate, and the Nissan Soto had borrowed or stolen was in the same place it had been the night before.

"Hey, Sandro!" Matt called as he went in through the office. "Hey! You awake? The relief is here!"

There was no answer. He came into the warehouse itself and saw the blood. After that he saw Soto.

Soto's gun was still lodged in his waistband. His shirt was a sodden, shredded mess. Blood had expanded beneath him into a pool almost six feet across. Little flies were already buzzing around the rich, dark red liquid, looking to feast.

A long trail traced back to where Chapado had been held. Matt's heart seized in his chest when he saw the chair empty, the shiny gray duct tape hanging limply. "Oh, shit," he said.

He advanced into the circle, unable to take his eyes off the chair, as if he could magic Chapado back into place if only he concentrated hard enough. Cold sensations passed through his arms and legs. Sweat sprang up on his face and trickled down from his pits, as though he had run a mile in the heat.

Matt looked back toward Soto, then whirled around on the chair again. Chapado still wasn't there. He glanced downward toward his feet and saw a yellow letter on the concrete: a capital C.

The message CALL ME was large and spray-painted in careful print. Underneath the letters was a telephone number. His pulse beat in his temples, and he pressed the heels of his palms against them to contain the pressure that built there. Matt knew he was breathing too quickly. Everything had a silvery sheen to it, the sign of hyperventilation. He turned around and around.

Only when the moment had passed did Matt bring out his phone. He looked at the number a second time, then tapped it in. He listened to the line ring. He recognized the bitch's voice the moment she answered. "Hello, Matt," she said.

"What the fuck have you done with him?" Matt demanded.

"With who?"

"You know goddamned well who! What did you do with Chapado?"

"I knew you'd care more about him than about your friend."

"Oh, I'm thinking about him. I'm thinking you're gonna die screaming. I saw you killed Sandro before he could get to his piece."

"He was dead the minute he tried for it," Camaro said. Her voice was flat.

"You are nuts. You don't know who you're dealing with."

"I think I know exactly who I'm dealing with. And now you know I'm serious."

"What do you want?"

"I want you to squirm," Camaro said.

Matt gritted his teeth. His jaw muscles stood out, and he felt a stab of pain in his head from the strain. He forced his mouth open. "What good is that gonna do?" he asked.

"It's going to make me feel better," Camaro said. "And when I'm ready, I'll tell you exactly what to do."

"I want to talk to Chapado."

"No."

"I want to know he's still alive and that you have him," Matt insisted. "If you don't prove it to me, then you can go fuck yourself. Do it, or hang up!"

She didn't say anything for almost a minute. Matt checked to see that the call was still live. "Just a minute," she told him.

Matt strained his ears to hear anything at all in the background that would tell him where Camaro was. He did not hear so much as a television. There was a mumble of quiet voices for a moment and then Chapado spoke. "Mr. Clifford," he said.

"Is that you, asshole?"

"I have nothing to say to you."

"I'm gonna find you. I'm gonna kill that bitch. And I'm gonna take you back, and you'll wish you never saw my face. I'll cut your whole arm off this time. I'll peel your skin like a grape."

"You will never touch me again," Chapado said.

"I *will!*" Matt said. "I'll make you *suffer!* You hear me? You *hear* me?"

"He's gone," Camaro said.

"You are so dead," Matt told her. "You're dead right now, and you don't even know it."

"I could have sat on Chapado and waited for you to show your sorry ass," Camaro said. "You'd be dead right now. The only reason you're still alive is because I allow it."

"Do it! Come at me! I'll show you what I can do."

"You'll hear from me," Camaro said.

Matt gripped his phone until his knuckles ached. "You don't hang up on me! You tell me where I can get Chapado right now, and I'll be merciful! You understand me? I'll do you *quick!*"

"Good-bye, Matt," Camaro said.

The line went dead. Matt moved to dash the phone against the floor but stopped himself. He screamed instead, and his scream echoed in the space. *"Bitch!"* he bellowed. But there was no one to hear him except the body of Sandro Soto.

CHAPTER SIXTY-TWO

IGNACIO ARRIVED FOR his shift and ate an early lunch of a burger and fries at his desk. He was still clicking his way through his emails when he felt the man at his back. Ignacio pushed the mouse pointer to the corner and the screen saver activated automatically. He turned away from the screen. "Can I help—" he started.

The man brandished FBI credentials in Ignacio's face. "I'm Special Agent John Mansfield. We spoke on the phone."

"Oh," Ignacio said.

"You are Detective Montellano, right?"

"Yes. It's only . . . well, I didn't expect you to come all the way down here to talk. Another phone call would have been okay."

"I like to work face to face," Mansfield said.

Mansfield seemed about fifty, his hair completely white. He wore a blue suit and a red tie with a golden tie tack. A large college ring was on his right hand. His left had a simple gold band. Ignacio saw all this in a moment. "Okay, that's fine with me. Why don't you pull up a chair?"

"Actually, it's better if we had somewhere more private to sit down. Do you have a conference room?"

"Sure. It's right over there."

"Let's go then."

Ignacio stood up from his desk, abandoning his food, and led Mansfield to the small conference room. It had chairs for six and whiteboards on two walls. A rolling rack with a television on top and a DVD player underneath was crammed into one corner. The white-boards were both stained with pinks and grays from long use.

"Close the door, please," Mansfield said.

"What's with all the secrecy?" Ignacio asked.

"Everything I told you on the phone was pretty general," Mansfield said. "Now we're getting into the serious stuff. I'd like to know that we're keeping this compartmentalized. In fact, I'm going to have to ask you to sign a confidentiality agreement."

Mansfield had a briefcase, and he put it on the table. The locks popped open and he lifted the lid. The agent passed a form across to Ignacio and then a pen.

"What's in this?" Ignacio asked.

"It's a non-disclosure agreement for sensitive, but not classified, information. What I'm going to tell you is background for your investigation, so anything you use will be subject to review by the relevant agencies—in this case, the Federal Bureau of Investigation—before it can be utilized in public documents, such as an indictment."

Ignacio sat down and looked at the form. It was dense, but it was at least only a single page. "I feel like we're getting into some James Bond stuff here."

"It's nothing like that. But it *is* the sort of thing we don't talk about on the nightly news. Please sign."

He signed and let Mansfield take the form back. It went into the briefcase, and then Mansfield sat down opposite him. "Now what?" Ignacio asked.

"Now we talk about Alpha 66."

"We already talked about Alpha 66. They're a Cuban militant group. They're small. They don't do a whole lot. The FBI isn't interested in them."

"Some of that's true, and some of it's not," Mansfield said. "They are a militant group, and they are small, but they do carry out operations, and the FBI is interested in them. We've been interested in them since 1961. They're an intriguing bunch of reactionary zealots."

Ignacio watched as Mansfield brought out a file. From inside the manila folder, Mansfield produced a series of black-and-white and color photographs, which he laid side by side on the table. Most of the men in the pictures were old, but some of them were young. Ignacio recognized one of them immediately. "That's Pablo Marquez. He was murdered last night."

"Right. And over here is a man named Hugo Echave. He's the nominal head of Alpha 66 these days, along with Carlos Molina. And this is Álvaro Sotelo and his son, Ulises. The rest of them you can see for yourself, but here's the core of the organization, minus Marquez."

"Five guys?"

"Ulises is new to the inner circle, we think. Total membership in Alpha 66 is something less than a hundred. Maybe below seventy-five. Not many, and most of those people are simply fundraisers or the kind who give speeches in front of special-interest groups. The hardest of the hard core, though . . . they're still dangerous and are very active."

"What do these guys do? Are they still training out in the Everglades?"

"Sometimes. The younger ones like to play soldier. But for the most part Alpha 66 funds radical action inside Cuba. And when I say 'radical,' that's what I mean. We're talking about murders, bombings, and things like that. They'll put money into protest signs, but they're more interested in racking up the bodies of dead communists."

Ignacio picked up Hugo Echave's picture. The man was distinguished looking, like a wise family patriarch with many, many grandchildren. "I read that they're terrorists."

"They are."

"If they're terrorists, then why aren't they in prison?"

"Because their targets are overseas. Let me give you an example. In 1976, a pair of timed explosives took down Cubana de Aviación flight 455. They were traveling from Barbados to Jamaica. Alpha 66 was involved, along with another group called Omega 7 and a few other violent factions operating under the Coordination of United Revolutionary Organizations. The bombing killed seventy-eight people. For a long time it was the worst airborne terrorist attack in the western hemisphere.

"Now, some people went to prison for it, but that was only outside the country. In 2005, one of the Alpha 66 bombers reentered the United States illegally. He was caught. Would you like to know what happened to him?"

"He got deported?"

"No. He went right back to his life. Pressure came down all the way from the president to make sure he skated on everything he might have been charged with."

"How? Why?"

"Alpha 66 and the other American groups in CORU are our pet terrorists. They attack targets we don't give a damn about. Or targets we don't mind seeing taken out. Cuban functionaries? Who cares? A cop or two in Havana? So what? Don't let the kind face the president put on the situation fool you. We may trade bananas with these people, but Cuba's still not our ally. And as far as certain elements in the United States are concerned, the enemy of our enemy is our friend."

Ignacio sat back. "That's screwed up."

"So the question is, what's going on with your investigation. Shoot-outs? Throats cut? Are they cleaning house internally, or is someone picking them off from the outside?"

"I don't care about all that Cold War crap," Ignacio said. "I want to clear murder cases."

"These are your people," Mansfield said. "The roots of this go deep."

"I'm Puerto Rican," Ignacio said. "I was raised in the Bronx."

Mansfield smiled. He gathered up the photographs. "Well. I'm authorized to give you the information you need to locate and question the members of Alpha 66, including those that have stayed mostly off the radar. But I'll tell you, investigator to investigator, that your best bet is to go straight to the top."

"Hugo Echave."

"He's visible in his community; he's politically active; he's everything that says fine, upstanding American. Which means that if he's mixed up in something bad, he's going to want it put behind him as quickly and as neatly as possible. Go to him. He'll crack."

"What if I find out this is some kind of terrorist thing?" Ignacio said. "What do I do then?"

"Then you come back to me, and we make it a Bureau matter. It'll be off your hands."

"Or swept under the carpet. If people find out there's still spying and killing going on, they're not going to think making nice with Cuba was such a great idea. It'll be a scandal."

"Maybe," Mansfield said. He slipped a sheet of neatly typed names, addresses, and phone numbers out of the file folder and gave it to Ignacio. "So make sure you don't have to call me."

CHAPTER SIXTY-THREE

Matt sat in the chair where Chapado had been held and rocked back and forth with his head in his hands. His mind raced ahead of him, skipping across ideas and plans and discarding them almost as soon as they occurred to him. He kept coming back to the knowledge that he had nothing and Camaro Espinoza had everything.

After he had run through every permutation of rape, torture, and murder that he could imagine, he was forced to turn toward more feasible ends. The corpse of Sandro Soto wasn't getting any fresher. Neither was the situation. He had to settle on something concrete and follow through on it. Otherwise he was lost completely.

Slowly his mind settled. He breathed more easily. The nervous sweat was gone, replaced with the simple perspiration of being in the hotbox interior of the warehouse without so much as a fan to stir the air. He took out his phone and dialed.

"Mr. Clifford," Hugo Echave said when he answered. Matt heard the barely contained rage once more. "What do you want?"

"There's been a change of plans," Matt said.

"What change of plans? You assured me last night that the exchange would go ahead on the schedule you set. This is what you *said,* Mr. Clifford! And now you call to play more games!"

"It's not like that," Matt said. "I'm calling because the place where I was going to set the meet is no good. We can't go there. There will be cops all over. I have to find somewhere new, or we're both gonna get caught up in something."

"This cannot go on forever, Mr. Clifford. We must come to a conclusion. You've killed eight of us and one innocent. We believe you will harm Señor Chapado if we push you. We're ready to *deal.* All you must do is agree to make the exchange."

Matt cursed silently. "I need another day or two."

"No! We must move forward. Or are you going to commit another murder?"

"I didn't kill that guy and his wife!" Matt said. "How many times do I have to tell you that? It's got nothing to do with me. Believe me, all I want is Chapado off my hands and the money in my bag. It's just going to take a little longer than I thought. It's not the end of the world."

He could feel Echave seething. "Señor Chapado is dead," the man said finally.

"What? No, he's not dead!"

"Let me speak to him."

"No. No, you can't talk to him. He's asleep."

"Wake him up!"

"I'm not letting you talk to him, okay? I have him and he's *fine.* You don't have to worry about anything. We're going to do this in a few days. Everybody will be happy."

"I want a photograph of Señor Chapado—*alive*—with a copy of the *Herald.* A current copy. You have twenty-four hours to produce this photograph, or we will consider Señor Chapado dead and our deal at an end. You won't get a single day to enjoy your money before we find you and kill you."

"You were going to kill me anyway," Matt said. "You said so yourself."

"Yes. You are going to die, Mr. Clifford."

"Then screw you. I'm not sending you any picture. You *will* wait for me to set a place and a time, and you *will* bring me my money.

And maybe in the meantime you can get your shit straight and stop blaming me for killing people I didn't kill. If I did it, you would know."

"We do know, Mr. Clifford."

"Whatever. See you around, Hugo."

Matt hung up the phone. His body trembled all over. He clasped his hands around the phone to still himself.

CHAPTER SIXTY-FOUR

CAMARO SLEPT, AND in the bathroom the man was also sleeping in his spot beneath the sink. Lauren was thirsty, but she didn't want to disturb either of them with the sound of the water. So she sat and watched the clock count away the minutes until she decided it was late enough.

Before she went, she took one of Camaro's phones, the cheap-looking one, and some of the cash left on the nightstand. Lauren didn't know how much these things would cost, so she took a hundred dollars. That should be more than enough, with more left over for something to eat and drink.

She let herself out of the room quietly and walked down the length of the motel to stay out of the sun for as long as possible. Mosquitoes and flies buzzed around, the former lighting on Lauren briefly before she flicked them away. She'd read somewhere that mosquitoes liked the smell of feet, so she expected there would be bites around her ankles by the time she got back.

Away from the motel, she stayed to the grass and gravel at the edge of the road. Eventually, she walked far enough that the motel disappeared, but other shapes were coming into view ahead of her. It occurred to her that all she had to do was keep going, that it would be as easy as calling 911 and asking to be taken away from here, but she did neither of these things. The police were the first step toward foster care, and she did not want to go back to that.

Thoughts of foster care returned her to memories of her dad. The pain was still raw and fresh and would be that way for a long time. At least now she didn't cry uncontrollably whenever his face appeared to her. Even now she had only a single tear, and she wiped it away. She sniffed a little, but kept the rest inside. That was where it had to stay for now, until she was gone from this place and somewhere the system could not lay its hands on her.

Lauren tried to imagine her dad and Camaro together, but she couldn't. They were completely different. Her father had always had an air of defeat around him, a sadness no amount of hugs could lift. Camaro was like a wall, with everything she felt hidden behind it. Lauren knew no one could touch Camaro through that wall if she didn't allow it. At some point she must have let Lauren's dad have that access, and this was the end result. Lauren was aware that in the end Camaro would kill the man she once called Uncle Matt. This did not bother her at all. And in the meantime, she would be like Camaro and build a wall of her own.

The drugstore was next to an auto parts store that was next to a hardware store that was next to a small family grocery. Lauren went to the drugstore first, exactly as Camaro instructed her, and took a handbasket to carry her things. She went down the short list, browsing the aisles until she found everything, and then she took it all to the cashier.

The man behind the register was old, and he smiled at her as he rang up her purchase. "Keep cool now," he admonished her when she walked away.

The grocery was compact and nothing like a grand supermarket, but it had things to take the edge of hunger off. Lauren bought a few pieces of fruit—oranges and apples and bananas—and a two-liter bottle of Coke. She lingered awhile in the bread section, thinking about making sandwiches, but there was no cool place in the motel room to keep the baloney and cheese safe to eat. Eventually, she settled on a box of cookies and some saltines.

The woman who rang her up bagged her purchases in paper and made change. Lauren thanked her but got no reply. She headed outside again.

An awning stretched out along the front of the hardware store and provided some shade. Lauren put her bags down and looked at the phone. From her other pocket she took a crumpled sheet of paper with Richard Story's information on it and called the phone number.

At first she thought he wouldn't answer, but finally he did. He sounded out of breath, as if he had been running or lifting heavy things. It was the middle of the day. He was probably working. "Hello?" he asked.

"Is this Richard Story?"

"Yes, speaking. Who is this?"

"I'm your niece. Lauren."

Richard was quiet for a long moment, and then he said, "Lauren? How did you get my number?"

"I looked it up on the Internet."

"I haven't seen you since you were about four or five. How old are you now?"

"Fourteen."

"Wow, fourteen. How's your dad?"

Lauren hesitated. There was no other way to say it. "He's dead."

She might have heard him gasp. She didn't know for certain. "Dead? How? When?"

"It was a couple of days ago," Lauren said. "I think he was shot."

"You think? Jesus, Lauren. Where are you now? Are you okay?"

"I'm fine. I'm staying with a friend of my dad's. But I need someone to come and get me."

"A friend? Aren't the police looking after you?"

"It's kind of hard to explain," Lauren said. "But I'm safe. The police are trying to find out who did it. I need someone to pick me up, Uncle Richard. You're the only one who can. If you don't, they're going to put me in care."

"Put you in care," Richard said. "What does that mean? Like protective custody?"

"No, like a home for kids with no families. I have a family, though: you."

Richard sounded less breathless now. "Lauren, I'm all the way out in Texas. Are you and Parker... I mean, are you still in Miami?"

"Yes. I really need you to come, Uncle Richard. I know it's been a long time, but I don't want to go back into care. I want to be with a real family."

Emotion welled up in her. She remembered Camaro and placed a barricade between her outward self and her inward self. This was hard enough without bawling into the phone.

"I don't know how I'd get there," Richard said. "I want to, but I don't have money for a plane."

"*Please,* Uncle Richard. I need you now."

"Shit," Richard said.

Lauren poured all the energy she could into her next words. "Will you come?"

"Aren't the police going to want you to stay put?"

"They won't stop me from going with you," Lauren said.

"I have kids of my own, Lauren. There's not a lot of room at home."

"I have to get out of here," Lauren said. "Please."

A long, long time passed. Lauren clung to the phone with both hands. "I can drive," Richard said at last. "But it's gonna take a while. A couple of days maybe. Can you hold on that long? Will you be safe? They won't try to make you go anywhere, will they? Not if they know I'm coming?"

"I won't go anywhere."

"Where are you, so I can find you?"

"I'm not sure where I'll be in two days," Lauren said. "Call this number again when you're close to the city. I'll tell you then."

"Lauren...am I walking into some kind of trouble there? Your dad..."

"It's okay," Lauren said. "Everything will be okay if you come."

"I'll leave as soon as I can get home and get packed," Richard said.

The tension fled her. "Thank you, Uncle Richard. You're saving my life."

"Just don't go getting yourself into trouble. Steer clear of whatever the police are doing. I'm going to want to know all about it when I get there."

"I'll tell you everything," Lauren said. "Good-bye, Uncle Richard."

"Take care, Lauren."

They hung up. Lauren clasped the folded phone between her hands as if praying, and then put it away. She picked up the bags from the drugstore and the grocery and went back to the motel.

CHAPTER SIXTY-FIVE

CAMARO WOKE AT the soft knock on the door. She brought her pistol with her as she checked the peephole. In the bathroom, Chapado was awake and watching. Lauren stood outside. Camaro let her in.

"I got what you needed," Lauren told her when she put the bags on the bed. "And some other stuff."

"How did it go?" Camaro asked her. She put the Glock at the small of her back.

"No one cared I was out there," Lauren said.

"Good. Did you see anyone hanging around? Watching the motel?"

"Nobody."

"Okay," Camaro said. She looked in the plastic bag from the drugstore. All the things were there. She went to the bathroom and brought out the key to the handcuffs.

Chapado exhaled with relief as she let him loose. His wrists were red, despite the relative looseness of the cuffs, and Camaro was reminded that long use of cuffs like these could cause nerve damage. If she'd had another way to secure him, she would have used it. But that was not going to happen.

The man shook his hands out and rubbed at his wrists. "Thank you," he said.

"You're going back in them when we're finished. Sit on the edge of the tub."

He did as he was told. Camaro brought the supplies in. She ran the sink until the water steamed and washed her hands before filling the basin. She soaked a small towel in it. When that was done, she indicated that Chapado should put out his injured arm and let her lay the towel on it. He hissed when the hot cloth touched the raw wound.

"That's just to soften things up a little bit," Camaro said.

She let the cloth sit for a couple of minutes and then lifted it off and cast it into the sink. The white was stained by leakage from the wound. If it was not cleaned thoroughly, it would get worse.

A pair of medical scissors were in a plastic bubble on a piece of cardboard. Camaro popped them out. There was no sterilizing them, but she let them rest in the sink until they were warm to the touch, then washed them in isopropyl alcohol. Two pieces of skin had been peeled free of Chapado's forearm. Camaro scissored them away, exposing the raw layer underneath, and then put the scissors aside.

There were cotton balls in the bag and hydrogen peroxide. Camaro let a couple of balls absorb the liquid. Then she knelt in front of Chapado to apply the peroxide to the wounds. Immediately, there was a sizzle and white foaming. "It stings," Chapado said.

"It might a little. But it'll help bring up any debris down in the cuts."

The stink of Chapado was still intense, especially so close. Camaro ignored it. Once the bubbles died down, she used a washcloth steeped in the scalding water to wipe down the injury. Chapado made a low, pained noise, but that was all.

More cotton balls, this time carrying a charge of the alcohol, gave the wounds a second cleaning. Chapado kept his silence then, though Camaro knew this must have been the most painful thing of all.

She was applying a layer of antibiotic ointment when Chapado spoke again. "You are a nurse?"

"No."

"You were a soldier?"

"I was once."

"It was there that you learned this?"

"Yes. I can take care of a lot worse."

"I thought you might be a soldier. The way you killed that man. No hesitation. No remorse."

Camaro glanced up at him. He was watching her closely. "Killing somebody is easy," she said. "You pull a trigger."

"I think we both know that is not the case."

Camaro washed her hands again before opening up a package of gauze. "It doesn't matter. I did what I had to do to get you out of there."

"But why? To get money from Clifford?"

"I don't want any of his money."

"Then money from my people?"

"I don't want their money, either," Camaro said.

"Then what is it? Why don't you let me go?"

Camaro covered the wound with a double layer of sterile gauze and then used medical tape to secure it on all four sides. "I'm doing something I don't have to explain to you. All you need to worry about is getting to your friends in one piece. When all of this is over, that's what will happen."

"When?"

"Soon. I have things to take care of first."

"I'm not afraid to die," Chapado said.

"Are you sure about that?" Camaro asked. She looked him in the face.

He turned his head. "I try not to be afraid."

"There's no harm in being afraid. I'm afraid."

"You don't seem to be."

"That's the difference between you and me."

"If I must die," Chapado said, straightening, "then I would prefer to die on my feet. Not begging. Can you promise me that will happen?"

"Nobody's going to die," Camaro said. "Nobody we care about, anyway."

"Then who?"

Camaro stood up. She brought out the cuffs. "Time for lockup. Get down on the floor."

Chapado did as he was commanded, and Camaro cuffed him in. "I never learned your name," he said.

"No," Camaro said. "You didn't."

CHAPTER SIXTY-SIX

IT HAD TAKEN only two phone calls to get a return call from Hugo Echave. The first calls had been brief ones, the people on the other end guarded when they learned Ignacio was calling from the police. But eventually they had given him a number where Echave could be reached. Ignacio was forced to try three times before he finally got an answer. "Mr. Echave, my name is Detective Ignacio Montellano of the Miami Police Department. I have some questions concerning the death of Pablo Marquez."

"I have nothing to say," Echave told him.

"I thought you might say that, but I think you do."

"I'm telling you I don't."

"Then how about this: you answer my questions about Alpha 66."

Echave went silent. At long last he said, "We should not talk on the phone."

"Then where?"

"Come to my home this evening. Five o'clock."

"Just tell me the address."

Echave did and Ignacio wrote it down. After that it was simply a matter of waiting until the appointed hour.

Echave lived on Palm Island in Miami Beach. Driving through the neighborhood made Ignacio feel like the poorest man on earth. Great gates and walls cordoned off huge houses, and palm trees sprouted everywhere, making a lush jungle of greenery that spread out on every street.

He found Echave's home without trouble and stopped his car at the gate. A box with a button and a grille on it stood waiting by the drive. A camera watched from the wall. Ignacio pressed the button and waited.

"Who is it?" asked a man's voice from the grille.

"Miami Police Department. I have a meeting with Mr. Echave."

"What is your name?"

"Ignacio Montellano."

"Please wait."

A minute passed in silence. All the air conditioning escaped from Ignacio's car, and now he sweated. He pressed the button again. "I have an appointment," he said.

"Please wait," the voice replied.

Another minute passed. Ignacio was poised to press the button again when the gates began to swing wide. There was no further instruction from the voice.

He went up the curving drive to a white house with ceramic tiles on its roof. It had large windows designed to be thrown open wide and catch the breeze, though there was no breeze today. A black Mercedes sedan was parked near the front door. It was identical to the one left in Liberty City, the one owned by Álvaro Sotelo's dealership. The Álvaro Sotelo who was a part of the upper ranks of Alpha 66.

An obvious bodyguard in a suit emerged from inside as Ignacio unfolded himself from his car and came up the steps. The bodyguard held the door for Ignacio. Inside it was wonderfully, blessedly cool, almost to the point of chill. The foyer was broad and long and tiled with a beautiful pattern that circled around a centerpiece table with a perfect bowl of fruit in its middle. Ignacio took off his hat.

"Wait here," the bodyguard said and left Ignacio.

It was close to five minutes before the bodyguard returned. With him was Hugo Echave. The man was older than in his photograph, expensively dressed, his wide body tailored into an immaculate suit. "Detective Montellano," Echave said. "Welcome to my home."

They shook hands. "I'm here," Ignacio said.

"Yes. Come into my study. We will talk there."

The study was in the north wing of the house. Ignacio immediately saw that it was a shrine both to old Cuba and to a new life in America. Echave waved him into a leather chair before taking his own. The bodyguard stood by the door.

"Before we begin, could I have something brought for you?" Echave asked. "Lemonade? Tea? Coffee?"

"I wouldn't mind a lemonade."

"Nicolao, fetch the detective some lemonade."

"Yes, sir."

The bodyguard left, leaving the door partly open. Ignacio glanced at the empty space that promised the man's return. "Is he part of Alpha 66?" he asked.

"Yes," Echave said. "His grandfather was a good friend of my father's. They both came from Cuba after Batista was driven out."

"Old times," Ignacio said.

"For some. Not for us. You are Cuban?"

"No."

"Then you wouldn't understand."

"I'd like to," Ignacio said.

"It's not something that can be taught," Echave said. "You must be born to it."

"Okay, then, let's forget about learning the history. It's not like there's a whole lot to catch up on anyway. Cuba's full of communists. You hate communists. Sometimes you have Cubans killed, and other times you play soldiers out in the swamps. Is that about the size of it?"

Echave frowned. "There's no need to be rude, Detective."

"Sorry. My BS levels are way off the charts this week."

"It's true that we hate the Castroites," Echave said. "And it's true that people have died. I will not admit to the killing of anyone, not even a Cuban national. So if you've come to arrest me for committing the crime of murder, you will be disappointed."

"Maybe you didn't commit murder, but some people under your employ did," Ignacio said. "That shoot-out in Liberty City? And we have a couple of dead bodies we pulled out of a self-storage place that I bet I could trace back to you if I tried. Guys in suits getting shot aren't too common around Miami these days."

"The men of Alpha 66 aren't my employees," Echave said.

"What are they then?"

"They are my *brothers.*"

"Well, somebody's killing off your brothers by the barrel. Like Pablo Marquez. I'd like to know why. And don't give me a whole bunch of runaround, because I know more than you think I know."

The bodyguard, Nicolao, returned with the lemonade. He put it on a coaster at Ignacio's right hand, on an antique table that could have cost thousands of dollars.

Echave sat with his hands folded across his belly until Ignacio finally took a drink from his glass. "Do you think Cuba is a great friend to the United States?"

"I don't know what to think. We're friends, we're not friends . . . it's not really my department. People seem real happy to get their hands on Cuban cigars."

"So they are. As if that's all that matters. Business and tourism. While the communists squeeze Cuba more tightly than ever."

"Like I said, I don't know anything about it. I'm all about clearing cases in Miami, not about what's going on two hundred miles away in another country."

"What I tell you is not to be used against us," he said when Ignacio was finished.

"I'll be the judge of that."

"I could tell you nothing."

"Then I'd start hauling your asses downtown to face charges of conspiracy to commit murder, just for starters. Like your friend Álvaro Sotelo, who supplies your vehicles. Yeah, that's right, we figured that one out."

Echave looked pained. "We are acting as patriots."

"American patriots or Cuban patriots?"

"Both. Cuba's interests are America's interests."

"Tell me," Ignacio said, and brought out his notebook.

CHAPTER SIXTY-SEVEN

It was only after a long while that Camaro decided it was safe enough to leave Lauren alone with Chapado. First she gagged the man with a clean washcloth, and then she admonished Lauren to run if there was any sign of trouble. She rode off to Homestead then and stopped in a discount clothing store, buying an outfit she thought might fit Chapado, plus clean socks and underwear. After that she swung through a McDonald's and bought food for all of them.

She came back to the same scene she had left. Chapado had not moved, and Lauren was watching TV. Camaro dropped the food on the bed and went to Chapado. She ungagged him, uncuffed him, and gave him the clothes. "Change into these. We'll throw the others out."

"You are too kind to me."

"Maybe. I'll close the door for a few minutes so you can use the toilet, too. Take a shower if you want. Just keep that dressing dry."

With the door closed, Camaro went to the bed and sat next to Lauren. They ate and had some of the warm bottle of Coke Lauren had bought at the grocery. Chapado ran the shower for five minutes, and then she heard him dressing. He opened the door carefully, slowly when he was finished.

She gave him food. "Sit on the floor and eat," she told him. "When you're done, I'm locking you up again."

"I won't run."

"I can't take that chance. Eat."

He was eating when the call came from Ignacio. Camaro cursed quietly and then answered. "I don't have anything else to say," she said.

"I do," Ignacio replied. "What do you know about Sergio Chapado?"

Camaro froze. She closed the door. "Where did you hear about him?"

"Never mind that. I asked you a question."

"If you're asking me, then you already know. Matt Clifford has him."

"Does he? Or are you and he working some kind of scam together?"

"I'm not working with him," Camaro said.

"Do you know where Matt has Chapado?"

"No."

"You have to stop lying to me sometime, Camaro," Ignacio said. "I'm way out on this one. *Way* out. You wouldn't believe how far. And now there's kidnapping involved? This is FBI shit. Pardon my language."

Camaro sat on the edge of the tub. "What does the FBI know?" she asked.

"You're asking me to be truthful with you now?"

"Yes."

"Okay, I'll trade. I tell you something, and you tell me something. How about it?"

"You first."

"The FBI knows something's going down involving a bunch of Cubans that call themselves Alpha 66. They don't know exactly what yet, but they know people are getting killed, and they know it's big. Right now I'm the only one sitting on the whole story."

"Which is what?"

"No. Now you tell me something."

"I know where Matt and Chapado are going to be in two days," Camaro said.

"Where?"

"If I tell you now, you're just going to send some cops to stake the place out, and it'll ruin everything. I'll call you on the night it's supposed to happen, and you can have them both if that's what you want."

"And how exactly did you come by this information?"

"I'd rather not say."

"I've said it before, but I'll say it again: you are playing with fire."

"Hey," Camaro said, "I know exactly what's at stake here. It's *my life*. Now I'm promising to give you Matt Clifford on a silver platter, and all you have to do in return is hold off for forty-eight hours."

"I should tell you something," Ignacio said.

"What?"

"Lauren Story is officially classified as a missing person. If a cop, *any cop,* catches you with her, you're going down for false imprisonment at the very least."

"Would it help if I told you she's safe?"

"It would help if you turned her over to the authorities so we can take care of her. What if you go off and get yourself killed doing whatever it is that you're doing? What happens to her? What if Matt Clifford gets his hands on her? You know as well as I do that he's bad news for little girls."

Camaro's voice dropped. "He's not going to touch her."

"You can guarantee that?"

"He'd have to kill me first."

"I'd like to believe that."

"Two days, Detective. That's all I need, and you'll have it all."

"You're gonna go to prison," Ignacio said. "You know that, right?"

"Two days," Camaro said, and she ended the call.

CHAPTER SIXTY-EIGHT

MATT DISCONNECTED THE smoke detector in his room at the Econo Lodge when he got back from buying his crank. He had a glass pipe he carried with him most places, and he put on the television and cooked off the meth with the heat of his lighter so he could breathe the smoke.

Some tweakers snorted it. Some injected it. Matt did not like needles, and snorting the stuff made him feel like he was carrying around a bad cold. Maybe he didn't get the biggest high for his dollar, but it was good enough for his purposes. And maybe it was a little healthier than sticking his veins full of holes or destroying his sinuses one sniff at a time.

Colors became more vibrant, and he heard the TV more clearly than he ever did when he was straight. Within minutes he was too fidgety to sit any longer. He paced the room before finally abandoning it to drive the streets of Homestead until he found what he wanted.

The hooker wasn't the best-looking one he'd ever had in his car, but she would do. Matt pulled off into an alley behind an abandoned Blockbuster Video and had her blow him, but even after he'd popped his nut he was still hard. He offered her twice the rate to go back to the motel with him. She agreed.

He did her on top of the sheets with half their clothes on because he could not wait to be in her. The condom tore from the roughness, but he ignored her complaints about putting on another. When he was all finished, he thrust money in her face then kicked her out of the room entirely. She could walk back to where she came from.

The high spike of the drug was wearing down. At least in the aftermath of sex he was able to sit, though his head was still awhirl. He thought about Echave and Chapado, and most of all he thought about Camaro. She was hot, and she had a fine set of tits, and everything he'd done to that hooker he would do to Camaro, except it would take longer and she'd hate it more. Maybe she'd even like that she hated it. Some chicks were twisted like that.

Matt decided to count the money he'd taken from the Cubans. There was still plenty of it left and no one to share it with, so it didn't matter that the amount didn't divide neatly in two. He turned away from thoughts of Camaro and instead considered what he'd do when this was done, when he'd gotten Chapado back and made the deal with the Cubans and gotten the other hundred grand.

It was enough to start over somewhere new. He could buy a small parcel of land in Georgia or somewhere and build a house. With that money, he could get involved in raising animals for their meat or whatever. He'd once heard about a guy in Georgia who raised ostriches and had a steady income from selling ground ostrich and ostrich feathers and ostrich skin. Maybe he didn't know anything about ostriches, but it was something he could learn. How hard could it possibly be? An ostrich was basically just a big chicken, and chickens were easy.

With the television still blaring, he started to drift off, carried down the long, slow slope into a crash. The crank never lasted long enough. Then he was asleep, dreaming of ostriches.

CHAPTER SIXTY-NINE

Now there was only silence between them. Camaro watched the late-night show, and Lauren watched it with her. Camaro thought for a moment about insisting that Lauren sleep again, but there was only so much she could force on the girl before Lauren pushed back. Teenaged girls were like that. Camaro thought of her sister when she was that age.

Lauren did not look at her when she spoke. "I called my uncle."

Camaro turned the sound down on the TV. "When?"

"Earlier today. I told him my dad was dead and that I needed him. He said he would come for me."

"Is he flying in?"

"No, he has to drive because he's broke. It'll take him two days to get here."

"We can wait two days," Camaro said. "Two days is perfect."

"I'm afraid to go to Texas," Lauren said.

"Why?"

"I've never been out of Florida."

"There's nothing in Texas that'll hurt you."

"Nothing or nobody?"

"Nobody," Camaro said.

"Do you really think they'll let me stay with Uncle Richard?"

Camaro shrugged. "It doesn't hurt to try. And the important thing is that you'll be far away from any crap that comes down after all of this is over with. It takes a lot to get things done between states. I figure they'd rather let you go than do the paperwork."

"Do you think you'd like living in Texas?" Lauren asked.

"I don't know. I've never really thought about it."

"Do you know where Del Rio is?"

"No."

"I hope it's near the coast. I like the water."

Camaro nodded slowly. "I like the water, too. But it's more about how you live than where you live. Wherever you go, you'll settle down. You're not like me."

"What are you like?"

She considered her words before speaking. "Wherever I go, I'm always looking out behind me to see what's coming up. I may not even stay here after this. I'd like to change that someday. Just live and not worry."

Lauren was watching her now, and Camaro did her best to ignore the stare. "You don't worry about anything," Lauren said.

"I worry all the time."

"Do you have people who want to hurt you?"

"Now, or always?" Camaro asked.

"Whenever."

"It's complicated," Camaro said. "I've done some things in my life that put me in front of some bad people. I always tried to do right, though. That's all you can do."

"You told me you've killed a lot of people."

"I have."

"Was it when you were a soldier?"

Camaro looked at her. "Who told you I was a soldier?"

"I heard you talking to that man."

Camaro turned back to the television. There was a comedian on the couch next to the host's desk, cracking wise about something. It was only half-audible, and Camaro didn't care anyway. "I killed people when I was a soldier. I killed people after that, too."

"Did you like it?"

"Nobody in their right mind likes killing anyone."

Lauren's voice was solemn. "When is Matt going to die?"

"Very soon."

"I wish I could be there to see it."

"That's nothing you want to see," Camaro said.

"He deserves it."

"He does, but that doesn't mean you have to be a part of that. By the time it happens you're going to be gone from here. And that's a *good* thing. A girl like you shouldn't have to deal with that kind of thing."

"What do you mean a girl like me?"

Camaro shook her head. "You aren't like me. You're just getting started in your life. It might not seem like it, but you have a long, long way to go, and you're never going to make something of yourself if you get caught up in the life that brought your dad down. All of that starts by you getting out of here and not looking back. You leave Matt to me, live or die. That's how it should be."

"What about that man in the bathroom? Is he going to die?"

"Not if I can help it. You get to go to your new home and he does, too."

"Where is he going?"

"I don't know, and I don't really care," Camaro said. "As long as he's out of my life, that's all that matters."

"That's not what you think of me, is it?"

Camaro turned to her again. "No," she said. "It's not."

"I wish I knew you before. I wish my dad had brought you home to meet me."

"I'm not really the kind of girl who gets brought home to meet the kids," Camaro said.

"I wish it anyway."

"You go ahead, then. I won't stop you."

Camaro got up from the bed and stretched. "Where are you going?" Lauren asked.

"I'm going to walk around outside for a little bit. If you need something, come get me. I won't go far."

"Okay."

She let herself out onto the long porch that ran the length of the motel and waited a long minute before stepping off onto the gravel of the parking lot. Out here, away from the clustered lights of the metro area, it was possible to see the stars in a sky that retained its darkness. Camaro turned in place and sought out the Big Dipper and Orion's Belt, but couldn't find the latter. She found Venus and Mars and the North Star. Doing it reminded her of late nights out on the sea with her dad, waiting for their fishing lines to be drawn tight and the fight to start, learning the constellations and the planets and even the features of the moon. In that moment she missed her father more than she had in a long time, and she felt the threat of tears before she pushed them back down inside herself.

Now wasn't the time for crying. Not now and not anytime. She was grown, and the past was the past. If she kept it away, it could never overtake her.

CHAPTER SEVENTY

"THIS IS JOHN Mansfield."

Ignacio held the phone to his ear and ignored the day-shift talk going on at the desks around him. "Agent Mansfield, this is Ignacio Montellano over at the Miami PD. How are you doing?"

"I'm doing just fine, Detective. How are things going with your case?"

He took a breath and steadied himself. "I got a chance to meet face-to-face with Hugo Echave," he said.

"How did that go?"

"He told me everything," Ignacio said.

Now it was Mansfield's turn to pause. Ignacio thought he heard the riffle of paper on Mansfield's end as the man hurried to find something to take notes with. "He was up front with you?" Mansfield asked.

"Totally. I couldn't have asked for a better interview."

"I assume you're calling me because something came up that's outside your purview."

"A little bit," Ignacio said. "Echave told me that his group was involved with an illegal entry into the United States of a Cuban citizen and that this guy they paid to bring in has been kidnapped by the people who were supposed to deliver him. As soon as I heard the word *kidnap* I knew I had to let you in on it."

"We talked about this, but I can see why you'd get in touch with me," Mansfield said. "Tell me about the victim."

"I didn't get a whole background on him, but his name is Sergio Chapado. He was some kind of Alpha 66 mover and shaker in Cuba, so they had to get him out before the government could find him and arrest him."

"Or kill him."

"Yeah, that, too. Do you know anything about him?"

Mansfield made an affirmative noise. "I've heard the name here and there. If I recall correctly, he was behind some embarrassing pro-democracy activism over there. Not exactly blowing up government buildings, but still more dissent than the authorities are used to. I can see why they would want him gone and why Alpha 66 would be hot to get their hands on him. A real live revolutionary is worth big bucks if he's put in front of the right donors."

"What about the whole illegal entry thing?" Ignacio asked.

"Oh, that? That would be glossed over. A man like Chapado would get asylum status easily. Pretty much anyone who asks gets a free pass into the system unless they turn out to be a straight-up criminal or a minor with parents back in Cuba who want him returned. You remember that whole mess from back in 2000."

"Elián González," Ignacio said. "I remember."

"You and every Cuban in the country. People who didn't even care about Cuba before were turning out to protest Elián's repatriation. Once you get the average citizen stoked up about communists, they'll go wild. Lots of Cuban exile groups made serious money off that disaster. Alpha 66 as well. Of course, someone like Chapado isn't anywhere near as cute as a seven-year-old boy, but like I said, he has value."

Ignacio flipped through his notes, hastily scribbled down as Echave unburdened himself in their interview. Now that he was on the phone with Mansfield, he felt strangely reluctant to part with all the details, knowing that his homicide cases could be caught up in an expanded FBI investigation and wrested from him. If they went, Matt Clifford went, too. He wanted to put the cuffs on Clifford himself. "Alpha 66 offered a hundred thousand dollars to an independent contractor to bring Chapado out of the country. Now he's holding out for another hundred thousand. They're paying through the nose."

"Who's the bad guy here?"

Now he must tell. "His name is Matt Clifford. He's a convicted felon with a pretty hefty sheet. I think he's good for a triple homicide that got pulled off four years ago, and he's *definitely* on the hook for the deaths of seven Alpha 66 guys, plus a higher-up in the organization and his wife. Maybe he didn't kill them all himself, but he's up to his neck in it. He has at least one accomplice: a guy named Sandro Soto."

"Can you send me what you have on Clifford and Soto?"

"Sure. I'll email it all to you."

"Where are they now? Did Echave have any idea?"

"*Nada*. Clifford's been in touch, but the number is for a disposable cell we haven't been able to pin down yet. Echave asked him for a current photo of Chapado, but Clifford wouldn't give it up. Chapado may be dead."

"Then he just bumped himself up to the death penalty," Mansfield said. "That's not a problem with me. Listen, Detective, what would you like me to do with this?"

"What do you mean?"

"Well, you know as well as I do that given what you've learned from Echave, the Bureau can take control of this entire thing. You'd be consulted, but we'd be the lead. All the credit would flow our way. And depending on the way the political winds happen to blow, it might get filed away somewhere in a dark place and never see the light of day again. Are you ready to give this thing up?"

"What's my option? This is federal stuff. I'm just a cop in the Homicide Unit."

"The federal end can be handled eventually. You have what you need, right? You can send me what you have, and I'll sit on it for seventy-two hours. I can make an excuse for not getting on it right away. Lost in all my emails, you know? Do you think you can clear this thing in three days?"

"I know I can," Ignacio said.

"Good enough for me. You follow the rulebook, and I'll pretend I did, too. This phone conversation didn't happen."

"Right. I never talked to you."

"Good luck, Detective."

"Thanks."

Ignacio hung up the phone. He checked around to see if anyone had overheard the conversation, but no one looked his way. He gathered up the files pertaining to the case against Matt Clifford and Sandro Soto and zipped them before attaching the compressed folder to an email and sending it off to Mansfield.

He had three days. And even if Mansfield chose to go back on his word and push his way in, he did not have what was in Ignacio's head and not written down. He'd made no notes that mentioned Camaro Espinoza's name. She was a hidden asset, and she promised him results in two days. The clock was running. If she could not deliver, he'd be out and the feds would be in. The whole thing would be lost.

The screen on his phone had gone dark. Ignacio saw himself reflected in the glass. Camaro was a phone call away, but she was the one who decided when and if it happened. He poured his will into the phone, wishing it to ring and produce her on the other end. She did not call.

CHAPTER SEVENTY-ONE

GALDARRES WALKED FROM his hotel to a restaurant with a view of the beach. All the buildings along the drive were painted in pastel colors and by night they were alive with neon. The sidewalks crowded with tourists and locals alike, the young ones clad in as little as they could safely get away with, the old ones draped in summer clothes that conspired to hide the frailty of their bodies.

They seated him on the patio. The morning sun pelted down around him, though the umbrella shaded him at his table. He ordered eggs, ham, and potatoes and coffee as well. Every table was served a pitcher of juice, either orange or grapefruit. Galdarres chose the orange.

He'd been waiting five minutes for his food when the cell phone Davíd had given him trilled in his pocket. He brought it out, flipped it open, and pressed it to his ear. *"Bueno,"* he said.

"Señor Galdarres, it's Davíd Ocampo."

"Good morning, Davíd. I was enjoying your Miami sun."

"We have word from our man inside."

Immediately Galdarres was alert. He sat upright in his seat and spoke quietly into the phone. "What has he learned?"

"The group is in disarray, just as you hoped. Accusations between the man who took Chapado and Alpha 66 are flying. They're holding him responsible for Marquez's death, but he's denying it. They don't believe him."

"Then this man, Matt Clifford, he must be anxious to make his deal quickly."

"No," Davíd said. "Something else has happened."

Galdarres scowled. "What has happened? Both sides have been pushed to make the exchange as soon as possible."

"It's happened the opposite way. Clifford is asking for more time."

"More time? For what?"

"Echave and the others suspect he might be hiding the fact that Chapado is hurt, perhaps even dead. If that's the case, he has no choice but to make delays."

"Delays," Galdarres cursed. "The man is a fool. This only gives Echave's group more time to find him. This is not what was intended."

"I know, señor. We're all very upset."

"Is our man inside pushing for a quick resolution?"

"He doesn't have that much authority, though he's doing what he can and is putting pressure on Echave to act decisively. He hopes to convince Álvaro Sotelo to push Echave into violent action. But there's worse news."

"What could be worse?" Galdarres demanded.

"A policeman spoke with Echave. Our man doesn't know for certain, but he thinks Echave may have talked. How much he revealed to the authorities, we don't know. But there was definitely a meeting, and it lasted for more than an hour. The suspicion is that Echave gave up details about Clifford and what he's doing."

"The last thing we need is the authorities being involved," Galdarres said. "This puts us under a heavy time constraint. You tell our inside man that I want to be informed *to the minute* about changes in this situation. No waiting. We have to be ready to move the moment we have an idea of Chapado's location. Do you understand?"

"Yes, I understand, señor."

"Good. See to it."

Galdarres snapped the phone shut and stuffed it into his pocket angrily. He took a glass of orange juice and downed it in two swallows, then poured himself another, the juice slopping over the edge. All the while, he fumed and swore to himself every swear word he knew in Spanish and English.

It would have been so much easier in Cuba. In his country, everyone was an informant, and the mechanism of the state a powerful and omnipresent thing. If a situation like this arose in Cuba, all it would take was the distribution of subtle pressure in the community before someone would break and tell the DI everything. After that it would only be a matter of swooping in to gather up the wrongdoers and see them to imprisonment. Once they were there, other forms of persuasion could be applied, resulting in still more information and still more arrests, until the entire, festering sore was cleaned out and only healthy flesh remained.

He did not know with whom he was angrier, the invisible Matt Clifford or the fat pig Hugo Echave. Echave styled himself a revolutionary, but he was too soft and too used to having his whims indulged to make truly hard choices. Had it been Galdarres in charge of Alpha 66, his people would scour the city looking for any sign of Clifford until they had either come up with the man or exhausted all possibilities. Instead, Echave kept himself hidden away in his palatial home, afraid to do anything but wait for orders from a common criminal.

Perhaps Matt Clifford had killed Chapado or allowed him to die. If that were the case, Galdarres still had to know. But it would also mean that he would not have the pleasure of dealing with Chapado and Alpha 66 in the same action. Gathered all in one place, the whole knot of them could be disentangled with bullets, with no one left to cause trouble in Cuba again. Poor, frightened Echave would never dare flex the diminished muscle of Alpha 66 in the face of such a crackdown.

The food came finally. Galdarres ate without tasting any of it.

CHAPTER SEVENTY-TWO

SHE FELT BETTER about leaving Lauren alone with Chapado. The man had shown no inclination toward escape attempts, and Lauren was wise enough to stay clear of him. The only time Camaro let him out of the bathroom was on those occasions when she or Lauren had to use it, and during those times he had not gone for the door. Camaro did not think he was broken, but he was clearly patient, waiting for what would come next without lapsing into despair.

He was still gagged when she went out, but that was a small concession to the situation. Chapado did not resist this either. Had there been a second bed, she might have been persuaded to let him sleep on it and not the hard tile floor of the bathroom.

When she came to the hardware store near the grocery, she went hunting for lightbulbs and found nothing but compact fluorescents on display. She tracked down the store's only employee, finding him sorting boxes of screws and bolts into bins at the back of the store. "Excuse me," she said. "I'm looking for something."

"What do you need?" asked the man. He was only in his fifties, but he wore heavy glasses. They did not jibe with the denim overalls and work shirt he wore.

"I'm looking for lightbulbs. Incandescent lightbulbs. You have any?"

The man nodded. "Yeah, sure. Got some in the back. I don't put 'em out anymore because people like the squiggly ones better. How many do you need? What kind?"

"Sixty-watt is good. A couple dozen," Camaro said.

"That many?"

"Do you have them?"

"I think so. Give me a minute."

He vanished into the back and then returned with two white cartons. At the counter up front, he opened the cartons and showed her the lightbulbs, packed away in twos. There were twenty-four altogether. "I'll take them," Camaro said. "And a few shop rags if you have them."

She paid for them, and the man told her to have a good day. Out at the bike, she carefully put one carton in each of the Harley's saddlebags and padded them with the red shop rags before stoking the engine and riding away. She went south.

The compound of warehouses was still secured with the chain and padlock for which Matt held the key, but by now Camaro was comfortable slipping in and out through the hole in the fence. She brought the lightbulbs and the rags with her, and soon she saw Soto's abandoned hatchback.

Matt had done nothing to lock up the place since she'd taken Chapado from him. She guessed he never intended to return. He'd left Soto's body where it lay, and already the sick-sweet odor of decay had begun to cloud up around it. Flies clustered on his wounds, supping on rotting tissue and laying their eggs. In days, Soto's flesh would be full of maggots.

Camaro laid the shop rags out on the floor and then opened up the cartons of lightbulbs. Unpacked from their sheaths, the lightbulbs went down on the rags, eight to a rag. When that was done, she gathered the rags up into bundles and then proceeded to stomp on them with the heel of her boot.

She did not want the pieces to be too small, so she did not grind them. They had to have a little more crush to them, and left this way they did.

The warehouse had three person-sized entrances: the side door she used, the path through the office, and a door in the back. There were the roller doors, but they were all locked from the inside with no way to open them from outside the building. Camaro took the first bundle of shattered bulbs and went to the office.

She scattered the glass over a three-foot span just inside the door. The rag kept the edges from cutting her hands. The second bundle provided a shower of bits around the side door, and the third covered the last door. When she was all done with each, she tossed the rags away. There was no further use for them.

Now she surveyed the towers of crates that populated the warehouse floor. Some were too tall and heavy to maneuver, but others were lighter and could be disassembled and restacked. She did this, building up a three-sided hide with a clear view of the center of the warehouse and the empty chair where Chapado had been held. To stay behind it she would have to crouch, but she wanted something she could hurdle without difficulty.

The crates she used had heft to them, but they were still made of simple, thin wood with slightly thicker reinforcements at the corners. Depending on what was inside, a bullet might punch directly through her cover and reach her. But if things transpired as she imagined them, she would not have to test the bulletproof nature of any of the wooden boxes.

Once she was done with the hide, she stepped out and approached the center of the warehouse from each of the three entrances. Even with daylight filtering through the ceiling panels, her position was hidden from all three angles. In the dark, even if she were exposed a little bit, she would be all but invisible.

Camaro checked the battery-operated floodlights Matt had left behind. She clicked them on and off to see if they still had juice. They were dimmer than they had been. But they were enough. She left them dark and went away from the warehouse, careful not to step in her own fields of splintered glass.

CHAPTER SEVENTY-THREE

The library in Homestead was just off the South Dixie Highway on a partially wooded lot. The grass between the trees was dry and yellowing at the edges. Camaro parked her bike and went inside.

She had hoped for computers, and the Homestead Branch had some. Camaro settled in front of a keyboard and pecked out the URL for Facebook. At the site, she plugged in the search term *Alpha 66*. There was a quick hit and she clicked through. Alpha 66's Facebook presence appeared.

The first thing she noticed was the banner at the top of the page, with a quotation from someone named José Martí. It was something about the courage to sacrifice and how those who didn't should shut up. Camaro didn't know who José Martí was, but the sentiment seemed understandable. She had sacrificed while others stood by and complained. She would have liked a few to shut their mouths.

The next thing she noticed was how few "likes" the page had. There were less than two hundred. The posts underneath were not inspiring, either, being mostly images with messages about Cuban liberation on them. A few seemed totally out of place, like a picture of US soldiers on patrol in Iraq. There were videos, too, including one demanding the impeachment of the president for betraying American interests and embracing the communists. A large picture of Fidel Castro had a red NO slash through it. Camaro shook her head at that. Fidel Castro was something like ninety years old now, not the fierce-looking, bearded revolutionary of the photo. Looking at Alpha

66's page was like looking through a cracked window into a world where people were afraid of their grandparents' boogeymen.

Camaro did not want to use her own account. She opened a second window and created a Gmail account with a false name she plucked out of the air. After that, she used the email address to set up a matching Facebook account. She left the personal picture area blank. She did not plan to use this page more than once.

She clicked the link to send a message to the owner of the Facebook page. A blank square of space opened up, the cursor blinking. She typed.

Matt Clifford does not have Sergio Chapado anymore. I do. He can't bargain with you about anything. Don't believe what he says.

I'll send you confirmation that I'm holding Chapado once you send me an email. He's alive and healthy. I will keep him that way. When you contact me, we'll make arrangements for him to be turned over to you. You can also have Matt.

Don't go to the police. Don't tell Matt you know he's lying. If you do either of these things, the deal is off.

Camaro didn't sign the message, but she included the address of the fake Gmail account she'd set up. As a final note she added, *Don't wait long to contact me,* and then she sent the message on.

She logged out of Facebook and then cleared the browser history completely before leaving the computer behind. Outside the library she squinted in the sun until she slipped on her sunglasses and the worst of the glare went away.

It was getting on toward an early lunch hour. Camaro circled around to point the bike south and cruised out of Homestead. Halfway back to the motel in Florida City, she stopped off for food, at a Burger King this time to break up the monotony. Within fifteen minutes she was on the road past the hardware store, kicking up dust in her wake.

The motel still looked deserted when she approached it. In the time they'd been there, she'd heard no cars coming or going or even a hint of other guests. She kept the Do Not Disturb sign on the door and went to the office for fresh towels. The manager seemed to have no problem with the arrangement so long as she paid.

Camaro let herself into the room. Lauren was there, and Chapado lurked beneath the bathroom sink. He breathed deeply when she plucked the towel from his mouth and flexed his jaw. "It's almost over," she told him.

"What is happening?" Chapado asked.

"I got in touch with your friends in Alpha 66. They know you're with me now and not with Matt. I told them to get in touch. As soon as they do, we'll work out the arrangements. You're more than halfway home."

"If I promise not to flee, will you allow me some freedom?" Chapado asked. "Keep me in the handcuffs, but let me at least sit on the bed. Anything except this floor. I'm not a young man, and my joints hurt."

"You guys in Alpha 66 think you're soldiers," Camaro said. "A soldier can handle sitting on the floor for a while. Trust me, it could be a lot worse."

"I need to urinate."

"Okay. And I have some food for you."

She released him from the sink and set the bag with his food on the bathroom floor before pulling the door closed. When she sat on the bed, she found she was ravenous, so she unwrapped her burger quickly. It had not cooled off but had been kept warm in the baking oven of the saddlebags.

"Is it true?" Lauren asked her.

"Is what true?"

"That it's almost over?"

"Yes, it's true."

"When will it happen?"

"When you're gone. Not before."

"Is that because you're worried you might die?" Lauren asked.

Camaro nodded without speaking. She finished off her burger swiftly and took up the fries. The salt was making her thirsty the way the summer heat had not.

"You won't die," Lauren said.

"You sure about that?"

"I'm sure. You won't let them kill you."

Camaro allowed the slightest of smiles to play on her lips. "I wish it was that easy," she said. "It's not really up to me."

"You won't die," Lauren said again. "I won't let you."

Camaro looked at her and put her hand on top of Lauren's. "Okay," she said.

CHAPTER SEVENTY-FOUR

Echave's hands shook as he looked at the printout. He was aware of Ulises Sotelo looking at him, waiting for his reaction, judging the exact level of concern he should feel. In this moment, whether the organization scattered into panic or moved forward steadfastly was bound up in Echave's response to this thing in his grasp.

"When did this come?" Echave said. He kept his voice level.

"It arrived this morning about ten thirty," Ulises said. "I found it when I checked my email. I supervise the page, so all messages are forwarded to me by the site."

"Have you responded?"

"No. I thought that would be best left to you, señor."

"Good. Good. You were right to wait," Echave said. "I must share this with Señor Molina."

"Should I step outside?" Ulises asked.

"No. Stay here. Sit."

Echave put the Facebook message flat on his desk and turned to the phone. He put it on speaker and dialed Carlos' private number. He was relieved when his old friend answered. "Hugo," Carlos said. "What has happened?"

"How do you know anything has happened?" Echave asked.

"I only guessed as much. You rarely use this line."

"Something *has* happened," Echave said. "We must discuss it."

He went through the short story as Ulises had told it to him. Then he read the contents of the message aloud. Carlos was quiet on the other end when Echave had finished and was slow to speak. "This is troubling," he said.

"This explains why Clifford wouldn't send us the proof we asked for. Who knows how long Chapado has been out of his hands?"

"Yes. And who is this person? Anita Lopez? I've never heard the name before."

"It's probably fake," Ulises said.

"Who is that?" Carlos asked.

"Álvaro's boy," Echave replied. "He's still with me."

"Ulises? Ask him if there's any way we can find out the real name of the person holding Señor Chapado."

Ulises shook his head when Echave looked at him. "There is no way. The address she gave is completely anonymous, and so is the Facebook account. She could be anyone. She may not even be a she. I can't imagine any woman taking Señor Chapado away from Clifford, a hardened criminal."

"A bluff within a bluff," Carlos said. "This could also be Clifford playing more games with us."

"We have to contact this woman," Echave said.

"Yes. Send her an email. We must tell her we're willing to do anything."

Echave nodded, then swiveled his chair to face his computer. He copied the email address from the message and carefully composed a reply while Carlos waited on the line and Ulises watched him. There was silence, save for the clicking of his keyboard. He sent the email.

"It could be hours before we hear from her," Ulises said. "Days."

"She seems anxious to do a deal with us," Echave said. "We may not have to wait long."

"We should gather," Carlos said. "It's better if we wait together."

"I will call my father," Ulises offered.

"Do that," Echave said. "In the meanwhile we—"

Echave's email pinged and silenced him. He looked and saw a new message in his in-box. The sender was Anita Lopez, and the address was the one she had given them. There was an attachment. Echave clicked to open the email and then the attachment.

The attachment was a picture from a telephone camera and showed Sergio Chapado sitting beneath a sink on the floor of a yellow-and-brown bathroom. A large piece of medical gauze was taped over his bare forearm. His wrists were red with the markings of handcuffs.

He hasn't been harmed by me, the email read.

Echave described the contents of the email. Carlos made a sound like relief and fear all at once. "That picture could have been taken at any time. Ask for proof of the date."

"Yes," Echave said, and he composed the response. *Show us today's date.*

Another email came quickly. A second picture of Chapado, only now a hand held a sheet of paper with the date written on it in pen. The hand was a woman's. "So she didn't lie about that after all," Ulises said.

Echave was about to answer when his email program chimed again. A third message from the woman calling herself Anita Lopez. No picture this time, but a simple trio of sentences: *He'll be yours in less than 36 hours. Matt Clifford, too. Keep it to yourself.*

"Ask her what she wants," Carlos said over the phone.

Echave typed. His fingers stumbled over the words. He sent the email. The response was nearly immediate: *Nothing. Don't test me. Do as you're told.*

We will, Echave wrote, and he sent it away. No reply came.

"We need to get the best men we have left," Carlos said. "We can't have another situation like Liberty City. This could be another trap. If we aren't ready, we'll be robbed again."

"She doesn't want the money," Echave said. "We won't need to take it. She only wants to hand over Señor Chapado and Clifford."

"Why?" Ulises asked.

"I have no idea, but I will not ruin the situation by overthinking it. We will go with weapons, but only to protect ourselves in case of betrayal. If we attempt to do more than that, this woman might do something to Señor Chapado, and all will be lost."

"I want to be a part of the team," Ulises said. "I'll retrieve Señor Chapado myself."

"That's not a good idea," Carlos said. "Álvaro would never forgive us if something happened to you. We have others who can go. It's too much of a risk."

Ulises addressed Echave directly. "Let me lead the way on this, señor," he said. "I swear I will do you proud. It will be my honor to bring Señor Chapado directly to this house, alive and unharmed."

Echave thought. He considered the words of the woman, the image of Chapado bound beneath the sink, and the chaos wrought by Matt Clifford on Alpha 66. Finally, he nodded. "I'll allow it. But take no chances. I will not have your death on my conscience."

CHAPTER SEVENTY-FIVE

GALDARRES SWELTERED IN Davíd Ocampo's garage with the others, waiting for the arrival of the last man. Their inside man. "He's late," Galdarres said.

"He'll be here," Davíd assured him.

Around Galdarres were the others—Peyrera, Icaza, and Pedro Maldonado—and they too perspired heavily. Davíd had switched on a shop fan to stir the air around, but with the garage door closed, all the heat of the day was trapped in the space with them.

Davíd's phone rang. He answered it and conferred quietly with the person on the other end before hanging up. "He's approaching now."

A button was pressed, and the garage door began to slowly rise. A gasp of blessedly fresh air breathed into the garage. Galdarres turned his face into it, but the moment did not last. A young man in shirt-sleeves and a tie ducked underneath the rising door to step inside, and Davíd pressed the button again. They were cut off from the outside.

Galdarres looked at the young man. Ulises Sotelo seemed barely out of his teens, despite the clean cut of his slacks and the neatness of his tie. His face was smooth-shaven, giving him an even more youthful appearance. A pomade in his hair made the black glisten.

"Señor Galdarres," Davíd said. "This is Ulises Sotelo."

Galdarres rose to shake Ulises's hand. "Come sit with us," he said.

A chair was made available to Ulises, and all of them sat in a circle. Davíd rubbed his hands together as if he were about to propose some kind of card game but said nothing. The others were sullen in the heat. Galdarres sensed frustration in them. They wanted to move ahead.

"It is done," Ulises said. "I've been placed in charge of reclaiming Señor Chapado."

"You and how many others?" Galdarres asked.

"Two. We have a shortage of capable men."

"And are they? Capable?"

"Yes. Military veterans. They will be well armed."

"We can take them out," Peyrera said.

Ulises's face creased, showing worry lines that seemed out of place on such young features. "Is that necessary? There must be another way."

"Are you worried we will also kill you?" Galdarres asked.

"No. I know you find me too valuable inside."

"And we do. You won't be harmed."

Ulises seemed relieved. "Thank you," he said.

"When is the exchange due to take place?" Davíd asked.

"We're not sure. We haven't heard back from the woman yet. She says soon, but she hasn't provided us with any details beyond that."

Galdarres nodded. "She will likely wait until the very last moment so you have no time to prepare. It's what I would do."

"You can rest assured that I will pass the information along immediately," Ulises said.

"I believe you. Your father must be very proud."

"My father is an idiot. Only a fool hangs on to a grudge for fifty-six years."

"I see," Galdarres said. "Will you excuse me? Davíd, please come with me."

Galdarres left the garage and went into the air-conditioned house.

He was soaking wet beneath his arms and in a patch down his back. The cool on his face was like the welcome touch of a lover. Davíd followed behind him. "Yes, señor?" Davíd asked.

"Be certain the door is closed," Galdarres said.

Davíd checked. He pulled the handle firmly. There was no give. "Yes," he said.

"How long has this man, Ulises Sotelo, been working with us?"

"A little over two years."

"And has he been useful?"

"Sometimes. His information is always good."

"We can't allow him to lay his hands on Chapado," Galdarres said.

"What? Why not?"

"There is something I have learned through many years in Cuba," Galdarres told Davíd. "And that is that anyone who betrays one person will easily betray another. As far as we know, Ulises may be claiming to work with us, but his allegiance may still lie with his father's people in Alpha 66."

"There's no evidence of that," Davíd said quickly.

"It doesn't matter. Once we have the information from him, we will move ahead with the operation on our own. We will be certain Chapado is dead before this young man or any of Alpha 66 have a chance to take him from the woman holding him. And after that, we will do away with Ulises Sotelo altogether."

Davíd's face paled. "Kill him?"

"Yes."

"But why? He's a valuable asset."

"Once we've killed Chapado, it will be only a matter of time before Alpha 66 deduces who betrayed them. How many people do they have left? How many are privileged enough to hold this information? He will be the first and most obvious choice. He's seen all of our faces. He knows too much about us. He needs to be eliminated."

Davíd said nothing.

"Go back in there and assure him that all is well," Galdarres said. "Make him feel like the valuable asset you say he is. But don't forget: once our enemy, always our enemy."

He let Davíd go before bringing out the phone the man had given him. He dialed a Miami number that went directly to a voice mail box. The tone sounded.

"The operation will conclude shortly," Galdarres said. "I will make arrangements to return in five days. All should be settled by then. Preparations should also be made to burn this cell after my departure to prevent leaks. Good-bye."

Galdarres hung up the phone. He weighed it in his hand for a long moment, thinking. Once he was done, he put the phone back in his pocket and turned toward the garage. He passed through the door into the heat with a smile and made all present feel confident about what was to follow.

CHAPTER SEVENTY-SIX

RICHARD STORY CALLED about midday. Camaro took the call. "May I speak to Lauren?" he asked.

Camaro passed the phone over. Lauren took it in both hands and held it to her ear. "Uncle Richard?"

"I'm coming into the city now. Are you okay? Where are you?"

"I'm..." Lauren said, and then she looked at Camaro. "I'm not sure I should say."

"Let me talk to him," Camaro said.

She took the phone back. In the background she heard wind and traffic. Richard was driving with the windows open. If he was from a town close to the Mexican border, out west of San Antonio, he would be used to the heat, if not Miami's cloying humidity. "Hello?" he said.

"I'm here," Camaro said.

"Who are you?"

"I'm a friend of your brother's."

"Why do you have Lauren?"

"I'm keeping her safe."

"She wants me to come and get her. Where do I go?"

"We'll meet you in Florida City. It's south of Miami about half an hour or so. There's a Denny's right off US 1. You'll see it from the highway."

"How do I get there?"

Camaro told him and had him repeat it back to her. "I'll give you an hour. Don't be late."

"I won't."

She ended the call and turned to Lauren. "It's all set. You're on your way out of here."

Lauren looked around her. "I don't have any bags to pack."

"I'll see if I can find a laundry bag or something."

She searched, but there was nothing of the kind. In the end she stripped the case from one of the pillows, and they filled it with the clothes Camaro had bought her. With the pillowcase slung over her shoulder, Lauren looked like a street kid. Camaro wouldn't wish that on anyone.

"There's something else," Camaro said.

Camaro brought the attaché case she had kept from Parker's house out from underneath the bed. She unzipped it and emptied the case out onto the mattress. Lauren gasped when she saw the bundles fall. "What is all that?" she asked.

"Your dad's money," Camaro said. "It's forty thousand dollars."

"How did he get forty thousand dollars?"

"It doesn't matter. All that matters is that it's yours now. Put it down deep in that pillowcase. Don't let anyone see it. Hide it somewhere when you get where you're going, and don't spend it unless you have to."

"What about my uncle? He should know."

Camaro put her hand on Lauren's arm. "Don't tell anyone. Ever. They'll ask questions you don't want to answer, or they'll try to take it from you. It's the secret that you keep."

Lauren nodded then. She gathered up fistfuls of cash and crammed them into the pillowcase among her things. Only when it was all gone did Camaro step away.

Chapado waited in the bathroom. Camaro crouched down to see him eye to eye. "I'm going out, but I'll be back. Tonight's the night. You'll go to your people, and we'll never see each other again."

"Please don't gag me," Chapado asked.

"You'll yell and scream if I don't."

"I promise you I won't. I have no desire to go with the police. I only want to be with my brothers in arms. They will take care of me."

Camaro took a washcloth from the sink and kneaded it in her hand, thinking. "I can't cut you loose of the sink," she said.

"I don't expect you to."

"I'm trusting you," Camaro said.

"I know. You can. You have never hurt me. I know what you do, you do for that girl. That it helps you is only your second concern."

She put the washcloth back in the sink. "I'll be gone no more than ninety minutes. I expect to find you here when I get back."

"You will," Chapado said.

"Okay."

Camaro stood up and closed the bathroom door on the way out. It was not a heavy door, but if he screamed, there would be that little bit more insulation between him and the outside world. She only hoped no one had taken the room next door sometime in the night.

"I'm ready," Lauren said.

"Let's go."

They left, and Lauren rode on the pillion seat with her arms around Camaro's waist, the pillowcase held fast in its place behind her. Camaro took the long way, and on a stretch of empty street, she carved a gentle slalom between the curbs. Lauren laughed at that and Camaro smiled.

When they reached the Denny's, Camaro parked the bike around back so that it was not visible from the road. They went in and asked for a booth for three. The server brought them water and seemed annoyed when they ordered nothing else. "We'll wait until our last one gets here," Camaro told him.

Camaro caught sight of Lauren's hand trembling on the tabletop, and she put hers on top of the girl's to still it. "I'm nervous," Lauren said.

"I don't blame you. You don't know your uncle."

"I don't remember him from when he came here last."

"When was that?"

"About ten years ago, I guess. My dad said they didn't talk much because of Dad's trouble. He always said Richard was the better brother."

Camaro patted Lauren's hand and tried a smile. "You'll do fine. You're a good kid, and your dad was a good guy. His brother will be, too."

"And what if there's a problem? What if I need you?"

Camaro waved the server down. "Do you have a pen I can use?"

The server gave Camaro a pen, and Camaro used it to write a number and an email address on a napkin. She gave the pen back. She pushed the napkin toward Lauren. "Anytime you need me," she said.

Lauren took the napkin and looked at it. She folded it in half and put it in her pocket. "Okay," she said.

Time passed. When she saw the battered pickup truck enter the parking lot, she knew it was Richard Story. When the man got out and put on his straw cowboy hat, Camaro thought she might have seen a little of Parker in him, but not much. The hair she glimpsed was dark and not fair. Parker had been broader at the shoulder, not rangy like his brother in his plain blue work shirt and faded jeans. Richard wore boots.

He came into the restaurant and looked around for them. Lauren twisted in her seat and signaled him with her hand. He came to the booth and stood there without sitting down. "Jesus, Lauren, you're all grown up," he said.

"Yeah, I guess," Lauren said.

Richard turned his gaze on Camaro. "You're the friend?"

"That's right. Sit down."

He did so slowly, sliding in beside Lauren and facing Camaro across the table. Up close there were features in his face that were exactly like Parker's. Richard was clearly the younger brother, maybe thirty, but sun-dried and tanned from long hours outdoors. Parker had the look of a surf bum. Richard looked like a workingman. "Where are the police?" he asked.

"Not here," Camaro said. "And they won't be. You need to take Lauren out of here, and only when she's at least a state away should you call them. If you do it before then, they'll want to take her. Don't make it easy for them."

"What happened to Parker?"

Camaro saw the waiter coming. "It's hard to explain," she said.

Richard seemed as though he were about to say something more, but the waiter arrived to take orders. Camaro asked for a club sandwich. Lauren had a burger. Richard told the man iced tea was good enough. It was only when the waiter was gone again that he found his voice. "I just drove sixteen hundred miles to get here," he said. "I want some explanation."

Lauren's expression turned pleading. Camaro knew she wanted all to go well. "You know your brother didn't always earn an honest living," Camaro said.

"I know."

"He got mixed up with some bad people. Real bad. They put him in a situation he couldn't get out of and he died. But he knew it could happen, and he asked me to look after Lauren and make sure she got to you. I did that. If you want more of the story, there's a cop I can put you in touch with, but you have to promise me you'll wait."

Richard examined her face as if searching for some lie. Camaro made her expression blank. "Did you kill him?" he asked her.

"No. I tried to save him."

"And these bad people . . . they'd hurt Lauren?"

"They might. Do you want to risk it?"

They sat still, looking into each other's eyes, until Richard looked away. He turned to Lauren. "Are you sure you want to come with me?" he asked.

"I'm sure."

"Where do you go from here?" Richard asked Camaro.

"It's better if you don't know."

Richard grunted. "We should go now."

"I'll walk you out."

They got up, and Camaro put money on the table to cover the food they wouldn't eat, plus a tip for the waiter's time. Outside, she sent Lauren to get her pillowcase of clothes. They all stood by Richard's pickup. He shifted on his feet, visibly searching for words that would not come.

Camaro looked to Lauren instead. "Be safe," she said.

Lauren came to her and hugged her, and after a moment Camaro allowed her arms to fall around Lauren's shoulders. She patted the girl's back. When they parted, tears shimmered in Lauren's eyes. "I won't forget what you did."

Camaro glanced at Richard. He had his keys in his hand. "Go make new memories," she told Lauren. "Better ones."

"Good-bye . . . friend," Richard said.

"Good-bye. Don't look back."

She waited until they were in the truck and Richard had pulled out of the parking lot and onto the road. Within a minute they were out of sight and Camaro was alone. She brought out the prepaid phone. She called Matt's number.

CHAPTER SEVENTY-SEVEN

"MIDNIGHT," CAMARO SAID without greeting.

"You whore," Matt said.

"You want to end this or what?" Camaro asked.

"I'll end it with a bullet in your head. Where do I give it to you?"

"Right where I left your friend."

"You're using my own spot," Matt said.

"You weren't using it for anything."

"I'm gonna kill you."

"That's what you said. You can try."

"Oh, yeah, you're dead."

Camaro looked around the Denny's parking lot. She tried to imagine where Matt was. She hoped it was comfortable, because it was the end for him. "The smart thing for you to do is take that money you stole from the Cubans and run, Matt."

"Run from *you?* I don't think so."

"Just remember I gave you a chance."

"Go fuck your—" Matt began, but she cut the call short.

She went to her bike and sat in the saddle as she typed in an email for the men of Alpha 66. She gave them the place, and she gave them a time: two o'clock. There was a warning not to come early or the deal was off. Maybe they wouldn't listen, but she believed they would be gun-shy after Liberty City. They would do as they were told.

Only then did she call Ignacio through the main switchboard at the police station. He picked up after a transfer. "Detective Montellano," he said. He sounded exhausted.

"It's me," Camaro said.

"Camaro," Ignacio said, audibly awakened. "Why are you calling?"

"Tonight's the night Matt Clifford's passing Chapado to his friends."

"When? Where?"

"Early morning. I'll let you know where."

"Tell me now."

"You know I can't do that."

"Goddamn it, you have to give me something to work with here! You've been stringing me along this whole time. Where is Matt Clifford, where is Chapado, and where is this all going down?"

"I'll tell you tonight," Camaro said. "But be ready. You won't have much time."

"Camaro, don't leave me hanging."

"I have to go. Remember what I said: be ready."

She closed the line and turned off the phone.

With Lauren's weight gone from the bike there was a strange lightness to her ride. The helmet she had bought the girl was held to the pillion seat's backrest by the chinstrap. Camaro didn't know what she would do with it.

There were no police at the motel when she returned, and she heard no noise from the room when she approached. She let herself in and went to the bathroom. Chapado sat there quietly. "You see?" he said to her.

"It's time to go," Camaro said. She crouched and unfastened the handcuffs. "You can ride with the cuffs on or off. It's up to you."

"I will go without if it makes no difference to you."

"Fine," Camaro said, and she put the handcuffs in her back pocket.

She fetched the shotgun from its place by the bed and checked through the partly opened door for watchful eyes before stepping out with the weapon. It went behind the saddlebag, and she and Chapado went on the bike. She pressed the starter, and the engine revved into life. "You try to jump off, or if you give me any problems . . . ," she said.

"I understand."

It was not far to the warehouse complex, and Chapado made no protest when they parked in the concealment of a tall Brazilian pepper and Camaro armed herself again. They walked side by side, not like captor and captive, and went through the hole in the fence one after the other.

"Watch your step," Camaro told him when they reached the side door of the warehouse. They crunched into the broken glass on the other side, and she showed him how to knock his toe against the floor and shake off the larger bits. "You don't want to end up kneeling in any of that."

Camaro showed him her hide and motioned for him to sit down. She went to the center of the warehouse and switched on the floodlights. The batteries would last at least long enough to get them through what she had to do.

When she was done, she sat down next to Chapado in the hide and put the shotgun across her knees. "Now we wait," she said.

"For what?"

"For Matt to cheat. I told him midnight. He'll be here by eleven. No later."

"A long time from now."

"You're used to waiting," Camaro said. "Wait a little bit more."

They let the hours slip past them. Camaro sweated in the oppressive heat of the warehouse. Chapado's face was wet with perspiration. A sauna would have punished them less, and the reek of Soto's corpse was pervasive.

The illumination from the plastic ceiling panels dimmed, as did the light through the warehouse windows. The sun went down completely. The night sounds began.

She heard an engine somewhere out on the road about ten thirty and knew it was Matt. He would come through the front gates as quietly as he could and creep up on the warehouse, watching it for movement and listening for a hint of sound. There would be none. Then he would come closer, his weapon out, until he was at the door. He would pass through.

Matt's foot crunched in the broken glass near the office. Camaro rose to a crouch and put a finger to her lips. Chapado nodded. She heard Matt curse and then the quiet footfalls of a man trying his best not to be heard.

Camaro came out of the hide and slipped through the shadows of the stacked crates. She could hear him and feel him moving toward the center of the warehouse, drawn inexorably toward the light like some kind of stupid insect.

She stepped out of cover at Matt's back and closed the distance between them with the shotgun up. "Stop right where you are," she told him.

Matt froze. He raised his hands, with his pistol still in his grip. "Don't shoot," he said. "You got me."

"Gun on the floor."

Camaro waited as he crouched down and placed his weapon lightly on the concrete. "You knew I'd come early," he said. "So you came earlier."

"Kick the gun away."

He did. "Now what?"

"Turn around."

Matt turned to face her. He was silhouetted by the brightness of the floodlights. The empty chair where Chapado had been held was like a waiting torture rack. "You gonna shoot me? Just like you shot Sandro?"

"I should."

"Go ahead then."

"No."

"So...what? We gonna stare at each other all night? Why don't you put that gun down, and you can show me how tough you are. Bitch."

Camaro felt the handcuffs in her back pocket. She looked at the chair. "You're stupid," she said.

"And you're nothing without that shotgun. Come on, lady, show me what you got."

Camaro let her hand slip from around the pistol grip of the Mossberg and held it by the forend. "You want to see how you do against me?" she asked.

A thin smile danced around Matt's lips. "Let's do it. One on one. I don't have no gun, and you don't have one. I'll put you down in a second."

"Okay," Camaro said.

She squatted to the floor and laid the shotgun down flat before standing again. Matt lowered his hands and rolled his shoulders. His hands made fists. "You just made a big mistake," he said.

"I don't think so," Camaro said.

She drew the Glock from the small of her back and shot Matt in the stomach before he had a chance to move from his spot. He folded in half at the waist, and his knees buckled. His body teetered. He toppled onto his side. Blood escaped between the fingers he clutched around his belly.

Camaro put the Glock away and grabbed Matt by the arm. She dragged him across the floor past Soto's body and into the center of the warehouse. "Get up," she said. "Into that chair."

Matt mumbled as she muscled him partway onto his feet and then into a seated position in the chair. Camaro took out the handcuffs and secured his wrists behind the chair's stiff back. Matt bled into his lap. "You cheatin' bitch," he managed to say.

"Don't complain," Camaro said. "You could be dead. It'll take you a long time to bleed out from that wound. And by then you won't be my problem anymore."

"Fu-fuck you."

"Just shut up and sit still," Camaro said. "You don't have to—"

A foot crunched on the glass near the entrance. She saw the first man appear in the space between two stacks, a submachine gun gripped in his fists. He opened fire.

CHAPTER SEVENTY-EIGHT

CAMARO THREW HERSELF to one side as the submachine gun barked. She tucked her shoulder as she hit the floor and rolled, coming up by the standing sentinel of a floodlight. The Glock slipped into her hand and then she was moving, even as a second man came storming forward. His bullets chewed a crate to flinders and thudded on the objects inside.

She turned as she fled, firing twice at the exposed gunman and catching him high in the chest. He spiraled to the ground, a quick flash exploding from the muzzle of his weapon as his dead finger convulsed on the trigger. Camaro faded into the shadows, aware of the rush of feet moving around the warehouse, a spreading fan of armed men.

The hide was a place to go, but then she would draw the enemy directly toward Chapado. Instead, she dodged back and back again, burying herself more deeply in the maze of boxes and crates, even as the men shouted to one another in Spanish.

One appeared in her peripheral vision, and she ducked before a flurry of slugs cut the air where she had just been. Camaro snaked around the corner of the stack, looking for a clear shot and failing to find one.

They were in front and behind. Camaro heard a shout less than ten feet ahead of her. She reversed direction, keeping low. A man with a shotgun passed through her field of vision, but he did not glance her way. Camaro surged forward and made the corner in time to see his exposed back. She raised the Glock to fire, but he sensed her at the last moment and turned. The barrel of his shotgun hit the Glock and sent it spinning from her hand. Camaro stepped in, past the muzzle as the shotgun detonated. She punched the man hard in the face and he staggered.

His grip slackened on the shotgun. Camaro grabbed it in both hands, and they wrestled for it, the weapon between them. He twisted the gun, but they both lost their grip, and it struck the floor. Camaro's stunned ears barely heard the clatter of it on the concrete.

The man punched, but she blocked it away, moving inside to drive an elbow into his stomach. He grunted and laced an arm around her throat, hauling her backward and clear off her feet. They fell together to the ground.

Camaro scrambled over onto all fours. The man caught her by the neck of her shirt and knotted his fingers in the material. He punched her with his other hand, and instantly she bled from the nose.

She got a leg over his hip and drove down with her elbow again and again, the point of bone cutting deep gashes on the man's forehead. Blood gushed from her nostrils, raining onto his face. Her nose was broken.

There was the flash of silver in the corner of her eye, and she put a hand out just fast enough to catch the man's wrist as he stabbed a knife toward her side. He wrenched her off her knees by her collar, the material giving way, and drove the point of the blade downward into her exposed thigh. Camaro screamed and pressed a thumb into the man's eye, gouging deep into the socket until she felt hot wetness. Now he screamed, too.

Camaro lunged away from the man toward the fallen Glock, her shirt tearing down the front. Her hand closed around the butt as the man stabbed her in the leg again. She fell on her side and shot him in the ear twice. He was still.

Two were down, but she did not know how many there had been to begin with. There were still at least three distinct voices, but the sound of their running footfalls made them sound like many more. She struggled to stand up.

"*¡Ahí está!*" called a man, and Camaro realized one had slipped behind her. She spun and nearly toppled. He raised his submachine gun, the weapon black on black. Camaro emptied her pistol into him. He danced with the impacts, tripped over his own feet, and collapsed.

The Glock was useless. She dropped it and swayed on her feet. Men were closing on her from two directions. Camaro limped to a short stack of crates and clambered up onto them, feeling the hot blood pulsing down her leg. Her mouth was full of the salt taste of it. She made it to the top of the stack, and for a moment she saw a pair of men in motion, armed with automatic weapons, navigating the warren formed among the towers.

She dropped down on the far side and her leg gave way. She clawed at the crates nearest her for handholds and stood again. She cut to her right, but finding the breaks too small to wedge through, she channeled toward the rear wall of the warehouse. The men were shouting to each other again, voicing confusion. Camaro went to her boot.

The karambit was five ounces in her left hand, nearly weightless as the adrenaline coursed through her. At the end of the row, she circled back, homing in on the raised voices, hobbling on her bloody leg. She could identify them by sound now: a young man and an older man, the latter's voice roughened by cigarettes. Camaro closed on the young man, tracking through the stacks, sweat slicking her skin and her heart thundering. She spat blood from her lips.

They nearly collided as they reached the same corner at the same moment. The young man's eyes bulged in the shadows, showing white, and he swung the muzzle of his submachine gun around. Camaro caught the weapon in her right hand and ripped with the left.

The karambit laid the man's throat open deeply, and there was a hot shower of red in the air as his carotid erupted.

The older man appeared at the end of the row, and Camaro let the karambit slip and fall. She seized the dying gunman by the shoulders and dragged him around even as his comrade opened fire. Bullets crashed into flesh, most of the impacts absorbed by the meat of the young man's chest and belly. Other bullets streaked by and another punched through, caroming off bone to strike Camaro in the hip. She felt the bite of the bullet as it slashed her.

Camaro's hand closed over her shield's right fist. She brought his arm and his weapon to bear in the same motion, triggering finger on finger and letting the submachine gun explode into a fully automatic blaze that lit the narrow row.

Slugs tore at the crates around the older man, but others sank home. He staggered under the shots and fell back against a tower. It teetered at the collision and then fell over, raising a riot of noise as wooden cases shattered and their contents spilled.

Both men were dead. Camaro let her shield crumple. Camaro fell, too. She put her hand on her hip and felt where the bullet had laid open the flesh but missed the bone. She gathered up her blade again and listened, but there was no further sound.

"Chapado?" Camaro called. She sounded weak.

"I . . . I am here."

"Stay where you are. I'm coming to you."

Getting up took all her effort. She stumbled to the hide and saw Chapado curled up in the shelter of the crates. His eyes widened when he saw her. "The blood," he said. "You're hurt."

Camaro wanted to collapse on the floor beside him. "I'm alive," she said.

"They are all gone?"

"I think so." She gripped Chapado's arm. "Come with me."

"You are hurt. I should help you."

"Just come on," she said, and she hobbled through the stacks to each of the dead bodies in turn, Chapado in her wake. "Is this one of Alpha 66's?" she asked him every time. He shook his head.

They came to the last, the older man she'd heard among the others. She lifted his head by the hair and showed his face to Chapado. "Is he one of them?"

"No," Chapado said. "But I know him."

"Who is he?"

"He is Cuban. Intelligence Directorate. His name is... Galvan. No, it's Galdarres."

"They're not even your guys," Camaro said.

"They came to kill me. I owe you my life. But it doesn't matter. You're bleeding."

"Help me sit."

Chapado helped lower her to the ground. She stripped off the ragged remains of her shirt and tore it into pieces. "Put pressure there," she said, pointing at her leg. "You do that one. I'll do the others."

Long needles of pain lanced through her when the wounds were pressed on. Camaro felt faint and clung to Chapado's sleeve when her vision flickered. They stayed in place for a long time, breathing together, as the torn fragments of her shirt slowly soaked with blood.

After a while, she took pressure off her hip and the blood didn't flow. Her nose was stuffed completely, but the streaming had stopped. She let go of the knife wound on her thigh. It oozed only slightly. Chapado did the same. They still bled, but the worst was past. "You need a doctor. Stitches."

"I'll worry about that," Camaro said. "I need to get up. I need my gun."

Chapado provided a shoulder, and Camaro searched through the warehouse until she found her gun. She tucked it away. "What now?" Chapado asked.

"Matt."

They went to him. Matt slumped in the chair, his stomach and legs sodden with blood. The bullet wound in his forehead was perfectly round and placed directly over the left eyebrow. His eyes were open.

"Son of a bitch," Camaro said.

Chapado was there. "Is he...?"

"Yeah, he's dead. I wanted him alive for your friends."

"I will tell my people you tried to give him to them."

The karambit came into her hand. Camaro stepped into Chapado and brandished the blade against his throat. He froze. "You don't tell them anything about me. You never saw my face. You never heard my name. You don't know who I am or where I came from. If you owe me your life, then you will swear I was never here."

Chapado swallowed. "I saw nothing. I know nothing."

Camaro stepped back. "Your people will come for you," she said. "You just have to wait."

She wiped the karambit clean on Matt's shoulder and put it away. Then she brought out the throwaway phone and called out. She waited until Ignacio answered. "Camaro," he said.

"It's time," she said.

"Are you okay? You don't sound too good."

"Just come and get them."

"Where?"

"You're a smart guy. You figure it out," Camaro said. She cleaned the phone on her T-shirt without ending the call and let it fall to the floor.

She picked up her shotgun from where it lay and left the warehouse behind, dragging her leg as she went.

CHAPTER SEVENTY-NINE

SHE WAS ON the flybridge of the *Annabel* when she saw Ignacio coming down the pier. It had been three days. He waved to her when he saw her, but she did not wave back. Ignacio stopped beside the boat and looked up at her. "Pardon my language, but you look like shit."

She lowered herself down the ladder gingerly, her leg and hip stiff. She had tape across her nose. "It's just my day off," she told him.

"So you're not taking any passengers today?" he asked.

"No," Camaro said. "I don't have any charters booked for the week."

"I went by your house, but you weren't there. I didn't think I'd find you."

"I was just waiting to say good-bye," Camaro said.

"Taking a long trip?"

"Something like that," Camaro said. She looked Ignacio over. He seemed relaxed. There was no sign of cuffs.

"I'm glad we got to see each other first," Ignacio said. "I wanted to tell you how things went the other night. I thought I knew the whole story, but now that I see your face..."

"You found Chapado. You found Alpha 66."

"Good guess. We found Matt Clifford, too. Unfortunately, his Cuban friends had already made sure he wasn't in the mood for talking by the time we got there. Or maybe it was the other six guys we found lying around the place that killed him."

"Sounds like a bad scene," Camaro said.

"It's not all bad. Turns out we matched prints off two of the dead guys with a double homicide where a man and his wife had their throats cut. And with Señor Chapado telling me all about how Matt Clifford and his buddy Sandro Soto kidnapped him and shot a few Alpha 66 members while they were at it, I'm closing cases all over."

"That's good," Camaro said.

Ignacio took off his hat and fanned himself with it. "You got anything cold to drink? This day's killing me."

She thought a moment, then she nodded. "Come aboard."

They went inside the cabin, and Camaro took water bottles from the refrigerator. Ignacio wiped his brow with the cold plastic before cracking the seal and drinking deeply. He exhaled and sat down. "That's just what I needed."

Camaro took a drink. "Is there anything else you wanted to tell me?"

"Only that I got a call yesterday from a man named Richard Story. He's Lauren Story's uncle. Lives out in Texas. He says she took a bus there to see him after her father got killed. So I guess I was all wrong about you taking off with her. Funny how that works out."

Camaro didn't answer. She drank again, waiting.

"There are a few other things, of course," Ignacio said. "I almost hate to bring them up. We pulled a lot of bullets out of a lot of bodies in that warehouse. Got a lot of 9 mm, like you'd expect, but there were some .45 lugs, too. Took both out of Matt, in fact. And then there were the .45 GAP casings. I seem to recall you telling me your piece was a .45 GAP."

"I don't have that gun anymore."

"That's too bad. I know some people who would have loved to get their hands on it. Did you sell it, or did you just forget where you put it?"

"I sold it."

"Oh, well. We don't really *need* it, because we can still pull partial prints off cartridge casings. Which we did."

Camaro put the water bottle on the counter. "What did you find?"

"It's weird, but there was some kind of mix-up, and they weren't ever put in the database. And then the print evidence ended up getting lost between the Florida City PD and Miami. The casings, too. So now we'll never know who fired that gun. It's a real shame."

"Yeah," Camaro said, and something dark inside of her went away.

Ignacio drained his bottle and put it down on the seat beside him. "I guess what I'm saying is: if you don't want to run, you don't have to run."

"What about New York? Aren't they going to want to talk to me?"

"I told you before: taking care of other cities' business isn't really high on my list of priorities, even if it is my hometown. They'll have to get in line."

Camaro collected his empty bottle and put it in the wastebasket. Ignacio's eyes were on her. She looked back at him.

He got up from the seat and went out of the cabin, with Camaro behind him. When he was back in the sun again, he put on his hat and shaded his eyes. "Did I ever tell you this is a really nice boat?" he asked.

"You might have mentioned it."

"I might like to try fishing off a boat like this one. How much does it cost?"

"Rates start at forty-five dollars a person, and I can take up to ten," Camaro said.

"That sounds real fair," Ignacio said. "See you around, Camaro."

"See you, Detective."

He looked at her and smiled. "Call me Nacho. It's what my friends do."

"I'll remember that."

Ignacio stepped onto the dock. Camaro cast off fore and aft and clambered back up to the flybridge to stoke the engine. She gave the *Annabel* some throttle, and the boat eased forward into the slow rise of the water. She didn't look back.

A quarter mile offshore she was still getting a cell signal. Her phone chimed for a text message, so she dug it out of her pocket. She didn't recognize the number.

There was a picture attached to a line of text. In the picture, she saw Lauren standing somewhere dry and hot with a horse looking sidelong into the camera.

His name is Gomer, said the attached message.

Camaro nodded at the phone and smiled only a little. Then she put it away.

Today she had no calling but the sun and the sea. The morning air stirred her honey-brown hair. She laid on more throttle and headed for deep water.

ACKNOWLEDGMENTS

I would like to thank a few people for their help in bringing Camaro to the world.

First and foremost, credit must go to my wife, Mariann, and my agent, Oli Munson. Without either of them, *The Night Charter* would not have made it into your hands. Thanks also go to the readers who bought the first Camaro stories in the summer of 2013 and convinced me the character had real potential. And finally I'd like to thank everyone at Mulholland Books for taking such good care of Camaro right from the outset. May she go far.

ABOUT THE AUTHOR

Sam Hawken is the Crime Writers Association Dagger-nominated author of *The Dead Women of Juárez, Tequila Sunset,* and *Missing.* He makes his home in Maryland with his wife and son, and is represented by Oliver Munson of AM Heath Literary Agents.

MULHOLLAND BOOKS

You won't be able to put down these Mulholland Books.

CLOSE YOUR EYES *by Michael Robotham*

UNDERGROUND AIRLINES *by Ben H. Winters*

SEAL TEAM SIX: HUNT THE DRAGON *by Don Mann and Ralph Pezzullo*

THE SECOND GIRL *by David Swinson*

WE WERE KINGS *by Thomas O'Malley, Douglas Graham Purdy*

THE AMATEUR'S HOUR *by Christopher Reich*

REVOLVER *by Duane Swierczynski*

THE EXILED *by Chris Narozny*

SERPENTS IN THE COLD *by Thomas O'Malley, Douglas Graham Purdy*

WHEN WE WERE ANIMALS *by Joshua Gaylord*

THE INSECT FARM *by Stuart Prebble*

CROOKED *by Austin Grossman*

ZOO CITY *by Lauren Beukes*

MOXYLAND *by Lauren Beukes*

Visit mulhollandbooks.com for
your daily suspense fix.

Download the FREE Mulholland Books app.